ALL I WANT FOR CHRISTMAS IS YOU

ERIKA KELLY

ALL I WANT FOR CHRISTMAS IS YOU

Erika Kelly

ISBN: 978-1-955462-32-7

Copyright 2023 EK Publishing II LLC

Cover design and Formatting by Serendipity Formatting
Editing by Sharon Pochron
Editing by Kelli Collins www.kellicollins.com
Proofreading by Karen Hrdlicka

Titles by Erika Kelly

The Calamity Falls series
KEEP ON LOVING YOU
WE BELONG TOGETHER
THE VERY THOUGHT OF YOU
JUST THE WAY YOU ARE
IT WAS ALWAYS YOU
CAN'T HELP FALLING IN LOVE
COME AWAY WITH ME
WHOLE LOTTA LOVE
YOU'RE STILL THE ONE
THE DEEPER I FALL
LOVE ME LIKE YOU DO
TRULY, MADLY, DEEPLY
ALL I WANT FOR CHRISTMAS IS YOU
NEVER IN MY WILDEST DREAMS

Have you read the Rock Star Romance series? Come meet the sexy rockers of Blue Fire:

YOU REALLY GOT ME
I WANT YOU TO WANT ME
TAKE ME HOME TONIGHT
MORE THAN A FEELING

Sign up for my newsletter to find out when NEVER IN MY WILDEST DREAMS comes out! #surprisebaby #hockey #sportsromance #holidayromance

Also, get PLANES, TRAINS, AND HEAD OVER HEELS for FREE! I hope you'll come hang out with me on Facebook, TikTok, Twitter, Instagram, Goodreads, and Pinterest or in my private reader group.

Aim your cell phone camera at the QR code to get links to all the places you can find me!

This book is dedicated to the kind, generous, and savvy women in my monthly mastermind group. I'm so glad to have you all on my side.

Acknowledgments

- To Superman, thank you for the way you love me and take care of me. You are my one true love.
- Thank you, Sharon Pochron, for your friendship. I'm lucky I get to do life with you.
- Erica Alexander, you are seriously the best. You're smart, you're kind, you're generous, and you're endlessly patient with me.
- Thank you to Melissa Panio-Peterson for understanding my brain and for gifting me with your artistic brilliance.
- Melissa Martin, you are such a relief! I'm so glad I can count on you. Thank you!
- Thank you to Kelli Collins for putting a shine on this manuscript!
- To Karen, thank you for that final pass. You're awesome!
- And thank you to the readers, bloggers, reviewers, and all my author friends who make this job so richly rewarding and worthwhile.

Prologue

ALL THROUGH HER SHIFT, MARGOT HODGES KEPT glancing at her watch. Anticipation jangled her nerves, making time move like sludge through a straw.

Her fellow barista handed over the next ticket and did a double take on her fingernails. "Well, look at you. All gussied up." He took her hand to examine the shell-pink polish. "What's the occasion?"

Margot smiled as she measured out the espresso beans. "It's my birthday."

"For real?"

"Yep." Normally, she didn't share much personal information. No one wanted to hear her sad story. But today, she was excited. For the first time in over a year, she'd get to see her kids.

Well, she hoped so.

She was pretty sure.

"Did you just say it's your birthday?" The manager swept in and pulled the cup out of her hand.

"Yep." Margot tried to take it back, but the woman

shook her head.

"Get out of here. We got this."

"I can't just leave. We're slammed." Though, really, she'd love to get home. In her twenty-seven years of marriage, no matter how busy her husband was, he'd always taken off for her birthday.

Today, though, he hadn't said a word. No flowers, no card, nothing.

And it made her think about the other things she'd noticed recently. Like last week, she'd caught him hiding in the bathroom, grinning during a text exchange. And the other day, he'd mentioned his new boss's connection to a senator. Normally, Margot would think *so what?* But if you added it all together, what else did you get but a surprise party?

Clearly, he was texting their kids and working with a senator to get her son home from his deployment. Delusional? Maybe, but what other conclusion could she make?

"Honey, you're my best and most reliable worker," the manager said. "You never take time off. Go home and celebrate. We'll cover for you."

Excitement bubbled inside her. "You sure?"

"Positive. Go."

She didn't need to hear it a third time. "Thank you so much." As she untied her apron, she headed into the break room to grab her purse. She couldn't wait to hug her children.

Scott needed this. Since her husband's career had tanked, he'd fallen into a slump. Seeing them would boost his spirits.

As she headed out the door, she breathed in the cool

April air, grateful for this break from work. Before starting her car, she checked her phone for messages. Nothing.

Yet more proof they were planning something. No way would they forget her today—not all three of them. Excited, she headed out of the parking lot.

It had been a rough seven years, but things were finally turning around. Scott worked in a volatile field, so he'd lost jobs before, but he'd always recovered. This time, his industry had collapsed. There were far fewer jobs, and in the game of musical chairs, there were no seats left for a middle-aged former titan.

They'd had to sell their home and most of their belongings. Their daughter, who'd just started college, dropped out because she didn't want to take on crushing student loans, and their son enlisted in the Marines.

As tough as things had gotten, though, Margot still had her family. Her kids and her husband meant everything to her. As long as she had them, she could get through anything.

As soon as she pulled into her apartment complex, she cut the engine and checked her phone again. Still nothing. Her son was stationed in South Korea, and her daughter worked long hours at a resort in Hawaii. All together, her family spanned three time zones—not the best for keeping in touch.

She flipped down the visor and checked her hair in the mirror. After a long day on her feet, she looked exhausted, so she fished around in her purse for her lipstick. Then, she got out, locked the door, and headed to the stairwell.

Scott hated living here. It was a constant reminder of how far he'd fallen. He'd tried every headhunter and job posting site, but no one would hire him. He was overqualified for the warehouse jobs and too old for corporations. She'd been a stay-at-home mom, so she didn't have much of a résumé, but it had fallen on her to bring in money. The barista job gave them a roof over their heads and benefits.

The hardest part of this whole situation had been watching her husband lose his confidence. He'd gone from a master of the universe to defeated and hopeless. Until this recent opportunity had come along, he'd barely been hanging on. Too often, she hadn't wanted to leave him alone when she went to work. It had been that bad.

She did everything she could to rally his spirits. Every night, she made him dinner, found ways to make him laugh, and regularly assured him of life's one and only guarantee: change. She believed wholeheartedly in the phrase, *This too shall pass*. A year, a month, a day from now, their lives could look entirely different.

Luckily, three months ago, he'd gotten a consulting gig. Attracted by his résumé, a woman found him on a professional social media app. She needed his expertise to help her develop a lithium trading company. Once they got venture capital money, he'd be the CFO, and Petra would be the CEO, and then, he'd get a salary.

Getting the job had energized him. He'd gone back to the gym and popped out of bed each morning. He'd found his purpose in life. She'd be forever grateful to Petra, a woman she'd never met but who'd offered her husband a lifeline. It might not come with income or benefits, but it came with a massive helping of hope.

On her way up the stairs, it occurred to her that by

coming home early, she'd ruin the surprise. She couldn't do that if Scott had gone to this much effort for her.

Margot: Good news! They let me off early. I'm coming home.

It had been so long since she'd squeezed her babies. Not only couldn't they afford airfare, but their apartment didn't have an extra bedroom.

When she saw he hadn't read the message, she figured he was probably setting up. Maybe balloons or crepe paper, as she'd done for all their birthdays over the years. She could imagine her daughter and son baking a cake together. *The mess they'll make!* Dancing to their playlists and fighting over who got to lick the beaters.

Oh, my God, yes. Please. Give it all back to me. All those blissful years of the four of them making cookies and sitting around the dinner table laughing and sharing stories about their day.

She missed her old life so fiercely. Not the house or fancy cars, not any of the designer clothes. Just her family, all together.

Hitching her purse onto her shoulder, she climbed the final three steps. Fortunately, she didn't need to worry about her clothes smelling like coffee or the makeup that had worn off since it would just be the four of them. Scott was estranged from his family, and her parents had died several years ago. Once they'd moved to this apartment—several towns over from where they'd raised their kids—they'd lost touch with all their friends.

She rounded the corner, and when she reached her unit,

she was a little surprised not to see balloons or a sign on the door.

Yeah, but that's something I would've done. They'll do things their way.

And it'll be fabulous.

She checked her phone one more time—just in case they needed her to stay away a little longer—but nope. No messages. And then, she shoved the key into the lock and stepped into the apartment.

The stillness hit her first. It smelled like it did every day when they were both at work and left the windows closed: the faint scent of last night's chicken and the stuffiness of recycled air. Which was odd since her daughter brought her signature coconut and vanilla scent wherever she went. Not to mention her chaos. All growing up, she'd come in shouting, kicking off her shoes, and dropping her hoodie on the nearest chair.

So, had she gotten it wrong? Had they actually forgotten her birthday?

Is Scott still at work?

From the entryway, Margot could see the kitchen. It was as clean as she'd left it last night. Except for that one glass.

One?

As soon as she shut the door, she dropped her purse. "Hello?" Maybe her husband was on his way from the airport? He'd have arranged for their flights to arrive close together. "Scott?"

"Yeah. I'm here." He sounded tense. Stern.

Her pulse quickened. *He's pretending.* They'd probably just arrived and hadn't had time to decorate. Maybe they'd bought a cake.

Who cares about any of that?

Unable to keep from grinning, she came around the short hallway and into the living area. But her spirits crashed when she saw her husband alone, still wearing his white dress shirt and suit pants.

Tall and fit, he was a handsome man. His graying hair only made him look more elegant. "We need to talk."

Shit. Something's wrong. Anxiety squeezed the air from her lungs.

He gestured to the couch. "Sit."

Oh, God. She needed answers immediately, so she did what he asked. "Just say it. Is it Owen? Tell me Emerson's okay."

"What? No. The kids are fine."

Oh, no. Petra let him go. Despair crashed over her. She couldn't bear to see him fall back into a depression. "It's okay. If you lost your job, don't worry. We're doing fine. I swear to you, a year from now, things will look different. I don't have a crystal ball, I can't see into the future, but we won't be in this situation. Something's going to—"

"Stop." He shook his head and pursed his lips as if he'd tasted something bitter. "Just stop trying to manage me. I'm a man. I'm not your son who didn't get into Yale." He drew in a breath, and for the first time, she noticed he had yet to look her in the eyes. "I'll get to the point. I've fallen in love with Petra, and I'm moving in with her. Tonight."

Ice water flushed through her veins. Her reality spun so wildly, so incomprehensibly, she felt nauseous. "Your boss?"

"She's not my *boss*. I'm consulting for her."

"That's…*God*." She pressed a hand to her heart as if she could soothe the rapid beating. *What is happening right now?*

"Are you telling me you're leaving your wife of twenty-seven years for a woman you've known *three months*?"

"Yes." Oddly, he didn't seem embarrassed or ashamed. It was more like he was dreading her outburst. "I know you're angry, and I don't blame you. But I'm finally *happy*."

None of his words landed. They bounced off the walls of her skull and slammed into each other. She could see shards of truth but none of the pieces fit together. "What have you done, Scott?" She didn't want to be vulnerable right now— *it's my goddamn birthday*—but she needed answers. "You don't love me anymore?"

"No, I do. Of course, I do. We've been together for nearly thirty years. We've raised kids. But at this point, we're nothing more than friends. You know that. With Petra, it's different. I feel alive for the first time—"

"In seven years. Yes, I know. I know, because I've had a front-row seat to your despair, your anger, and your complete unwillingness to reinvent your life."

"That's right." He spat out the words, his ugly side rearing. "I've hated my life. But now, I have a chance to get out of this fucking mess, and I'm taking it."

"And what about me?"

"I'll continue to pay the rent on this apartment and your car payment."

"That's not what I'm talking about. Jesus, Scott." She got up, studying him across the ottoman. He must feel shame… remorse…*something*. But she couldn't detect even a hint of it. He was dead serious. Her husband was literally abandoning her. "We've lost everything. We have no money in our savings account, and you're going to *leave me*?"

She waited for regret to wrench his features. For doubt,

hesitation…any normal human reaction. But he remained steadfast.

Panic got a grip on her nervous system and squeezed. "You don't abandon your family like this. I'm your *wife*."

"I know that. You think I don't know it's a shitty thing to do? But what's the alternative? What we're doing isn't sustainable. Your job in a coffee shop is not going to solve any of our problems. You think we can live off your hourly salary when we're in our nineties?"

"No. I think you can use your experience and your brains to create a business. Be entrepreneurial. You have to do more than apply for jobs."

"I have a job. And as soon as we get VC money, I'll be back on top."

"With Petra."

Let this be a cruel joke. Let him crack a smile and point a finger gun at her. "*Gotcha.*"

Let this be anything but her husband abandoning her when they had nothing but a garden apartment in Norwalk, Connecticut that ate up nearly half her salary.

With a patronizing expression, he tilted his head. "Come on. You know as well as I do we're basically roommates at this point. We both deserve better."

Rage set her in motion, and she rounded the ottoman. "*Roommates* don't do your laundry and make your meals. *Roommates* don't listen to every detail of your day and every conversation you had so you can feel seen and valued. They don't play cheerleader to make sure you don't fall into a depression you can't get out of. I am not, nor have I ever been, a roommate."

"Look, this is shitty, and I know it. But we're in a death

spiral, and I found an exit ramp. I have to take it." Through the crack in his stern demeanor, she could see desperation. His gaze wandered out the window, the skin around his eyes pinching with abject fear. "I *have* to." When he finally looked at her, he'd gone hard again. "And I hope you find one, too."

She opened her mouth to let him know he was a heartless, careless asshole, to explain what life had been like for her working nonstop just to keep a roof over their heads —and not just in the coffee shop, but nights and weekends on her side business selling Christmas ornaments—all while watching him seethe with bitterness every day, staring at the television instead of creating job opportunities for himself.

But what was the point?

He'd crossed a line, and there was no coming back from it.

She wiped her face clean of emotion. "Okay."

Oh, he liked that. He liked it a lot. His shoulders relaxed. "Right now, I'm going to pack a bag."

Words continued to spew out of his mouth, plans, details, but she didn't hear them over the roar of blood in her ears. Because this was happening. Her husband was leaving her.

With nothing but these four walls and the couch that still reeked of the beer someone spilled at one of Emerson's high school parties.

He strode to the closet like the boat was sinking, and he had to find the one single life vest they owned. His leather weekend bag hit the floor with a smack. The sound tapped the base of her spine like a mallet, sending fear radiating throughout her body.

We have no savings.
I'll be working every day for the rest of my life.
I am completely alone.

In the bedroom, drawers slammed shut and hangers whacked the wall as he pulled off his shirts. Minutes later, he came out with his bag bulging.

At the door, he stopped. "I'm sorry, Margot. I am." For a split second, remorse flashed in his eyes, but it died like a spark hitting the lake. "Like I said, I'll cover the rent and the car. The only thing I ask is that you're out of the apartment this Saturday, so I can get the rest of my stuff."

The moment he left, Margot got busy. First, she quit her job. Then, she made phone calls, looked at maps, and evaluated possibilities.

On Thursday morning, she packed her car.

They'd only taken enough from the Greenwich house to outfit a one-bedroom apartment. Everything else they'd ever owned had been sold, dumped, or shoved into a storage unit. Besides, she didn't need much anyway. She took her clothes, the fancy new television Owen bought them for Christmas, the toaster—because she was all about buttery bread—half the silver and dishware, her computer and office supplies, two sets of sheets and towels, and the lovely duvet she'd ordered from Switzerland for their twentieth anniversary.

And then, she blocked his number, walked out the door, and drove off.

Destination unknown.

Chapter One

EIGHT MONTHS LATER

Beau Gentry didn't know what it was about their server, but he couldn't stop watching her. There was something so genuine about her. She interacted with customers as if she truly enjoyed them—not because she was looking for tips.

And her scent—it was probably just perfume, but it stirred up feelings of clean sheets, warm bodies, and lazy Sunday mornings. Bagels and coffee in bed. Whispers and quiet laughter.

He shook his head. *What the hell?* He'd never thought about a woman that way before.

His daughter came back from the bathroom and dropped into her seat. "Do you want dessert?"

Normally, he wouldn't. He'd enjoyed his steak and potatoes with a side salad, and that was enough. But his girl had a sweet tooth, and since she wouldn't get to come home for Christmas this year, he wanted to spoil her rotten. "You bet."

"Oh, good." When she opened the menu, her long,

curly hair spilled forward, and she had that intense look of concentration she'd had as a little girl trying to figure out where to put a puzzle piece. "The salted caramel cheesecake sounds yummy." Her eyes widened. "Oh. Chocolate lava cake?"

Beau smiled. He didn't care what she got. He was just happy to be here with his princess. The bluegrass band played a lively tune, the decor in this historic lodge was festive, and if he didn't have to get home, he'd stay in town longer. He didn't want to leave her all alone over the holidays. But with a few weeks to go until she earned her master's degree, she had to stay in Merry Falls to finish her thesis, and it required work in a lab.

"Then again, that trio of gelatos sounds amazing." Jessa's forehead creased with concern.

Knowing his youngest was overwhelmed with stress, Beau reached across the table and closed the menu. "Let's get one of each."

"Really?" In that moment, she might as well have been ten years old, trampling down the stairs to see whether Santa had brought the mountain bike she'd requested. "I can get one of each dessert on the menu?"

He smiled. "Merry Christmas, sweet pea." He picked up the server's scent before she came into view, and he didn't understand his body's reaction. Smell and emotion were stored as one memory, so he had to assume she wore the same perfume as someone from his childhood. Though he couldn't imagine who.

"So, what did you guys decide?" She gave them a warm smile.

While other staff wore name badges, this woman didn't.

Then again, she didn't seem to have one specific job here. When he'd checked in, he'd noticed her scattering salt on the driveway in anticipation of snow. The next morning, he'd found her in the lobby café working on her laptop. That same afternoon, he'd come upon her on his walk through the woods.

Maybe she owned the place?

Honestly, he didn't know why he was so preoccupied with her.

"Apparently, my Christmas present is one of each dessert." His daughter had a teasing glint in her eyes as she handed over her menu.

"Lucky girl," the server said. "Coffee with that?"

The simple question triggered the realization that he knew exactly what this woman would order. Each morning, when he got some work done at the coffee bar, he noticed she ordered two drinks: a skim decaf latte and a vanilla chai latte.

His ex's biggest complaint had been that he didn't pay enough attention to her, so what the hell was he doing noticing what a stranger drank?

"I'll have a cappuccino," his daughter said. "Make it a double, please. I'll be up late tonight."

"Lots of presents to wrap?" The server looked to be about his age. Her shiny dark hair tumbled down her back in soft waves, and she had warm hazel eyes.

"I wish." Jessa's expression fell. As the youngest, she'd missed out on the most. Her older siblings had aged out of Easter egg hunts and building gingerbread houses at a time when it mattered to the littlest. He'd built and hunted with her, but it hadn't been the same. "I have a ton of work."

"Student at Whitney?" the lovely woman asked.

"Yep."

"I went there." A grin brightened her face. "Loved it."

There's a clue. Maybe she'd majored in hospitality. She probably did either own or manage the lodge.

"I love it so much, I stayed for my master's," Jessa said. "My mom says I'm afraid of the real world, so I'll just keep staying in school—"

"But the truth is," Beau cut in, "Jessa's passionate about making mining sustainable." He would not let anyone get into this perfect child's head. "She's going to change the world one day."

The woman gave him a smile filled with admiration but turned her focus to Jessa. "Mining, huh? That's unusual."

"Well, my dad owns a mine, so I'm creating a way to extract the minerals from the water, making it less harmful to the environment."

"That's fantastic. I'm impressed." The server hugged the menus to her chest, her upbeat spirits flagging. "Well, let me get the rugby team out here to help deliver your five hundred desserts. Be right back." When she started off, he felt the strangest tug in his chest. He didn't want her to go. But she surprised him by turning back around. "What about you? Coffee, tea? An after-dinner drink?"

"Nothing." *Except you can tell me what made you sad just then.* "Thank you, though."

The woman rallied with a smile. "Oh, you'll need something to go with all that goodness."

"My dad doesn't have coffee after two o'clock, and he rarely drinks booze." His daughter rolled her eyes, but he knew how much it mattered to her, since her mom overindulged in everything. "He's incredibly boring."

"Or *maybe* he's got a whole other secret side." The server gave a playful lift of her eyebrows.

"No. She's right. I'm just boring." He reached out his hand. "I'm Beau." He gestured to his daughter. "And this is Jessa."

"Nice to meet you both. I'm Margot. I hope you're enjoying your stay at the Merry Falls Lodge." And then, she was gone.

"That was weird, right?" Jessa asked.

"What was?"

"The way her mood changed when I talked about my job. Did I say something?"

"No." It was just like his girl to blame herself. Which was why the divorce had been so damn hard. Growing up in a small cabin, the kids had gotten a front-row seat to the fighting and indifference of two people ill-suited for each other.

He'd read a lot about the impact of divorce on kids and learned they often blamed themselves. He didn't want that for his open-hearted little girl. "We don't know anything about her life."

"We knew she was happy, and then I talked about my plans, and she got sad."

"We can't read her mind, so the only thing we can do is be kind to her."

The band stopped playing, and the microphone screeched. He turned around to find an older woman on the stage. "Sorry about that." She laughed. "Happy holidays, everyone, and thank you for joining us at the Merry Falls

Lodge. I'm Lucy Gibbins, the proprietor, and these are The Lost Ridge Ramblers."

While Beau joined in the applause, his gaze roamed in search of the server. "Margot." Even though his voice went unheard over the shouts and whistles, he said the name out loud, testing the sound of it on his tongue, feeling the movement of his lips on the M and the O.

She stood behind the bar, her dark hair gleaming in the overhead lights, her expression full of affection for the speaker. *Huh.* Related somehow?

"In case you haven't noticed, this is our favorite time of year." Ms. Gibbins made a sweeping gesture to indicate the strings of white lights, the fresh boughs wrapped around the exposed wooden beams, and the sprigs of mistletoe dangling from the low ceiling. Each table had a pine wreath wrapped around the base of a glass votive, giving off its sharp scent. "So, we're glad you're here to share it with us."

"It's a wonderland," his daughter said to him, her voice rich with awe.

"We'll get back to the music in a moment," Ms. Gibbins continued. "But I do need to let you know about the travel advisory that just came in. There's a big storm coming, and it doesn't look good. With Christmas only two days away, you might want to rethink your travel plans. North Carolina's not set up for big snowstorms—even this far west in the woods. No worries if you're staying with us through the holidays. We've got you covered. Plenty of food, booze, and music. Now, it's time to give the band a break and get into…" She opened her arms wide to the audience.

"Sunday Karaoke," a good number of people shouted.

"That's right. Okay, I'll let Felix take over from here."

While the rest of the band left the stage, the bass player took the mic and looked at the sign-up sheet. "All righty, folks. Let's see which brave souls are up first. Mark and Stephanie Evans?"

Beau turned to face his daughter and couldn't miss her mischievous expression. His stomach dropped. "No."

"No what?"

"You didn't go to the bathroom, did you? You signed us up. *Jessa*." He was an engineer. He was comfortable with data and research. He solved problems all day long.

That's what I'm good at.

He didn't perform. And he definitely didn't sing.

"Thanks for coming out here, Dad. It means a lot."

"I wouldn't want to be anywhere else. I'm sorry I can't stay through Christmas." His son and grandson were waiting for him at home. The two-year-old's mother wasn't in the picture, and he deserved as big of a family as they could give him. Beau would move heaven and earth for that little boy.

"No, I know. I wouldn't have time to see you anyway."

"You've worked hard for this, Jessie. I'm proud of you."

She touched the red velvet bow on the wreath. "Are you still going to make me work for someone else before you hire me?"

"Absolutely. You understand things theoretically. Now, you need to get in the field and apply your research. When you're ready, Gentry Mining Corporation will be waiting for you."

"I mean, it doesn't seem fair, does it? Walker's only twenty-six, and you're letting him basically run the place."

"Different situation. He studied mining engineering like

I did. Plus, he's worked there since high school. Your role is different. You'll help us be cleaner and more efficient."

"I want to work *with* you—not join after you retire. Well, if you actually do ever stop working."

"Hey, now. I've already started transitioning to the new development." His family's biggest complaint about the mine was its remoteness. With its location on the outskirts of Calamity, they'd felt cut off from the town and their friends, so he'd spent the last decade developing the property. He had a lodge, a place for tourists to pan for gold, and a Wild West gift shop. Most recently, he'd built a shopping mall. After the New Year, he'd start looking for business owners to lease the spaces.

"Dad." She laughed. "That's still work. I want you to have more in your life than that."

"I have my kids." He was close to the younger two. The oldest—well, she had a massive career, and he hadn't seen her much over the years. "And my grandson."

"I know, but we're all adults now."

He knew that. Eventually, Walker would get married and move out. Jessa would get a job in another state. And then what would he have? Like she said, *work.* "Where's this coming from?"

"I just worry that you're letting Mom get into your head."

Funny. I worry the same thing about you. "In what way?"

"She basically tells everyone who'll listen that you were a terrible husband, a bad father, and that you screwed her out of all the money."

His wife left because he wouldn't give up on the mine, wouldn't move her out of the small cabin, and stubbornly held on to his "worthless" dream. She'd divorced him before he'd discovered gold. "Do *you* think I was a terrible husband and bad father?"

"No." Her grin told him she knew she was her daddy's little girl.

She was born a bold, confident, happy little girl, and he was so damn proud of her. "Then, that's all that matters to me."

"I know, but you don't date. I don't want you to become some bitter, angry man who refuses to love again."

He weighed the two emotions inside himself. "I don't feel bitter." He wanted his kids to have a good relationship with their mom, so he had to be careful what he said. "I'm angry about what she did to me and Lorelei." His ex had lied to their oldest about him. She'd made it sound like Beau was so preoccupied with *his* dreams that he didn't support his daughter's, when the whole time he'd been the one paying for singing lessons, an in-home studio, their move to Nashville, and even her first tour.

Fortunately, the truth was out now, so he'd had the summer to reconcile with her. "And it's not that I *refuse* to love again." He toyed with the pepper shaker, wondering how much he should tell her. He supposed at twenty-three, she was mature enough to hear the truth. "I'm just not sure I'm wired for it."

"What does that mean?"

"I love my children with every fiber of my being, but I've never felt romantic love."

"You didn't love Mom?"

The kids knew they'd married because she'd gotten pregnant. "Not the way I should have. And I know that because I saw what happened to you when your relationship blew up. I've never loved anyone enough to be destroyed like that."

"Oh. That's sad."

"Well, since I don't know what I'm missing, it's probably okay." What Jessa had gone through was bad, but his oldest had suffered a horrible betrayal. He didn't need to experience anything like that.

"But, Dad, you'll never know passion. And sure, my ex hurt me badly, but I wouldn't have known that kind of pain if I hadn't felt the highs that come from wild love." She leaned across the table. "Don't you get lonely?"

He hated that she was so worried about him. "Not really. I like my work, I'm close to my kids...I'm good with my own company." He and Jessa talked every day. Walker and his son lived with him, so he had companionship.

He'd even gotten Lorelei back. As soon as she'd found out about her mother's lies, she'd signed on for a summer residency at the Owl Hoot Music Festival so she could begin repairing her relationship with him. They'd had two great months before her world had fallen apart. Not long ago, though, she'd gone to a remote cabin to regroup. He'd barely heard from her since.

"All right." Jessa swatted the air. "I'll stop getting into your business. You know how emotional I get when I'm stressed. After I turn in my thesis, I'll be a whole different person."

"I like this person." He set down the pepper and reached for her hand.

"This person's very different from you. I want love. I want passion. *I'm* not a lone wolf."

"And you'll find it. Probably when you least expect it."

Just as "We Are The Champions" ended, the server —*Margot*—returned with four plates. "All right. Here you go." She must've caught his daughter's disappointment because she quickly added, "Oh, don't worry. I'll have the next batch out in just a minute."

For some reason, she'd put her hair in a ponytail, and he had the strangest urge to pull the elastic and release it. He wanted to see that bounty of silky, shiny hair fall free around her shoulders. In the mornings when she worked, she sifted her fingers through it. When she reached the ends, she gave it a twist. It was a cute, unconscious habit.

She headed back to the kitchen, and he watched the sway of her hips, noting the way the fabric of her jeans cupped each round ass cheek as she extended a leg to walk.

Had he ever noticed the way clothing fit a woman before? No. He was sure he hadn't. Another server came out of the kitchen, handing some plates over. And then, Margot was on her way back to the table.

As she approached, his heart knocked against his ribs.

What is happening to me?

He pressed his hand to his chest, as if he had some external control of his body's response. She set down four more desserts, and when her arm brushed his, the strangest thing happened.

Goose bumps popped up on his forearm. He was so confused by his body's reaction that when the emcee called his name, he jolted, jerking around to face the stage.

"Beau and Jessa Gentry?" The musician used a hand to shield his eyes from the bright spotlight as he searched the room.

Beau whipped back to find his daughter grinning. "Dammit, Jessa. You know I hate karaoke."

"Please, Dad?" She reached for his hands. "Can this be my Christmas present?"

"Absolutely not. You know I already have one for you."

"Okay, then, my stocking stuffer. Dad, please, please, please? Come on. I'll be all alone on Christmas morning. I don't get to wake up to hot cocoa and bagels and cream cheese and a tree full of gifts."

She knew just how to punch his heart. "I don't sing." He had a terrible voice. Everyone knew that.

"Jessa and Beau Gentry?" the emcee repeated. "You here?" A floodlight zigzagged across the dining room.

His daughter popped up. "We're here. Coming." She threw her napkin on the table and reached for his hand, giving him the puppy dog look that got him every time.

He looked at Margot as though she could somehow help him, but all she had to offer was a kind, compassionate smile. "The things we do for our kids."

She was right. He'd do anything for his daughter. Pushing his chair back, he got up. "Cover your ears."

She gave him a pat on his shoulder. "You got this."

"You underestimate my ability to kill a song."

Margot leaned in close, her Sunday-morning-under-the-covers scent filling his senses. "Nobody cares, I promise. I've watched karaoke night for eight months now, and they're just here to have fun. No one cares whether you can sing."

He appreciated hearing that. With a nod, he turned to follow his daughter, weaving through the tables and climbing the steps to the stage. After Jessa told the emcee which song she wanted, she gazed up at him with so much enthusiasm, he had no choice but to go along with whatever she'd chosen. "Ready?" she asked.

"Sure thing, sweetie." But he took the microphone out of her hand and spoke to the audience. "Fair warning, I have the kind of voice that makes dogs hide under the bed." His daughter nodded with gusto. "I suggest you take this opportunity to use the restrooms. But if you choose to stay, dessert and coffee's on me."

Everyone laughed, and then the song got going. Once he recognized the pop tune, he shook his head. He was never going to reach those notes. But Jessa just laughed, enjoying every minute. She threw herself into the performance.

His daughter might not need to read the prompter, but he sure did. And once he joined in, it was apparent to everyone in the room that he wasn't exaggerating about the quality of his voice. He could see people laughing, covering their ears. It was all in good fun, of course. He knew that. But he hated being the center of attention almost as much as he hated singing.

The beginning of the song was the easy part. All too soon, though, it began ramping up. And the huge vocal range it required spelled disaster for him.

He'd just closed his eyes, knowing his voice would surely crack and bracing for the humiliation, when he felt warmth against his left side. Someone pulled the mic out of his hand.

It was Margot. She'd arrived at the exact right moment to take on an impossibly high note, saving him from sounding like a yelping dog.

And she held it. Even longer than his daughter.

Beau stepped out of the spotlight, watching as the two

women nailed the song, dancing and laughing and having the time of their lives.

Nothing made him happier than seeing his daughter so carefree. Because no matter how hard he tried to be a good father, Jessa had still gotten the shortest end of the stick. Her mom had moved to Nashville with her older sister, and her family had shrunk to the three of them.

When the song ended, the audience burst into applause. The two women hugged, and then his daughter dashed across the stage and threw herself into his arms. "That was so fun."

"I love you, Jessa girl."

"Thank you so much, Dad."

"Of course." But he knew she meant a whole lot more than enduring karaoke night. "There's nowhere I'd rather be."

The server was heading away, and he called out to her. "Margot?"

It was too loud to talk, but he held her gaze for a long moment. Overcome with a strange sense of panic at her leaving, he wanted to ask her to wait for him while he took his daughter back to her dorm, see if she wanted to grab a coffee.

But of course, she was just doing her job. She was kind to all the lodge's guests.

It's not about me.

So, he nodded his gratitude, and she gave him a soft smile on her way to resume her duties.

He was leaving tomorrow.

Nothing could come of this.

Chapter Two

MARGOT COULDN'T STOP THINKING ABOUT THAT MAN.

Which was crazy because she was a grown-ass woman—not a teenager. She'd noticed him the moment he'd handed off his rental car to the valet—his cheeks red from the cold, his overlong dark hair tousled from the wind.

And those eyes. She'd never seen a brighter blue. It was like staring into the heart of a fire.

Sure, he was handsome. So much so that everyone noticed him. Whenever he crossed the lobby or entered the restaurant, heads turned and conversations paused. But the world was full of good-looking people, and she didn't get a visceral reaction from any of *them*. No, there was something about him.

A goodness, a kindness. He exuded a humility that didn't fit with his expensive watch and designer clothes. That leather duffel bag had to have cost a fortune. She recognized it from her Greenwich days.

Given what she'd just endured—a divorce after the worst

kind of betrayal—she might've been able to ignore him. It would be a long time before she considered dating. Except that *he* noticed *her*. Every time he passed her in the lobby, he'd give her this stoic look, but his eyes burned with interest.

For most of her life, she'd gotten attention from men. She wasn't a beauty by any stretch, but she had a pleasant-looking face—approachable, friendly, whatever. She exercised regularly. Nothing grueling, but she made a point to walk every day.

But at some point, she'd hit a certain age and the attention stopped. She'd become invisible. She wasn't sure why. Honestly, she didn't even think she looked all that different. There was no question, though, that she didn't turn heads anymore.

Except his. Somehow, she was on his radar, and she couldn't for the life of her figure out why.

All of five foot two, her aunt Lucy burst into the kitchen with her big, commanding energy. She stopped when she spotted her. "What're you doing here?"

Margot held up a tray. "I'm bringing more scones out."

Twenty years ago, when all she'd wanted in the world was to get into Whitney, her parents had told her there was no way they could afford it. She'd understood, of course. It was an elite, private university, and she'd gotten into plenty of other schools. The state one would've been just fine.

But Whitney had the best Fine Arts program in the country. World-famous artists visited and worked with the students. She'd wanted it so badly. So, when her aunt Lucy had offered her free room and board—she didn't have to do a thing at the lodge because it was fully staffed—Margot had bawled like a baby. She'd wanted so little out of life, but to learn her craft and work with artists? It meant the world to her. She'd taken out loans, packed up her bags, and off she'd gone.

In a million years, she'd never have anticipated moving back into that little room intended for live-in staff. In her *forties.*

But here I am.

Her aunt marched over like she wanted to snatch the baked goods out of her hands, but once she stood in front of her, those pale blue eyes gazed up with concern. "Honey, go back to work. I've told you a hundred times, I don't need your help. You'll probably trip on the carpet and drop the whole batch anyway."

Margot laughed. She was plenty coordinated and wasn't prone to dropping things, but her aunt showed love with actions, not words. *Yeah, well. Same.* So, she moved around her, determined to help in any way she could. "I earn my keep."

"You want to know how to do that? Build your business so you can get the hell out of my hair. Now, go on. Get out of my kitchen and go sell some ornaments."

"Fine. *After* I drop these off. I'm working at the coffee bar this morning anyway."

The Merry Falls Lodge had been in the family for generations. Most of the Gibbinses had left western North Carolina to seek their fortunes in big cities, but not Aunt Lucy. She loved it here. Loved hosting families and couples, travelers, and workers.

She was tough as nails and had the biggest heart of anyone Margot knew.

At the kitchen door, Margot turned back. "You worried about the storm?"

"I'm not the one who needs to be worried. It's all those guests out there who think, 'Eh, it's the East Coast. They're set up for snow.' I'd hate to see anyone miss out on the holidays with their families."

Aunt Lucy had never married or had kids—well, she'd say she married the lodge, and she considered her friends in Merry Falls her family. Margot had always wondered why her dad had left only to become anonymous in a big city, where he worked a thankless job, when he could've run the lodge with his sister. "All you can do is warn them."

"We'll be okay. We've got the generator and a pantry stuffed to the gills, so at least we'll have enough food for everyone. Now, take those out there before they get stale. Go on." She made a shooing motion.

"Ugh. So mean." With a grin, Margot headed out of the kitchen into the lobby. The lodge was a historic landmark, but her aunt kept up with the times and had created a very cool space in the lobby with a fancy espresso machine, comfortable chairs, tables, and lots of electrical outlets and charging stations.

She set the tray on the counter. "Here you go."

The barista was busy but gave her an appreciative smile. "You want something to drink?"

"No, I'm good. I still have my chai." Margot sat down at her table. *Time to dig in.*

Despite the ordeal she'd endured the past eight months,

one daisy had pushed its way up through the concrete: she got to earn her living through art.

She'd chosen to stay home with her kids, assuming she'd get back to her work when they graduated high school. Unfortunately, her ex lost his job during Emerson's freshman year of college, so she'd had to put it off again. But she was so grateful she'd started her side business to make extra cash because now, she'd grown it into so much more. She made logos for business owners, book covers for small publishers and self-published authors, and even sold original watercolors online.

But her favorite thing of all—and the real money maker —was her Christmas ornaments. She'd only started it as a fun project to do at night while her ex watched TV—just to keep him company—but the response had been amazing. And now, thanks to Aunt Lucy not charging her room and board, she was building a nice little savings account.

Of course, it would never be enough for her to retire. She'd have to work the rest of her life. Fear stabbed the base of her spine, and she got jittery. *No, no, no.* She couldn't let negative thoughts worm their way in. She had to keep pushing forward.

Okay, where was I? She tried to sink back into her work, but every time the door to the lodge opened, she couldn't help looking over.

Is it him?

She should probably feel foolish, but this was the first time since getting married two decades ago that she'd felt that zing of excitement for a man. It was harmless, and nothing would come of it, so she wasn't worried. He was passing through, and she had a business to build so she wouldn't have to make espresso drinks for the rest of her life.

It was just… He'd been nothing more than a crush until last night, when one of the servers had called out sick, and Margot had stepped in. She'd finally gotten to meet him, and the real man was so much better than the fantasy.

Beau. Such a handsome man. Like an old-school Hollywood actor—all dark hair, strong jaw, and sexy mouth. She could imagine him on a horse, cowboy hat hanging low, hard expression as he surveyed the barren land around him.

And then, during karaoke, when he'd looked at her with such vulnerability, it had ignited interest into a full-blown obsession. Because she'd somehow convinced herself there was something happening beneath the surface. Like their souls were calling out to each other.

Ha ha ha.

Souls.

Oh, my God. You're a sad, lonely woman.

Go back to work.

She clicked on her sales tab for the tenth time that day. It might seem silly, but it was her only source of comfort these days. Every time she got scared of her future, she'd reach for that hit of reassurance that her business was growing. She was doing just fine. Better than fine.

Just as she sank into designing a commissioned set of ornaments for a small museum in Kansas, the lodge door swung open, and a family burst into the lobby. A little boy raced ahead, his dad shouting for him to slow down. A mom with a baby in a carrier strapped to her chest held the hand of a little girl. All of them had red cheeks from the cold mountain air and, while the parents looked harried, there was an air of contentment about them. Like they were right where they wanted to be in life.

I remember that.

She'd loved every second of raising her two kids.

This was her first Christmas alone, and it hurt. All those years of bringing the magic—the lights and decorations, the cocoa with marshmallows—were gone in the blink of an eye. No wrapping presents in the basement with her husband, laughing and talking the night away. No family gathered around the oven to see if the Yorkshire pudding had puffed up. And no one to ooh and aah as she brought the Yule log to the table, everyone excited to see how she'd decorated it.

The twist in her chest was so violent, it brought a sting of tears. She blinked them away. *Oh, come on.* It happened to everyone. Kids grew up and moved away. *It's called an empty nest.*

Emerson loved living in Hawaii and adored her fiancé. And Owen, her sweet, earnest little boy—in a million years, she could've never imagined him in the Armed Services. When she thought of how his deployments might change him, it scared her down to her bones. Still, he seemed to be doing all right.

The door swung open again, but this time, she was too damn sad to look up, so she kept her focus on the screen and worked on the project.

Moments later, two chairs scraped back at the table next to hers, and when she glanced over, her gaze locked with Beau's.

Adrenaline slammed her, colliding with her sadness and

sweeping it right out of her body. She felt alive in a way she hadn't in years.

His daughter sat down and, while he draped his coat around his chair, he asked, "Scone and cocoa?"

"Um." Jessa lifted half out of her seat to peer at the display case. "It depends on what kind."

"Oat date," Margot said. A wave of mortification crashed over her, making her hot and itchy. She might've chatted with them last night, but she'd been their server. Not their friend. She had no business barging into their conversation.

Jessa didn't seem bothered, though. "Are they good?"

"Yummy." Margot glanced at Beau, who was already on the move.

As he passed her table, he pointed to her drink. "Skim decaf latte or vanilla chai?"

Stunned that he knew what she ordered each day, she could only gape. It took a full ten seconds to get her wits about her. "No, no. I'm fine. I'm good."

"That one's gone cold by now." He pointed to her mug as he joined the line.

"How does he know that?" She said it to herself, but apparently, it was loud enough for him to hear.

"It's got the same lipstick stain on the rim as when I left to go pick up Jess." It was his turn in line, so he placed his order.

Wait a minute. "How would you know?"

Jessa rolled her eyes. "Oh, my dad's a total charmer."

Disappointment slammed her. She didn't realize how much her little crush had done to lift her spirits until it crashed and burned. Playboys were so not her thing. "I don't like charming men." She said it loud enough to turn heads from other tables, but Beau just grinned.

Now, she felt like an idiot. She really needed to focus on her work and not on some dude passing through Merry Falls. God, she'd actually thought he was vulnerable, that their souls were reaching out to each other. She closed her eyes to steep in her embarrassment.

Get a life, girl. He's a stranger passing through, and he noticed the lonely woman who kept checking him out. Maybe he was looking for a hookup, something to do when he wasn't with his daughter.

Well, you're barking up the wrong tree, buddy. She'd never had a hookup in her life. It just wasn't her thing. Mostly, because she got too emotionally involved.

"Women love him," Jessa said. "All growing up, my friends wanted to come to my house—and believe me, I know it was because of my dad because I grew up in the boonies. And their moms." She rolled her eyes. "When they dropped their kids off, they'd always come inside, hoping to see him. They all tried to out-flirt each other at my volleyball games."

"A real heartbreaker, huh?"

"No, it's not that. Honestly, he's oblivious to all the attention. He's an engineer, you know? Always lost in his own thoughts. Once, I kept trying to ask his advice about this guy I was dating, and he wasn't answering. I go, 'Dad. *Dad.*' And he, like, jerks to attention, and I said, 'I'm talking to you. What are you *doing*?' He goes, 'Thinking deep thoughts.' I cracked up because it's so true. He's not the guy who's wondering what he's going to have for dinner or what kind of plans he's got for the weekend. He's thinking about embedding sensors and optimizing material flow. But since he doesn't talk about that stuff, you just think he's this mysterious guy. My friend said it best. She said, 'Every woman wants to be the one he notices.' Of course, it doesn't hurt that he's rich. And handsome."

"I don't like handsome men." Margot practically shouted it, and when he and his daughter laughed, she had to smile at her outburst. Okay, fine. Maybe he wasn't a playboy, and maybe he wasn't hitting on her, but she didn't want to be like those other women, drawn to a handsome, mysterious man who didn't talk much.

Because red flag: mysterious only means he doesn't communicate.

Which his daughter just said is the case.

"I'm the same way," Jessa said. "I watched my mom and my sister date all the gorgeous men with big muscles, but they always wound up getting hurt. And I mean, you can't get more perfect than my mom and sister. They're beautiful, tall, fun, smart—super successful. If *they* could get cheated on, then I don't stand a chance. I have no interest in going down that same path."

"I don't know if it works like that." Was Beau a cheater? If so... *Whoa.* She'd misread him entirely. "My ex cheated on me, and it didn't have anything to do with his looks or muscles." She waved her hand. "I've got a whole theory about it, but you don't need to hear it when you're hanging out with your dad for Christmas."

"No, actually, I want to hear it."

"Are you sure? It's Christmas. We're supposed to be wrapping presents and drinking egg nog."

"I hate egg nog."

"Yeah, me, too." Though she'd made it every year for their annual tree trimming.

"So, come on. Tell me."

"Okay, well, keep in mind, I'm in no way blaming your sister or mom for men cheating on them—I've never even met them—but I think we're drawn to people based on our childhood wounds."

Jessa set her chin on her palm. "Explain."

Margot loved this girl's intensity. "Let me put it this way. Did your mom and sister have trust issues? Daddy issues?"

"Yes. Absolutely. My dad was hardly involved in my sister's life, and my grandfather was a real piece of work."

"Right, so see, if your mom couldn't get her dad's attention, then maybe she went after men with a similar nature, trying to get from them what she couldn't get from her dad."

"That makes sense."

"And the important piece in this theory of mine is that we shouldn't be looking at the men who cheat on us. We should be looking at ourselves."

"So, if we understand how we're wired, we can stop going after the kind of man who'd cheat?"

"Exactly. Instead of being bitter and deciding all good-looking men are bad, it's a better use of our time to look inside ourselves and make the kinds of changes that will enable us to find good, healthy relationships."

Beau set down his daughter's cocoa and scone.

"Thanks, Dad."

Oh, God. Had she just gone on a tear with this lovely young woman?

Had she blamed women she'd never met for the actions of their boyfriends and maybe him—the ex-husband?

She noticed Beau hadn't gotten her a drink, and she didn't blame him. He probably wanted to whisk his daughter away from the crazy lady.

Clearly, I'm not fit for social interaction just yet.

Go back to your room!

But instead of sitting down, he returned to the counter and got two more mugs, setting the vanilla chai latte in front of her. She did a double take when she saw the foam. Instead of the usual leaf, there was a heart.

Had he asked for that?

No way. *You're ridiculous.*

The moment he sat down and dragged his chair closer to the table, Jessa said, "Dad, she says it's your fault Mom's a gold digger."

Embarrassment sent a wave of heat through her body, burning her cheeks. "No, I didn't. That's not what I said at all."

But he threw his head back and laughed.

"In my defense, I've only recently emerged from my cave after a divorce. And, obviously, I should crawl right back in." Maybe this was why Aunt Lucy didn't want her help. She could see the cracks and fissures, smell the sulfur leaking out. "I'll leave you two alone now."

"No, no. I want to know what you said." His big hands cupped the mug, and he settled in for the conversation.

"I promise it had nothing to do with you and your wife—"

"Ex-wife."

She nodded. "It was more the lesson I learned from my

own experience. I'm just saying if I spend my life trying to figure out why my ex cheated, I'll be stuck as a victim. Obviously, we can't help doing a forensics on our relationships, but since we can't get into other people's heads, we might as well turn all that energy into figuring out our part in how it failed."

"So, it's our fault for being attracted to someone who cheats on us? Is that what I heard?" He asked the question genuinely.

A phone pinged, and his daughter read her screen. "Oh, okay. Dad, can I go up to your room for a few minutes? My advisor needs to go over a few things."

"Sure." He dug the old-fashioned key out of his pocket. "Here."

"Thanks." She grabbed her backpack and took off for the grand staircase.

Leaving Margot alone with the handsome stranger who might or might not be a cheating playboy. "I'm so sorry. You're here to spend time with your daughter for the holidays, and I'm fire-hosing you with my self-reflection."

"I'm actually interested in your theory."

"Oh, man. It might not be anything more than the ravings of a woman spending her very first Christmas alone."

"You sound pretty smart to me."

Two things. One, he didn't look at her with pity when she'd blurted out her sad story. Bonus points for that. (*Also, note to self: shut up*). And two, he'd kindly complimented her to ease the embarrassment of her outburst.

But he was waiting patiently for her to go on, so she figured she might as well make an attempt at sounding rational. "The first six months after finding out about the betrayal was a total roller coaster. At first, I was scared. I'm talking paralyzed by fear. But then, of course, anger set in. It was just so unfair. I'd been a good wife. I'd catered to his every need…" She pressed her lips together. He didn't need to hear the whole tirade. "Finally, I made the conscious decision to stop thinking about him at all. Because it was over. He'd shown me his true character, and that was that. The only thing I could control was my future, and if I ever wanted to fall in love again, if I wanted to be happy, I needed to figure out who I am in a relationship."

"That's smart."

"Because guess what? He never asked me to make him the center of my universe. It was my choice. I gave up my work to raise my kids. I gave it up a second time to support us when his career went sideways. All the choices are on me, so I can't be angry with him—"

"You can. You can absolutely be angry with him."

"You're right. I can. But I don't want to live like that. I don't want to be a victim, so, I decided I could either fume and seethe and plot revenge the rest of my life, or I could clear out all the negativity and just forge ahead with this new life." She smiled. "And make it sensational."

"I like that a lot."

"I swear I didn't say you're the reason your wife's—"

"Ex-wife." He shifted in his seat.

It seemed important to him that she hear it. "I'm sorry. Your ex-wife."

"But you're exactly right. I knew she was interested in a certain lifestyle from the start. I had a tough major in college, which meant I didn't have a lot of time to party. But when I did catch up with my friends at a nearby bar, she was there. Everyone warned me she wanted to marry an engineer, but I didn't care. Settling down wasn't even on my radar. But here was this fun and sexy woman who wanted to have a good time." His cheeks colored. "I know that makes me sound like an asshole, but I made it clear I wasn't looking for anything serious. I never led her on."

"I believe you. It sounds like you both wanted different things from the relationship."

"I wasn't looking for one at all. Not only didn't I have time, but I had a plan. But then, of course, she got pregnant. She said if we didn't marry, she'd move back home to her family in Michigan, and I didn't want my child to be raised in another state without me. So, yes, to your point, I knew who she was from the start."

"If I'm being too nosy, you can tell me to stuff it, but can I ask what your parents are like?"

He chuckled. "To be honest, I prefer this conversation to the weather, which is all anyone around here can talk about."

"Right? It's December, people. There's going to be snow."

"Yeah, exactly. My mom left when I was a kid, but my dad and stepmom are great."

"Were you close to your mom?"

"Uh, no. Not at all. It's hard to get close to someone who doesn't want to be there. My dad liked to say she had a 'restless soul.' I guess she wanted something that wasn't me or my dad or the town we lived in."

"And did you try to fix her?"

"I don't know about fixing her, but I did try to be good. I tried to make her smile." His gaze wandered across the lobby to the giant Christmas tree with twinkling lights.

"I guess I didn't know what to do to make her want to stay."

"To be *worthy* of her staying."

He swung back to look her right in the eyes. "Yes, that's right. I wanted to be good enough for her."

"So, I know you married your ex because she was pregnant, but is there any part of you that chose her because of what you were trying to fix with your mother? Like, maybe deep down, you thought you could find a way to keep an unhappy woman from leaving her family?"

Beau drained his mug, then stared into it. She couldn't explain how much she liked that he was giving serious consideration to her question. Her ex had only done it when she'd forced him. He was always doing ten things at once. And all ten ranked higher on his list of priorities than random talks with his wife.

This man took the time to sit and talk to her.

"I can see that. I did try very hard to make her happy, but she wanted the one thing I couldn't give her, so it was destined to fail."

It's almost Christmas, and I'm making him talk about depressing things. She smacked the table with her palm. "Speaking of fails, how about me as a conversationalist?"

He cracked a tiny smile. "My daughter says I'm an introvert, which means I'll take talking about this stuff over which ride-on lawn mower to buy. I don't have a lot of friends because most of the guys I know want to watch football on Sunday, and I'd rather tinker in my garage, so I promise, you're doing all right."

She was a firm believer in listening to what people told her. "Well, good. And I'm the same way."

42

He held her gaze for a long beat, but it wasn't uncomfortable. It was electric. It was an acknowledgment that they were connecting, and it was by far the most thrilling moment she'd had in years.

He broke the moment by reaching for his mug, tipping it, and finding it empty. "Yeah, so, my marriage wasn't good, and the only reason I stayed as long as I did is that I didn't want to be a part-time dad. But I think you're saying I didn't have to date her. I could've dated any other woman in that bar, but I chose her. Even though I knew she wanted something I couldn't give her."

Warmth spread through her. He'd listened. He'd heard her. It was such a simple thing, but it filled her with affection for this man she barely knew. "Yes. That's what I'm saying."

"And actually, if you want to know the truth, my ex gives the impression she's friendly and fun, but she's actually detached. Just like my mom. So, there you go. The little boy in me recognized his mom's attributes." Awareness lit his handsome features. "Damn."

"What?"

"My ex will tell anyone who'll listen I cared more about the mine than my own family. That I forced her to live in that 'crappy town' where she had no friends and couldn't do anything. So, there you go. My mom was the same way. I was just a kid, but I can remember feeling defensive of my dad. He was a good guy, and the idea that what he had to offer wasn't enough really messed with my head."

"Do you live so far from town that she couldn't meet friends for coffee?" She leaned back in her chair. "How far are we talking, Hermit Man?"

He laughed. "I'm not a hermit, trust me. And we're less than fifteen miles from town. Her real issue was that I didn't have money. It's why she left me."

"Wait, I thought Jessa said you were wealthy."

"Now, I am. I didn't get there quickly enough for her. But she found her own way to get rich, and she's still not happy, so there you go. Money doesn't buy happiness."

She thought of that tab she kept clicking on her laptop. "But it sure does buy peace of mind." One day, it would be nice not to check her sales five times a day.

"I can't argue that."

"Was it hard? Her leaving?"

"I don't talk about this much because it doesn't make me look good—"

"But since we're never going to see each other again..." She hunched a shoulder. "I'm safe."

"There's nothing safe about you at all."

She didn't know what he meant by that, but her body thrilled to the way his voice went deeper, more gravelly, when he said it.

"But yes, it was hard. She took my kids away from me. I had to share them, which meant duplicate bedrooms, sets of clothes, and toothbrushes. That pissed me off. On the other hand, it was a relief. Coming home from work was stressful. There's nothing worse than walking in the door knowing your wife is angry and ready to unleash on you."

She'd never talked so openly with a total stranger, and she loved it. It felt like a gift.

And it's probably the only one I'll get this Christmas, so I'm going to take it.

She dove right in, asking the hard question. The kind she'd never get to ask her ex.

"Were her feelings valid? Were you not giving her enough?"

"This is a little more involved." He gestured to the empty chair next to her.

Oh. He wanted to sit closer. "Please." She closed her laptop and slid it into the tote bag, freeing space at her table.

She'd been so lonely, so starved for connection.

Who would have imagined it would come in the form of this gorgeous, blue-eyed stranger?

Chapter Three

CAROLS PLAYED ON SPEAKERS THROUGHOUT THE HOTEL, and children chased each other around the Christmas tree, its limbs sagging with ornaments and gold garlands. Clusters of guests chatted, their shopping bags stuffed with shiny wrapped presents.

But for all the activity swirling around her, all the holiday excitement glittering in the air, Margot didn't want to be anywhere but with him.

Her pulse quickened when he took his empty mug and joined her. "So, like I said, I met Courtney my senior year at Colorado School of Mines, and she was twenty minutes away at the University of Denver. I didn't have a lot of time to date—"

"And see, she saw *your* red flag from the beginning, and yet she continued to pursue you."

He stilled for a moment before nodding. "There you go again." He shook his head in wonder. "Soundly proving your theory. You sure you're not a scientist?"

"Ha. I wish that was the reason." Instead of a traumatic divorce.

"That was her issue with me from the start. I wasn't calling her enough. I wasn't prioritizing her." He pressed both palms onto the table. "That first night we met, I told her my plans. She wanted to know what I was going to do after I graduated, and I told her everything."

"Just out of curiosity, what were your plans?"

His smile told her how much he liked this story. "Freshman year, I took Introductory Mining, and the professor's first lecture was about gold prospectors. He talked about lore, places around the world where people believe the mother lode of gold still exists. And this one place in Wyoming—that's where I'm from—caught my interest. Something about it rang a bell at the back of my mind. I called up my dad and asked him why it sounded familiar. And he said, 'That's our family.'"

"Really? That's fascinating."

"Yeah, so, apparently Sam and Joseph Gentry were part of a group of prospectors who found gold on a mountain outside the town of Calamity. They built a cabin for all six of them to live in while they worked, but they got attacked, and the brothers were the only ones to escape. They hiked into town and showed off their gold in a saloon—which is how the word spread about the cabin. Over the years, people tried to find it, but no one did, and it wound up becoming part of the gold rush lore."

"What happened to the brothers?"

"They formed another prospecting party, but they got killed on their way back."

"I can't believe that's your family story. And in all these years, no one found the cabin?"

"Not until me. After talking to my dad, I became obsessed with finding it. Courtney knew that, right from the start."

Really, it didn't surprise her that he was so willing to talk about his marriage. Even in the most amicable divorces, spouses still needed to process an upheaval of that magnitude. "But she was stuck on the idea of marrying an engineer and having a certain kind of lifestyle."

"Yeah, and I did get the job she wanted right out of college. It paid well, but I was saving every penny to buy the land, so she didn't get the big house and nice car. She also didn't understand why we couldn't live in the city while I was saving money, but I needed to be on the mountain so I could find the mine. I spent every lunch hour and Saturday morning at the county courthouse, pouring over tax assessor records and mining claims. After I got a sense of where the cabin might be, I spent my free time walking the land."

"And you had a baby by then?"

Lowering his chin, he nodded.

"Your ex must've loved that." Margot could relate. Her husband had worked seven days a week and bailed on most family vacations. She'd never minded, though. She'd understood the requirements of his job and wanted to spend time with her kids.

"I was preoccupied."

She could read the shame all over his handsome features, and she didn't like it. "Were you maybe a little resentful, too?"

"Resentful?"

"Well, you had to marry a woman you didn't love."

"It was my choice. I didn't have to marry her." He glanced over his shoulder. Maybe checking for his daughter? "We'd only been dating a few months, and since we were graduating, I figured we'd go our separate ways. So, when she came to me with a pregnancy test, I was knocked sideways. So, I guess you're right. It's fair to say I was resentful. Unfairly so." His features relaxed, almost as though he was relieved to say it out loud. "But still."

"I can understand that."

"I've never brought it up before because of my kids. I didn't want them to get any sense of negativity from me. But damn, it feels good to say it." He broke out in a grin. "So, have I convinced you it's not my fault my wife's a gold digger?"

Margot laughed. "One-hundred-percent. And hopefully, now that you see why you were attracted to her, you won't find yourself in a similar predicament the next time around."

He glanced down at his empty mug. "I don't think there's going to be another marriage. I'm not really cut out for romantic love."

Now, why would he say that? "Just because your first one failed?"

"No. Because I've never felt what my daughter calls 'wild love.'"

"Maybe you just haven't met the right woman yet."

He studied her. It went on long enough for her to grow worried.

Oh, no. Did he think she was implying *she* was the right woman? Flustered, she wanted to explain herself. She meant to say that kind of love didn't come along all that often, and since he'd married right out of college, maybe he hadn't been open to it.

But before she could say anything, he reached out. Her fingers were curled around the handle of her mug, and he brushed them with the back of his hand. It sent a hot current up her arm.

Both of their gazes locked on the point of contact.

Never in her life had a single touch made her sizzle.

What's going on here?

Desire awakened in a slow churn that softened her. For so long, she'd been in fight mode. Fighting to keep a roof over their heads, to keep her ex from sinking into despair, to build her business so she could support herself…

But there was something about this man…she couldn't explain it. A familiarity, a recognition. She could see beneath his good looks, the broad, muscular shoulders hidden by the heather gray Henley T-shirt, and the fancy, shiny watch on his wrist. All the way down to his core of strength, of calm, and she felt a trust that made no sense.

It was so weirdly easy between them. Yes, she was attracted to him, but there was a connection happening on a whole other level, one that didn't exist in the physical world. One where their souls recognized each other.

And it didn't scare her. Not one bit. Oddly, it energized her.

"I've never had that spark with anyone." He stuttered out a laugh, clearly uncomfortable. "But now, for the first time, I think I know what—"

A metal key clattered onto the table, and Jessa stood behind her dad. "Sorry to do this but can you take me back to school? I got the results I needed from the lab and have to analyze them. It's going to take a while."

"Yeah. Of course." Beau stood up and pocketed his key.

The idea of losing him sent a rush of panic through her. *Don't leave.*

Finish what you were going to say. For the first time what? Does it have to do with me?

She couldn't bear to lose this precious moment of openness, of trust...of connection. And his lingering gaze only reinforced that it was mutual. But really, what did it matter what they felt? This man was leaving. She had no other choice but to let him go.

Smiling, she waved them off, pulled her laptop out of her bag, and set it on the table.

She went through the motions like she was unaffected. But it was all forced. She couldn't concentrate. Not when every cell in her body strained to go with him.

Focus. Her finger hovered over the start button, determined not to look for him. Maybe if she were a stronger woman, she wouldn't have done it. But she wasn't. This man had tipped her world over and left her spinning. She couldn't stop herself from glancing over.

Walking alongside his daughter, he headed for the door. His worn jeans cupped his ass, accentuating the tight round globes, and his thick, dark hair hit the collar of his shirt.

He turned back to look at her, his expression wistful, his eyes full of longing. He gave her a hint of a smile.

And then, he was gone.

Dammit all to hell. For eight months, she'd run through the gamut of emotions. From being scared about her future to healing and finding her strength.

Now, she had something new to add.

Because she'd never felt more acutely alone than she did in that moment.

For the first time in her life, she had a true connection.

To a man she'd never see again.

As Beau drove through the historic town of Merry Falls, he took in the pine garlands wrapped around streetlamps, the festive wreaths with bright red ribbons adorning the businesses, and the shoppers tromping along snowy sidewalks to buy last-minute presents.

"I just wish she'd come home, you know?" Jessa asked. "I get it. I get she doesn't want the press camped out in front of our house. But it's Christmas. She should be with family."

"She should. But she's worried about Colt." He would never forget the little boy's terrified expression when the fans crowded around his famous aunt or the SUV that jammed on its brakes not a foot in front of her while she'd carried him across the street. It was her first time in the public eye since the band had broken up, and it hadn't gone well.

His daughter couldn't get away from the media. Not only were they speculating about her career, but they treated the bandmates who'd betrayed her the way they did Bigfoot, posting blurry sightings in random places like a health food store in Malibu and at a campsite in Glacier, Montana.

His daughter had once been on top of the world, cocooned by a team who'd sheltered and looked out for her, but it all turned out to be a lie. He didn't blame her for needing to regroup.

"It's too much. Her best friend, her boyfriend, *and* her mom? How's she going to recover?" Jessa turned to her dad. "How could Mom do that to her own daughter?"

And here's where it always gets tricky. He couldn't badmouth his ex, but he also wouldn't make light of what she'd done. "I don't think she had bad intentions. I think she was inexperienced and got in over her head. She was trying to manage Lori's career and signing the only contracts she could get at the time." But as it grew, the opportunities got better, and his ex wound up breaking the early contracts they no longer needed.

"I just wish I knew how she was doing. When I text her, she says she's fine or whatever, but I want to know the truth." Jessa turned her gaze out the window. Snowflakes drifted down from the sky, jerking with the gusts of wind. "Do you think she's writing new material? I mean, what's she doing all alone in that cabin?"

"She says she's blocked, so I think she's just figuring things out." Which made him think about Margot, how she'd hidden from the world for months, struggled with a whole range of emotions, only to emerge strong and healed.

Lorelei would come out of her cave empowered, too. She'd find a new direction, he was sure of it.

But he understood Jessa's concerns. Since retreating, his oldest had given him similar responses to his text messages: *I'm okay. I'm actually enjoying the time off.*

Was she though? He didn't know. "I'd do anything to help her, but she doesn't want it."

"But that's the thing." Jessa's tone turned anxious. "She doesn't need our help. She needs our love. She needs us to make her grilled cheese sandwiches and share a blanket with her on movie night and…and…play family games until she's laughing so hard her stomach hurts."

She was right about that. But what could he do? His girl was hurting, and there wasn't a damn thing he could do about it.

When they reached the university, he drove under the ivy-covered arch that read Whitney University, established 1842. He braked in front of her graduate housing dorm. "Here you go." He leaned over to give her a hug. "I love you, Jessie-girl."

"I love you, too, Dad." She reached for the door. "I like that woman in the lodge. Margot."

Her name rocketed through him.

What the hell was that?

His reactions to her made no sense. "She's nice, but don't go getting any ideas." Jessa would love to see him remarried. Or at least dating. "I'm leaving in the morning."

"I know, but it's too bad, right? The sparks were flyin', that's all I'm saying."

"Is it all you're saying, though?" He grinned at her.

"No, but I get it. Nothing can happen. It's just…she spends all her time at the lodge. Where's her family? I wonder who she's going to spend Christmas with. Do you think we should invite her to dinner with us?"

"If that's what you want, I can ask." He'd like more time with her, no doubt about that. While he'd told her his story, he hadn't gotten a chance to hear hers. And he wanted to. In fact, he was greedy for more, and he couldn't figure out why. But she only worked in the lobby for a few hours in the morning. By the time he got back to the lodge, she'd be gone. He might never find out more about her.

"I have to go, but ask her, okay?" Jessa got out of the car. "I'll see you tonight."

"Bye, doll."

After she closed the door, he watched her walk away. Of all his kids, she was the one who'd wanted to spend time with him. On the weekends, she'd crawl into his bed and snuggle with him. They baked cookies and muffins together. She'd sit on the sink while he shaved and talk about a movie she saw, a book she'd read, or something that had happened at school.

Lord, he loved that girl.

Before she reached her dorm, she turned back, motioning for him to lower the passenger-side window. She gave him a mischievous grin. "Don't forget to bring my present."

"Oh, you already got that. I sang karaoke with you, remember?"

"Yeah, but did you? Or did Margot? Hm, looks like your lady friend gave me something, but you...? Not so much. Good thing you've got one more shot to give it to me."

"The lodge has a gift shop. I'm sure I can find you something. Did you see those moose snow globes?"

"No way. Are you serious? That's what I got *you*." She laughed. "I know you, Dad. Whatever you got me, it's fabulous."

"Great. Now, the pressure's on." He pulled his phone out of the cup holder.

"What're you doing?"

"Seeing if I can buy you that pony you wanted when you were ten."

She cracked up, waving to him before heading inside the

building. The snow-covered campus was mostly empty. It had shut down for the holidays, and he hated knowing Jessa was alone.

Both of his girls were alone, but at least he'd had a few days with Jessa.

He needed to remind Lorelei he was there. Before heading back to the lodge, he texted her.

Beau: Hey, sweetheart. Thinking about you.

He pictured her in a cabin with no tree, no presents, no family breakfast. It made him want to track her down, haul her over his shoulder, and carry her to his house.

Beau: Come home for Christmas?

The moment Beau entered the lobby, his gaze went to the coffee bar. He'd known Margot wouldn't be there, so he shouldn't be this disappointed. Besides, even though Christmas was the day after tomorrow, he still had work to do.

And yet, instead of heading up the grand staircase to his room, he found himself wandering the hallways.

To find a woman he barely knew. And would never have the chance to know.

Nevertheless, there he was, checking the business center where an older man was printing out his boarding pass.

What the hell are you doing? Instead of chasing after some woman, he needed to check in with his son. A problem was brewing at the mine, and he needed to stay on top of it. Making an abrupt turn, he marched back toward the lobby and the stairs.

But he got a whiff of cinnamon and baking bread and thought she might be in the restaurant prepping for dinner. He'd take a quick look. As he peered into the kitchen, ten sets of eyes landed on him. All of them held the same expression. *What're you doing here?*

"Sorry." He quickly shut the door, utterly confused by his uncharacteristic behavior.

That was it. To avoid any more temptation, he headed down the long hallway at the back of the hotel. He'd take the smaller set of stairs where he had the least likely chance of running into her.

As he hit the first step, he heard a familiar voice.

"You sure I can't help?" It sounded like the owner, Lucy Gibbins. "Looks like you've got a lot of work here."

"Oh, this is the easy part." *Margot.*

An eruption in his chest sent a vibration through his bones. And his reaction to something as basic as her *voice* was just so damn unsettling.

What is going on with me?

"Thank you, though," Margot said. "As soon as I finish, I'll salt the back patio. The snow's already starting to come down."

"I don't know if you've got wool stuffed in your ears or if you're just stubborn as an old mule, but I have people on my payroll who're paid to salt, shovel, and trim my walkways. Now, if I see you out there, I'm going to kick you out on your ass."

"Oh, Aunt Lucy. You wouldn't do that. I have nowhere to go."

Even though she was teasing, his heart squeezed hard. Because he suspected it was the truth. Now, he was getting a clearer picture. She lived here, and to pay her aunt back, she pitched in wherever she could. And given Ms. Gibbins's tone, it seemed the older woman felt bad for her niece's predicament and wanted her back on her feet as soon as possible.

But how had Margot wound up with no place to live? Had she gotten nothing from her cheating husband?

"Well, what're you doing with all the money you're making?" Ms. Gibbins asked. "Don't tell me you're buying fancy handbags."

"Please. You know I can't afford those. At least not until I complete my Louis Vuitton luggage collection. I'm saving up for the rolling trunk."

"Oh, Lord. I come in here to see if I can lend a hand, and what do I get in return? Your sass. Maybe I will make you shovel the driveway." Ms. Gibbins stepped out of the room.

Shit. Fortunately, she kept her back to him. Maybe he could sneak up the stairs before she noticed.

"And don't forget," the older woman said. "We're baking cookies in half an hour. That, you can help me with."

He liked that Margot had an ally in this fierce woman, but when the lodge owner turned around, she spotted him. "Can I help you?"

Oh, Christ.

Chapter Four

Ms. Gibbins gave him a challenging look, and what could he say? He was caught eavesdropping. So, he gave her the truth. "I was looking for Margot."

Not me sounding like my son when he was ten and snuck an injured squirrel into his bedroom in a shoebox.

Her eyebrows shot up. "My Margot?"

"Yes."

The older woman's scrutiny had him running a hand through his hair because it probably still had snowflakes in it. For whatever reason, he wanted her to find him worthy of her niece's time.

After a painfully tense moment where he was ready to concede that, yes, he was irrationally interested in a woman he'd just met and all he wanted was a little more time to get to know her better, Ms. Gibbins gave him a curt nod. Then, she tipped her head toward the door she'd just exited. "She could use a hand." She arched one brow as though asking if he was the kind of man who'd spend his time helping out a stranger.

He waved his hands. "Ready and willing." He smiled, then dipped inside the room like he'd just convinced a cop to let him off the hook for speeding through a school zone. He found Margot in the middle of a conference table strewn with boxes, bubble wrap, and packing tape. "Wow. Your aunt wasn't kidding."

Her surprise at seeing him quickly flattened into confusion. "My aunt? Oh, don't tell me she asked you to come in here and help me. You're on vacation."

Oddly, there was nothing he'd rather do than be with her. He picked up a glass globe. The color was a rich blue that made him think of the depths of the ocean. "What is this?"

"That's one of my Christmas ornaments." She gave him a soft smile as she taped a box closed. "I sell off my remaining inventory to holiday stores." Her hands were full, so her gaze traveled the length of the table. "I know it looks like I've got a lot left over, but I made a ton extra just for this reason. I actually did really well this year. Thank God."

On closer inspection, he could see she'd hand-painted the glass. "I can see why." Some were basic snowmen, jolly Santas, and Christmas trees, but others were unique. Dark blue backgrounds with white sketches of a pine forest, or deep green with smoke curling out of a cabin. "These are beautiful."

"Thank you. I was an art major here at Whitney."

"Really?" He stood there awkwardly, embarrassed because he'd hunted her down. Not that she knew about it. But her aunt did. And it made him feel like a teenager with a crush. "They have one of the best programs in the country."

"They do."

"I know that because Jessa was originally looking at it." He set the ornament down and assessed the work. "What can I help with?"

"Nothing. I got it." She moved quickly and assuredly, and since the ornaments were glass, he didn't want to damage anything. "She switched to science?"

"Yep. Freshman year, she realized she liked art but didn't want it as a career." But if he couldn't help her out, what was his reason to stay?

"How does she feel about science?"

"She loves what she does. Especially now that she's found a way to work at the mine."

"That's nice that you'll have two of your kids working with you."

There it was again. That dip in her mood. "She'll have to get work experience first. It's one thing to read articles and do research and another to apply it."

"That makes sense." She set the box on the floor with the others and started packing another one.

"Did I say something?"

"No, why?"

"Last night in the restaurant, when we were talking about Jessa's major, your mood changed. And it happened again just now. What happened? What did I say?"

She lowered her wrists to the edge of the table and stared at him.

This was new territory for him, caring about someone enough to ask about her mood shift, so he wondered if he'd crossed a line. Maybe she didn't feel as comfortable with him as he did with her. He didn't know. But she wasn't answering. "I'm sorry. I don't have the best social skills." He forced a laugh. "Too much time analyzing data." He shifted uncomfortably. "Are you sure I can't help you? There must be something I can do."

"No, that's okay. I appreciate the offer, but I've got a system. I learned how to package after the first batch of angry emails from buyers who got nothing but shards of glass." She grimaced. "That was bad."

"Okay, well, then… I guess I'll leave you to it." Weirdly, though, he didn't go. He felt rooted to the spot. There was something soothing about the way she tucked the globe into a bubble pouch and then gently inserted it into the foam-encased box.

Everything she did was careful, thoughtful, and he really fucking liked that.

The tension grew, expanded, and neither seemed able to look away from the other.

Finally, she broke it. "You didn't do anything wrong." She blinked a few times, then went back to work. "I'm just surprised you noticed. And here I thought I was so slick."

"Jessa mentioned it, too."

"She did, huh? That's not good for a server. Or a barista. Better work on that."

"You don't have to work on anything." *You're perfect as you are.* He perched his ass on the edge of the table. "Jessa's the youngest, so she watched all the family dynamics at play. She's learned to read expressions." He didn't mention that his daughter never knew where she stood with her mom. Courtney could turn on her charm when she wanted something, but when she didn't need someone, she'd cast them aside. That person ceased to exist. Not easy for a child.

Hang on. Hadn't his mother been just like that? He was pretty sure she had. "All I know is I said something to bring you down, and I'm sorry for that."

"You didn't. You were talking about your kids and helping them find their passions, and I…" She let out a frustrated sigh. "My kids didn't have that chance."

· He felt like he was hacking away at a block of ice with a toothpick, desperate to form a clear picture of this woman. "Where are they now?" *And why aren't you with them for the holidays?*

"My daughter's in Hawaii, and my son's in South Korea."

"Well, that sucks. Are they in the military?"

"My son is. Marines."

That would explain why she couldn't be with him. "And your daughter?" He shouldn't be so pushy. Normally, he'd never ask something so personal. "I'm sorry. You don't have to answer that."

She set the box on the table. "No, it's only fair. You told me your sad story. I can tell you mine."

"Well, now, as much as I'd like to learn more about you, there's no tit for tat here. Talking to you helped me understand some things about my marriage, and I get the sense you've already done that work, so if you don't want to go there, I can just sit here and be with you." Did that sound creepy? He cleared his throat. "I like hanging out with you."

She pressed her hand over his. "I like hanging out with you, too. And I don't mind telling you what happened. My ex-husband was a coal trader. Right when my daughter went off to college, the industry tanked, and he lost his job. She didn't want to take out student loans because she didn't think she'd ever be able to pay them back with the kind of career she wanted. So, she moved to Hawaii and got a job in hospitality."

"Is she happy there?"

"Deliriously. She loves everything about her life. In fact, she's getting married in a few weeks." The skin around her eyes pinched, and sadness flashed across her features, but she shook it off. "And Owen, my son, he was a junior in high school when it happened. We thought he'd apply for scholarships or go to a community college. He'd wanted to be a veterinarian his whole life. When he was little, the only stories he wanted me to read him were the ones with animals in them. He even volunteered in a shelter outside of town." She gave a wistful twist of her head. "But he surprised the hell out of us by enlisting."

"That's a tough one. How's he doing?"

"It's hard to tell with him, but I think he's all right. He's twenty-three now, so his contract is up. I'm hoping he'll come home." She reached for the box, and he was pretty sure it was to cover her sadness. She had to be wondering where her son would go. He certainly wouldn't live at the lodge with her.

He pulled out a chair and sat beside her. He wanted to unlock the stories she kept hidden away, *help* her, but it wasn't his place. "And that's why you're here? Because your kids are away?"

"I'm here because I don't have a home anymore."

"I'm sorry, Margot." He didn't even know the story, and he could feel this woman's loss.

"It's okay. It's just every time I think I'm good, that I've healed, something comes along that brings it to the surface all over again. At some point, the well has to run dry, right? It's not bottomless."

"No, I don't think it is. I don't know all you've gone through, but I think you're doing great."

"Well, thank you for that." She inserted the ornament into the bubble pouch. "My aunt's been my saving grace. I don't know how I would've survived without her." Her features went soft with gratitude. "You know what got me out of my cave? I'd been here maybe five months or so, and I hadn't really left my room. I was working in my room all day, growing my business. It was the only thing I could focus on. I couldn't read, couldn't watch TV, couldn't be around people. One day, my aunt came in and sized me up."

"Unshowered, no bra, a nightstand full of empty cookie sleeves?"

She grinned at him with an expression that said, *Where did that come from?*

"Jessa had a terrible breakup. She was heartbroken for months."

"Oh, forget about my heart. My ex broke my trust, which is so much harder to repair. But no, I was able to shower and wear a bra." She cupped her breasts and gave them a shake. "My boobies are my one form of vanity." Releasing them, she laughed. "I actually do pushups every day to keep them perky."

Sensation burst inside him, releasing a wave of lust so powerful he went hot and hard. He wanted to fill his hands with her plump breasts, feel the heavy weight of them. He wanted her beaded nipples on his tongue.

Holy shit.

He didn't recognize himself. He'd seen plenty of women naked. He'd had lots of sex in his lifetime, but no one had ever excited him the way she did from just a jiggle of her tits.

"Anyhow, no, it wasn't the empty sleeve of Girl Scout cookies that worried her. I think she saw my fear. She sat on the edge of my bed and said, 'You're in a terrible season, my sweet girl, and I hate that for you.' And then, she got up to leave and said, 'I can't wait to see you shine in the next one.' And the idea that this inescapable pain was just a *season*. That it would be gone and replaced by something new…that there was something better up ahead…it literally changed my whole mindset."

"That's a great way to look at it. Where's your ex now?" He watched her expression, looking for traces of hurt and anger, wondering if she'd really let him go.

"He's living his best life with Petra." Nope. Not a single trace of either.

He settled back in his chair. "Can I ask what happened?"

"Sure. I'll give you the quick and dirty version. My ex was a master of the universe. He went to Harvard Business School, got a job on Wall Street at an investment bank, and then clawed his way to the top of a very competitive industry."

"What kind of dad was he?"

She cocked her head. "What a great question. I love that. You weren't wondering how big our house was or what kind of cars we drove. You wanted to know how he managed a successful career with raising his kids." Her hand landed on his arm and squeezed. "You're such a surprise."

The hard-on he'd tried so hard to suppress came roaring back. Just from a simple touch.

Fuck my life.

When she reached for the tape, letting him go, he looked at his arm, marveling at how much he missed the warmth of her touch.

"He was a good dad. I mean, he obviously worked long hours, but when he was home, he was there for the kids. No matter what he did to me, I'll never speak badly about how he parented."

"You're a good person, Margot."

Her cheeks turned pink, and all it did was make him want to kiss her. "Oh, well, thanks. Anyhow, over his career, he'd lost his job four times. The first three, he was young, and the market was sure to rebound, so he was able to jump back in. The last time, though, it had shriveled up, and he never recovered. He did the right thing, though. He put the house on the market, sold the cars, and we stopped spending."

"So, you're living off savings?"

"Ha. No. He blew through that on bad investments. People stopped returning his calls. He tried putting up his consultant shingle—like every other unemployed titan—but no one wanted his advice or experience. He had lots of meetings and lunches, golfed with his old colleagues, anything to stay in the game. And when they mentioned sure-thing deals in their portfolios, he'd want a piece of the action. He was desperate for something to take off."

"And nothing did?"

She shook her head. "We lost everything. I was a stay-at-home mom, so I didn't have much to offer the workplace, but I got a job as a barista, and we found a small apartment in another town."

"You lived off your income?"

"Yes. It wasn't much, but—"

"No." He placed his hand over hers. "It was everything. Did he do it, too, though? Get a job like that?" Because it sure sounded like she took over paying the bills while he tried to reclaim his glory days.

"No. He couldn't bear the idea of serving someone he'd once worked with. And that was okay. I understood that. He never stopped trying to get a job, and he always came up with business ideas—good ones—but for whatever reason, nothing panned out. Until Petra."

Ah, fuck.

"She found his résumé online and reached out to him. He was so excited at first, imagining himself as a CEO of her new company, but she was offering potential, not income. Still, he ran with it. He's a very determined man, and he was sure he'd get her the venture capital money she needed. He went from long hours napping on the couch to going back to the gym and being excited about his future."

"If you tell me he cheated on you with Petra, I'm going to flip this table."

"Why, because it's such a cliché?"

"No, because he got you into this situation and then abandoned you."

"That's exactly what he did." She said it firmly, resolutely. "And it knocked me on my ass. In my mind, we were in this together. No matter what hardship came our way, we could handle anything because we had each other."

He got a tug in his gut because he'd always wanted that kind of partnership. He'd had anything but that with his ex.

"I never gave up hope that we'd get back on track, but all he could see was doom and gloom. Living on my salary wasn't sustainable in our old age, so he believed we were in a death spiral." She ran her finger along the length of tape, securing it down.

His body could barely contain the rage billowing up from his core. The idea that this man would toss aside his wife because he couldn't rebound…that he'd left her with no money, nothing. His hands curled into fists. He was going to lose his shit.

The only thing tethering him to his composure was that it was her story. *She's the one who lived through it.* She didn't need to deal with his emotions on top of her own.

When he looked at her, he saw determination and strength, and he admired her more than anyone he'd ever met.

"Those were his words, by the way. He said, 'We're in a death spiral, and I found an exit ramp. I hope you do, too.'" She curled her hand over his fist. "Thank you."

"For what?"

"For being outraged on my behalf."

Oh, he was that, all right. Her ex was the lowest form of humanity. "I have a lot I want to say."

"But?"

"But you don't need to hear it."

"I do, actually. The only person who knows the whole story is Aunt Lucy. Who else can I talk to? It's not like my kids need to hear me rant about it, and we fell out of touch with our friends when we moved. I'm pretty sure they thought failure was contagious. Not that I blame them, of course. It's no fun to talk about your trip to Bora Bora with someone who lives off canned tuna until she gets her next paycheck. So, please, don't hold back." She gestured for him to speak. "Let 'er rip."

As much as she needed to hear an outsider's perspective, she didn't need him blowing up. It wouldn't be fair to unleash his anger on her. So, he kept his tone even. "He got hit with some of the most stressful events in life. Job loss, a move... Couple that with the destruction of his ego..." When he found himself getting riled up, he reined it in. Because yeah, her ex had gone through hell, but what about his wife? She'd been there right alongside him. And guess fucking what? Not all women stayed through the tough times. Some of them bailed. Margot hadn't. "Some people can manage through that compounded disaster, and others can't."

She burst out laughing.

"What? What did I say?" He thought he'd been fair.

But that only made her laugh harder. "You're trying so hard to be rational and reasonable." Hand over her heart, she dragged in a breath. "You don't have to do that. You can say what you really feel. I *want* you to."

"Okay, well, good. Because your ex-husband's a piece of shit. He's *not* a master of the universe. He's a fraud. A master of the universe doesn't fall apart during tough times. It doesn't matter how much is stacked against him, he doesn't yield. Your ex is a candy-ass who happened to fall into a bed of clover and that made him think he was a genius. Anyone can be strong when things are going well, but a person's true character comes out in times of conflict. And your ex showed you his soft underbelly." He couldn't keep the disgust out of his voice. "Abandoning his wife for a fucking 'exit ramp' is unconscionable."

She lunged at him, wrapping her arms around his neck and pressing her lips to his cheek. "Thank you. I needed to hear that."

He was enveloped in her scent, could feel her heat and her lush curves, and his body went haywire. He pressed his palms flat on the table so he wouldn't reach for her. Because if he did, if he hugged her back, he would lose control.

Because he'd never wanted anyone the way he wanted her. Everything about her appealed to him and made him fucking yearn for something he couldn't have.

So, he was glad when she pulled back. Relieved, frankly. He was too far out of his comfort zone.

She glanced at her phone. "And now, it's time to make cookies."

"Okay." Still worked up by her closeness, he felt disoriented by the shift in conversation. "Cookies?"

"My aunt's all about traditions. The Christmas tree goes up the Sunday after Thanksgiving. The lights go on December first. The gingerbread houses come out a week later. And two days before Christmas, she bakes a gazillion Moravian cookies."

"Moravia? Wasn't that a country?"

"Yes. It's now part of the Czech Republic. In the seventeen hundreds, the Moravians came to the New World. They settled in Bethlehem, Pennsylvania and Winston-Salem. It's a tradition in North Carolina to make these cookies."

"Oh, okay." It was hard to switch gears, but he supposed

he'd taken enough of her time. And of course, he had work to do. He needed to touch base with his son.

After he left the room, she shut off the lights and locked the door.

"I'll see you later." But he wouldn't, would he? He'd take his daughter out to dinner, come home and pack, and then head to the airport in the morning. He watched her walk down the hallway.

It's your last chance.

Tell her.

"*You're* the master of the universe."

"What?" She whipped around, clearly confused. "No, I never had a career. The money I make now is—"

He stalked toward her. "It's not about money. It's about a person's character. Who they are at their core. And you're... indomitable." A couple passed them in the hallway, and he lowered his voice. "I admire the hell out of you."

Her eyes flooded with gratitude. "Thank you, Beau." She blinked back tears. "It's so nice to hear that. It's been really hard."

"Did you know that's the first time you said that? You talked about how tough it was for him to lose his job and house and fancy cars, but it sounds like you were too busy taking care of your husband to deal with the impact on you. Did he ever take care of you?"

"No," she whispered.

"Of course, you were blindsided when he left. It's your nature to stand by the people you care about. I would imagine the hardest part of this whole situation was having to reconcile the man you thought you'd married with the shithead he turned out to be."

Her bottom lip wobbled, and her beautiful features wrenched in sorrow. He had no choice but to pull her into his arms. She didn't even hesitate to lean against him, giving him all her weight, and he loved it. For a reason he didn't understand, he wanted her to know he was strong, that he could take it.

That I'm not like him.

He wanted to line up all her troubles and bowl them down one by one. He wanted to free her of the pain that suffocated her. *But guess what?* This formidable woman had already done that. She had her own business and wasn't wasting her energy seething about her ex.

His T-shirt dampened from her tears. He didn't know how to make her feel better. There were no platitudes for what she'd gone through. So, he just held her, gently rubbing her back.

Voices came from the other end of the hallway, and she glanced over. When his thumb intersected a tear gliding down her cheek, she wrapped her hand around his wrist. "You have no idea how hard it's been to keep this all to myself. I've been completely alone, but you gave me the validation I've needed." As the couple reached them, she lowered their joined hands. Once they passed, she asked, "Have you ever baked cookies?"

"Sure. Plenty of times."

"Oh." Her features fell. "Okay, well, it was nice talking to you today. I'll be sure to make an extra special batch for you. Just so you know, you're going to see them everywhere. My aunt even has them delivered to every room. Milk and cookies before bed." She gave him a weak smile and then turned to go.

But he hadn't released her hand, so he gently tugged her back. When she nearly stumbled against his chest, their gazes locked, and sensation bloomed inside his chest. "But I've never baked them with you."

Chapter Five

THE KITCHEN SMELLED OF CINNAMON AND MELTED butter. Staff who weren't even on shift came in to help bake the thousands of crisp, wafer-like cookies Aunt Lucy liked to offer her guests. She kept a basket of them at the check-in desk and offered them for free at the coffee bar.

Everyone worked in teams. Some stood sentry at the ovens, ready to pull them out and set them on cooling racks, while others arranged them for delivery. Margot and Beau rolled out the dough that was made the day before and also made new batches for tomorrow.

Since the kitchen was so crowded, she'd found an out-of-the-way workstation. At the moment, she was alone. A garbage disposal had broken, and while everyone had flipped out—*what're we going to do? Can we even get a plumber this close to Christmas?*—Beau had stood quietly in front of it, arms crossed over his chest, head cocked, and then got down on the floor, slid his upper body under the sink, and began fixing it.

Why was a capable man so sexy? When she'd found

herself staring a little too long at his muscular thighs in those well-worn jeans and the patch of tan skin exposed when his Henley rode up—she quickly got back to work.

Only when she poured molasses into a Pyrex measuring cup did she notice her shaky grip.

I'm a mess.

She'd known a lot of people in her life, had made a lot of friends, and been married for two decades, but she'd never connected with anyone the way she did with Beau. But while that was nice, it wasn't what got her all worked up. It was because she knew the only reason someone could read another person so well was because they cared. They were paying attention to expressions, gestures, and tone of voice.

Which begged the question: *why* did he care about her?

She wasn't some beauty. She didn't have the body of a swimsuit model. So, clearly, the attraction wasn't based on the physical.

Which is good. It's great. Having a crush and connecting with a man was life-affirming.

But connecting with a man who was leaving TOMORROW MORNING...not so good. Terrible, in fact.

Do not get attached to this man.

You hear me, Margot Rhodes?

You've just come out of the most godawful season of your life.

Don't get in any deeper or it's going to hurt.

Beau finished his work, dropped the wrench in the toolbox, and washed his hands. When Aunt Lucy thanked him and then launched into the history of the Moravians in

North Carolina, he listened as though she were telling him the results of his DNA ancestry test.

He's not even from here, and he cares.

He was such a good man. So genuine and kindhearted. And God, to be with someone like that? She wanted it. Needed it. That hug he'd given her in the hallway should've been awkward and uncomfortable. She hardly knew him, after all.

But it hadn't. It was like the shape of him had been built especially for her. She'd felt so safe, so seen, that all the loneliness had bubbled over, and she'd cried like a baby.

"Lucy?" someone called, and her aunt dashed off to see what they needed.

Beau came back to her side. "Sorry about that. What can I do to help?"

"Don't be sorry. You fixed something. Everyone loves a handyman."

"It's the engineer in me. I like to figure out how things work." He gave a chin nod to the ingredients. "Can I make a batch?"

"Of course." She slid the measuring cup toward him. "I've only just started with the mise en place."

"The what now?"

She smiled. "It's when you measure out all the ingredients in advance." *And see?* Just like that, she'd stopped shaking, and she was comfortable with him again.

"Ah. Okay."

"You're going to dump all of these"—she gestured to the brown sugar, butter, and molasses—"in here." She lifted the pot. "And warm it until the sugar dissolves."

He did as she'd instructed and turned on the heat.

"You said you've made cookies before, and I know you don't have a sweet tooth, so that must've been for your kids?"

"Oh, you know that, do you?" He picked up the wooden spoon and stirred.

"Yep, Mr. Steak And Potatoes Man. You're the kind of monster who would've walked out of the restaurant two days before Christmas without ordering dessert." She shuddered.

"What does Christmas have to do with it?"

"Unless you're gifted with a magic metabolism, we all look for excuses to indulge. You get a vaccination? Grab a milkshake. You got an A on your essay? Awesome! Here's a slice of cake to celebrate."

"But it wasn't Christmas yet." He looked genuinely confounded.

"We pull the celebration card starting December first." Her tone said, *Don't you know that?*

"So, *twenty-five* days of indulging?"

"Of course not." She shook her head as though she couldn't believe he'd just said that. "New Year's is only seven days later. It's *thirty-two* days of celebrating."

When he grinned like that, dimples popped out on either side of his mouth. "There's a whole secret world of information I knew nothing about." It turned him from handsome to devastating.

Oh, Lord. She did not need him pulling that one out of his Ways To Make Margot Swoon arsenal. "Which explains the extra junk in my trunk." She patted her bottom. "We all have choices to make…" She popped a cookie into her mouth and chewed. "And this one's mine."

For the entire time he had his attention fixed on her ass, she wondered what he was thinking. This man revealed very little, but she couldn't miss the fire burning deep within his eyes.

"There isn't a man alive who'd question your choices."

Oh, Lordy, this man got her hot and bothered.

You better stop this right now.

It's not like you're going to sleep with him.

The shock that hit her body had her hair practically standing on end. Which made her wonder: *do you* want *to sleep with him?*

She needed to change the subject. Fast. "Have you tried one yet?" She offered him the half-eaten cookie in her hand.

But he didn't take it. Wrapping his hand around her wrist, he brought the cookie back to her mouth. "I'd rather watch you indulge."

Watch.

Me.

Indulge.

Even though he hadn't budged, it felt like he was crowding her, overwhelming her.

She tried to lighten the mood by gobbling up the rest of the cookie. "Mm. Yum." She chewed the spicy, crunchy cookie, then swallowed.

"So, what, exactly, are we celebrating right now?"

"Our friendship." She licked her lips.

He followed the path of her tongue, and he shoved a hand into his pocket. "Is that what this is?"

Holy crap. Was he… She glanced down to see an erection tenting his jeans. Excitement sped through her. *No, no, no. Shut it down.* "That's all it can be."

He swallowed. "It doesn't feel like friendship." His voice sounded gravelly.

"No, it doesn't." As they held each other's gazes, a bud of sensuality blossomed in the very core of her, and an image dropped into her mind of them in bed. His big, strong hands roaming her body, caressing, stroking, gripping. His tongue licking a trail across her breasts, down her belly, and right into her slick, hot cove.

She jolted, as if he'd actually stroked her clit.

What in the world is going on with me? She'd never been this attracted to a man.

Ever.

And it made her feel feminine. Sexual. Alive. She hadn't felt any of those things in ages. While she'd been in survival mode, she'd neglected a whole other side of herself. The part that made her feel like a woman. A desirable woman.

Oh, God, yes. She needed to be wanted. Maybe she could—

No. She knew herself. If she had sex with him, she'd feel terrible the next morning. And she couldn't afford any more emotional lows. "So." She forced herself to shut it all down and went back to her work. "You made cookies for your kids?"

He didn't respond right away, and she guessed they both needed a moment to settle down. "Cookies. Yes. We made them every year for Santa. In the beginning, it was just basic sugar cookies for Jessa to decorate. But the older she got, the more she wanted to experiment. We did just about everything."

"Except Moravian."

He chuckled. "Yeah, too bad, because I think she'd like these."

"Well, take some to her when you pick her up for dinner."

"Good idea. Actually, it's perfect, because I also used to make them for her when she was having a hard time."

"And spending Christmas alone is a gut punch."

He cringed, and she knew he was imagining his daughter waking up alone in her dorm room.

She handed him a smaller pot. "Okay, now, you're going to bring this water to a boil and then add the baking soda."

Once he tipped over the measuring cup, he turned on the flame. "I'll take some of this batch."

"Sorry?"

He chuckled as if he'd been caught saying his thoughts out loud. "No, just that it only makes her feel better if I make them. She doesn't want them if they come from the store."

Did his cheeks turn pink with that confession? *That's adorable.* "You two have such a special relationship."

"Yeah, we do." His eyes went warm with affection.

"Well, you can't give her any unless you've tried them. Come on." She reached for another one. "Soil that bodily temple." She yanked it back. "Oh. Sorry. It's not Christmas Day. You don't have anything to celebrate." She loved teasing him.

"I met you." He made a gimme motion with his hand. "That's reason enough."

"Did you forget I don't like charming men?" She offered him the cookie, but he was busy adding the baking soda, so she brought it to his mouth. "Taste." She hadn't considered the intimacy of feeding a man, but the way he watched her while he took a bite sent her pulse pounding.

"I wouldn't know how to charm if you paid me. I mean it. I'm glad I met you."

She stood so close that her hand itched to wrap around his big biceps. His masculine scent filled her senses, overriding the molasses and cinnamon. He smelled of clean clothes, expensive soap, and something uniquely *Beau*.

His dark hair gleamed in the overhead lights, and she was positive his blue eyes saw right through to her soul. "That's good."

Deep inside, she felt an emptiness, a carnal ache, that she instinctively knew only he could relieve. And so, she forced herself to step away. All these years, she hadn't missed sex. Not at all. In fact, she was relieved when her ex stopped asking for it.

But right then, she could see how utterly essential that kind of intimacy was. That urgent, grinding, wild passion that made a woman lose her mind with the yearning to get as close as possible to her mate. "They really are."

"Do you decorate them?"

"Oh, no. Aunt Lucy's a no-frills woman."

His eyebrows lifted as he gestured toward the kitchen where fresh garlands hung from the walls and wrapped around light fixtures and big baskets stuffed with cinnamon-scented pinecones rested on counters.

She couldn't help but laugh. "What can I say? She's a complicated woman. All I know is she likes the cookies plain." When the water started to bubble, she turned off the flame. "Okay, go ahead and dump the cinnamon, cloves, and ginger into the flour." She waited while he did it. "Perfect. Now, we'll add everything to the sugar mixture."

He poured the water and baking soda into the bowl of

flour and spices and stirred until it was all incorporated. "Good?"

"Yep. And now, we form it into a rectangle, wrap it up, and stick it in the refrigerator. They'll roll it out tomorrow and bake them."

"Got it." He dumped the dough onto a floured cutting board. "What's the one thing you miss most from your former life?"

She had the plastic wrap on the teeth of the box, ready to slice it off, when every muscle in her body squeezed. Wait —could he tell she was missing sex? Was it that obvious? But then, she laughed when she realized he was just making conversation. "That's an interesting question."

"I just can't stop thinking about what that son of a bitch did to you."

She never should've told him her story. The last thing she wanted from anyone was pity. She thought she'd made that clear. She owned her part in what happened. "Look, I'm not a victim—"

"No, I know that. That's why I can't stop thinking about it. Because it wasn't that long ago and look at you—you're happy and strong and *thriving*. You've gone through an incredible process of self-reflection, and you've come out the other side, and it's just so damn impressive. And I can't help but wonder, out of everything you lost, what do you miss the most?"

"I miss having my family together. I mean, I get it. They grow up and go out into the world, but isn't there always a home base, where they come for holidays or crash when things get tough? I told you my daughter's getting married the first week in January?"

He nodded.

"Well, I'm a guest. I'm not hosting it in my backyard or helping her find a dress or a venue. I'm just... a guest. So, that's it. I lost the thing I valued most in the world. A home base where my family can be together."

He nodded. "Makes sense." Finished wrapping up the dough, he lifted it. "I'll put this in the fridge."

As soon as he left, she started putting together the next mise en place. When he came back, she said, "I like how you don't try to make it better for me. You don't say, 'You're still a family. It just looks different now.' Or, 'You gave your kids all the tools they needed...' or whatever. You listen. You hear me. And you understand. Thank you for that."

He dumped the dry ingredients into a bowl. "And what about material things? Of everything in your old house, what do you miss the most?"

She was going to surprise him with her answer. "My ornaments. I know that sounds silly, but it's true. You probably expected me to say my grandma's armoire or my kids' baby books or something like that."

"I've never met anyone like you, so I don't really have expectations."

Oh, the things this man said. Had anyone ever made her feel so special? *Nope.* No one had. "I'm an only child, so I've got heirlooms that've been passed down from both sides of the family. Then, with my kids, every year, we'd make new ones of our own."

"Like gluing popsicle sticks into the shape of a star?"

"Yep. We've got those. But as they got older, we upped our game." She rinsed out a bowl. "When we sold our house, we rented a huge storage unit. It's stuffed to the gills with furniture and pots and pans and all the stuff I thought I'd need once we got on our feet again. We obviously never did, but the funny thing is I don't miss any of it. I don't even think about my designer clothes and scarves and shoes and purses, but I think about those ornaments." She handed him the measuring cup of water and tipped her chin to the pot.

"You still have them, right?" He dumped it and turned on the flame. "One day, you can get them?"

"Maybe. I don't know. I haven't talked to my ex since he told me he was leaving. He might've stopped paying for it. I have no idea."

Emotions crossed his handsome features, one after another. First, pain. And yes, not knowing if her ex had tossed out her ornaments cut deep. But then, confusion. "You mean you haven't talked about personal things, right?" After adding the spices to the flour, he used a whisk to mix it. "Because you went through a divorce, so you must've talked."

"Nope. We had no assets and nothing to divide. I did it all online."

He went hard. "Are you telling me he hasn't tried to reach out to you? To find out how you are?"

"Oh, no. He has." She poured the liquid into the dry ingredients. "But after the last thing he said to me, I was done with him. I blocked him."

"What did he say?"

"He said he'd continue to pay the rent and my car payment but he needed me to leave the apartment for a few hours on Saturday so he could come pick up his stuff." That request still had the power to enrage her. *The entitled son of a bitch.* "I packed up my car and was out by Thursday." She smiled. "I got a lot of satisfaction knowing he'd shown up and found me gone. Not a trace of me."

"Did he try to reach you?"

"Apparently. He kept texting the kids, demanding to know why I wasn't answering him. He wanted to know where I was, and if I was coming back."

"Did you ever unblock him?"

"I did, but only because he might have news about one of our kids. That's the only conversation he's worthy of having with me."

"Have I mentioned how much I admire you?"

"Once or twice." She grinned.

Just then, his phone buzzed, and he pulled it out of his pocket. "This might be Jessa. She's going to let me know when she's free for dinner." He studied the screen for a moment and then broke out into a grin.

He was so serious most of the time that when he smiled, his features transformed into movie star gorgeous. Those dimples, that jaw, those astonishing blue eyes... *Whew.* "Your girlfriend sent a boob shot?"

"What?" He barked out a laugh. "No. I think you know I don't have a girlfriend, and secondly, I leave my phone out in the open. You think I want my kids or my assistants catching an eyeful of that?" He shook his head. "No, it's my grandson. Look." He turned the screen toward her.

A blond-haired, blue-eyed little boy with a wide, wet smile stared at her. "Oh, my God. He's precious."

"He's hell on wheels." His tone was rich with affection.

"How old is he?"

His thumb brushed the screen, and she could see how much he missed him. "Two and a half."

"And they all live with you?"

His smile faltered, and he tapped out a quick response before shoving his phone back into his pocket. "Uh, not the mom. She's not in the picture."

"Can I ask what happened there?"

"Yeah, of course." He dumped the new batch of dough onto the cutting board and began forming a rectangle. "She was just twenty-one when she got pregnant, and she wasn't ready to be a mom. She actually wasn't going to tell my son about it. He only found out because he overheard mutual friends talking about it."

"Oh, boy. That's tough."

"He asked her to hold off on taking any action. He needed time to process." He hunched a shoulder. "Walker's like me. We need to ruminate."

"I'm the same way. I admire people who can size up a situation and make a snap decision, but I need time. I need to look at it from all angles."

"Yep. So, like you, he went into his cave, kept to himself. I knew something was up, but when I tried to talk to him, he clammed up. He's a planner. He had goals. And being a father would change everything. That's not easy for him."

"Wait, are you saying he didn't want to work at the mine?"

"No, no. He did. Eventually. But he loved travel, and he had a goal of visiting every continent. He kept a travel folder with ideas like going to Iceland to help toss the pufflings into the ocean and visiting the Turtle Festival in Velas Beach. But it wasn't just that. He'd hoped to win back his high school girlfriend and build a life with her, and he didn't know what she'd think of raising another woman's child."

"Whoo. Yeah, that's a huge upheaval. So, what made him finally decide?"

"His mother." His tone hardened, and he focused on wrapping the dough in plastic wrap.

"When he told her the situation, she said, 'Get rid of it.' It was the way she referred to his child—her grandchild—as an *it* that changed his perspective. He went straight to his girlfriend's apartment and asked if he could raise the baby himself."

"How did that go? If she didn't want to keep it, how did she feel about carrying a child to term?"

"She said it was her body, her choice, and he said, 'Yeah, but it's fifty percent my DNA.' They hashed it out, and eventually, she agreed to it. She signed away her rights."

"And you've never heard from her since?"

"Not a peep. But I think it all worked out in the end. Walker's a great dad, and Colt's a really good kid." He clearly loved his grandson. He looked around the kitchen where people were pulling cookies out of the oven, grabbing dough from the fridge, and making new ones at their stations. "One more batch?"

"Sure." She headed to the sink to fill the measuring glass with water. When she returned, she found he'd already begun setting up. "Quick learner."

"It helps that I watch everything you do." When she faltered, he stuttered out a laugh. "That sounded creepy. But you know, I *am* fascinated by you."

"But why? I'm just...average."

He looked like she'd shoved him. "Average? Are you serious? Look at you. Look at all you've been through. For seven years, you kept your spirits high—"

"Yeah, so my ex wouldn't sink into despair."

"But you did it. For seven years. And then, after the way he treated you, you're not bitter and angry. You're building a future. I'm in awe of you." He rubbed his clean-shaven jaw. "I saw your art, by the way. You're incredibly talented."

"Oh, well, thank you."

He tipped her chin. "Why did you do that?"

"Do what?"

"Look down and say 'thank you' like you thought I was just being nice?"

"Because I've never shown my work before. Not since college when I felt like I had the potential to become the next Monet. Since then, I've barely touched a canvas. And now, I'm basing my entire future on something that might not pan out."

"I think it will," he said quietly.

She hated to be so insecure, but she really didn't know. "Well, it's one thing to make pretty ornaments or book covers, but the art world is different. There has to be something special...avant-garde...*revolutionary*."

"Does there? I always thought art needed to make you feel things. And yours does."

"Like?" Sure, she was testing him. But he couldn't just make these statements without backing them up.

"Your watercolors are ethereal, but I get a strong sense of home. Of settling in by a fire. But also, the colors are vibrant, almost...I don't know...festive. So, they make me happy and comforted at the same time." He cocked his head. "They're you. They're totally and completely you."

"Thank you for saying that. That's really nice."

"Jessa did a lot of art programs as a teenager, and she

used to talk about finding her voice. If your work is an expression of your personality, your spirit, I'd say you've done that. In any event, what do your buyers think?"

She smiled. "There aren't a lot, but the ones I do have left pretty great reviews."

"There you go." His thumb brushed her cheek in the most darling way, and her knees went weak. She wanted to let go and just sink into him, but he got back to measuring the cloves.

He couldn't understand how his support impacted her. Sure, she had a few nice reviews, but the people who shopped on her site were faceless. Like bots. Having someone real look at her work and compliment her... She needed that.

But she didn't want to get all dramatic around him, so she steered the conversation in a new direction. "Well, in any event, there's still lots of time for Walker to travel."

He dipped the measuring spoon into the ginger. "You know, by nature, he's a real homebody. I've always wondered if his interest in travel comes from himself or from the stories he heard about my childhood." He cut her a look. "Mine was fairly unconventional."

"Unconventional?"

"Yeah. After my mom left, my dad changed. Basically, he said, 'Fuck this.' He'd played by the rule book, and it hadn't worked out. He started dating Annie—my stepmom who'd had a heart attack at thirty-five—so she was on the same page. They both agreed that a life of nine-to-five jobs and sitting down to a family dinner of roasted chicken and green beans was not what they wanted. So, they sold the house, bought an RV, and we hit the road."

"What about school?"

"They were both college professors, so they felt comfortable homeschooling me. I got to see the whole country. You ever hear of Dinosaur National Monument?"

She smiled. "I sure have. I took my kids there on the infamous eleven-thousand-mile road trip. My son was obsessed with dinosaurs, so I thought he'd love it. Boy, was I wrong. I was the only one who got a kick out of seeing those bones. But it's very cool that your parents showed you the world."

"In a way, it was. But it also sucked being a kid with no friends and not having roots. Eventually, my parents grew tired of life on the road, and they went back to teaching. It was an interesting childhood."

"So, you're helping raise your grandchild. What about your ex? Does she pitch in?"

"Not at all. She told our son if he went through with it, he'd have to take full responsibility, and he couldn't look to her for help. She'd already raised three children."

"Wait, so does she spend time with her grandson at all?"

"Not really. She's in her own world."

That's so sad. "I guess I can see her point of view." She could never imagine having that attitude with her children or not knowing a grandchild, but who was she to judge?

He gave her an affectionate grin. "You're very kind."

"No, I mean it. I do understand her perspective."

"But you wouldn't share it."

"I've never been in her shoes, so I can't say what I'd do, but I believe I would respect my son's decision and be there for him however I could. I don't have a lot of money, and I have to consider my future, but if he needed my help, I'd offer to live with him to share childcare and household responsibilities."

"That's what I figured." He wrapped the dough in plastic wrap. When he came back from the fridge, he asked, "We done?"

"We can be. I'm sure you have other things to do."

"I do." He glanced at his watch. "But, oh look. It's time for a vanilla chai latte. Let me buy you one."

She laughed. "I can't believe you know what time I drink my tea. I'm either shockingly boring or utterly fascinating."

"I think you know my answer." He brushed flour off her collarbone.

A shiver of awareness tripped down her spine. Which was an odd response considering it wasn't even a sexual gesture.

"I want to spend more time with you," he murmured.

"Oh." It all felt so delicious. The excitement, the fear, the anxiety he roused. None of it made any sense—*why* did this man want to be with her?—but she loved it. And maybe because it was a whole new suite of emotions than what she'd experienced the last eight months—no, eight *years*—she welcomed it. "Let's get that tea."

After a quick cleanup of their station, they headed out of the kitchen. As they crossed the restaurant, she breathed in the pine-scented air, and she smiled at a couple she'd served the night before.

His hand brushed hers, and her fingers flexed. She'd never been a big fan of hand-holding. It seemed awkward and forced. But she sure wanted to hold his.

"Can I ask you something?" he asked.

She steered them toward the lobby. "Of course."

"After what he's done, what's your kids' relationship to their dad now?"

"Oh, that's a tough one. I mean, the divorce obviously hit them hard. They'd always seen us as the couple who would stay together forever. They never gave a thought to us breaking up."

"Do they know the truth? What he did?"

She found an empty table tucked against the wall. "Hang on. Let me get us drinks."

"No, I got this." He didn't give her a chance to object, just strode off.

She didn't like to argue over money. If someone offered to pay, she just let them, figuring she'd get it next time around. Of course, with Beau, there wouldn't be a next time.

And she really had to stop thinking like that and just enjoy the time they had together.

After he put in their order and paid, he came back and sat down across from her. "Did he tell them the truth?"

"Absolutely. He used the same line with them as he did with me. He said we were in a death spiral, and he found an exit ramp, and he hoped their mom would find one, too."

"Jesus fucking Christ." He glanced at the table nearest them, but he'd kept his voice low enough that no one heard over the buzz of conversation and the Christmas carols playing on lobby speakers. "What a piece of shit." He shook his head. "I'm sorry. It's hard to keep my thoughts to myself."

"I love knowing what you're thinking." It enabled her to lower her defenses. And honestly, since the day her ex had walked out, she hadn't felt safe—not for one second.

She'd had moments of happiness, even glimpses of hope.

But no matter where she was, what she was doing, or how she was feeling, temblors quaked beneath the surface, a constant reminder that her future was uncertain. That she had only herself to rely on.

Which was why his opinion of her art mattered so much. Her steadily growing sales should've been proof enough that it could support her. Unfortunately, once the bottom dropped out of your world, the pieces never quite fit back together again.

He dragged his chair closer. "Have they seen him since he left you?"

"No. My son wants nothing to do with him, and my daughter's just confused. The wedding's going to be at her fiancé's family home, and while it'll be very simple, there are some traditions she wanted to uphold."

"Like having her dad walk her down the aisle?"

She nodded, imagining her ex in a tuxedo and her daughter in a designer gown. The way it would have been done before their world had changed so dramatically. Now, she couldn't picture it at all. "She said she can't do it. The way her dad bailed on me and left me with nothing sickens her."

His features tightened. "He doesn't deserve the honor."

She smiled in appreciation, glad he understood. "So, it makes her sad to think her father will be just another guest at her wedding. I feel bad for her, but I guess we're all having to adjust to the new normal."

"Beau?" the barista called.

He got up, grabbed their drinks, and set the steaming mugs on the table.

"Thank you." She wrapped her hands around hers, savoring the warmth.

He sat so close at this little table that their thighs touched. He could've shifted away, but he didn't. It was intentional. Such a simple gesture—and yet it had her heart fluttering in her throat.

Because it means he feels it, too.

It wasn't just a crush she'd blown up to fill her empty spaces. It was real.

"I think my kids are having a harder time processing what he did than I am. As weird as it sounds, I'm done with him. I seriously don't have any lingering feelings."

"That doesn't sound weird at all. He killed any love or loyalty, and you decided not to spend your energy on a man with a shitty character."

"Yes, exactly. More than anything, I think my kids are worried about me. They're afraid I won't be able to support myself into old age. They probably picture me as this old lady barista hobbling to work and getting scolded because she can't read the order right."

"They've got it all wrong."

"Oh, yeah? And how do you picture me?"

"A woman with paint under her fingernails, making hot chocolate for her grandchildren, and living in a…" He made a slow rolling motion with his hand as if waiting for her to finish the sentence.

"A cottage by the sea?" She shook her head. That didn't fit. "A cabin in the woods? A farm where I make my own butter?" She laughed. "God, no. My gnarled hands won't be able to churn that long."

He reached for her, turned up her palm, and held it as though it were a fragile shell. "These hands will be lovely, even when they're gnarled because they'll make beautiful art and delicious cookies, and they'll soothe cranky grandchildren."

"You make me feel things, Beau Gentry. Dangerous things." Even though it felt good, she pulled her hand away. Or, more likely, *because* it felt good.

"So, what about you?" he asked. "Are you worried about seeing your ex at the wedding?"

"That's hard to answer. I've built this fortress, so part of me can stand behind it and say I don't care about that piece of shit. But there's another part that dreads seeing him."

"With Petra, you mean?"

"Not really. Maybe if he'd left me for another nurturer, I'd be upset. But he didn't. Petra's my polar opposite. Now, there'll definitely be some resentment if their business got funding, and now they're rolling in cash. I'll feel a little sorry for myself. But it's more that I don't want to be forced to play the happy parents of the bride. I don't want to ruin my daughter's day, but I also don't want to pretend to be on good terms with him. Do you know what I mean?"

"I do." He leaned closer, gazing into her eyes. "How about this? I'll go with you and be your fake boyfriend."

"What did you just say?" She laughed. "How do you know about fake boyfriends?"

"Because my brilliant daughter Jessa reads romance, and she tells me about them."

"She talks to you about *romance* books?"

"We talk about everything. Well, she mostly talks, and I listen."

"But why would she think you'd want to hear about what she's reading?"

"It's not about the book. It's about what she thinks about the different situations. She gets all riled up because the hero did something unforgivable or the heroine's a doormat. Stuff like that. I could listen to her all day long just to get a glimpse into her mind."

"I've never met anyone like you."

I want to kiss you.

And peel that shirt off your shoulders. Unbuckle your belt, pop those buttons, and yank down your jeans, so I can run my hands all over your body.

I want to keep you.

He grinned. "I hope that's a good thing."

"Yeah. It's good."

The connection between them crackled and sparked, and she found his attention fixed on her mouth. Unconsciously, she licked her lips. His gaze tracked the slide of her tongue, and his hand fisted on his thigh. He leaned in, his scent filling her senses and making her dizzy. And right when he got a breath away from kissing her, right when her eyelids fluttered closed, his phone trilled.

He jerked away, fumbling as he answered the call. "Hey." A sheen of perspiration gleamed on his forehead. "Yeah, of course." He turned his wrist to read the face of his watch. "Don't worry about the weather. We're still having dinner together." He cut a nervous glance at Margot. "I don't know if that's a good idea. I'm on my way." He hit disconnect, but he didn't get up. He looked as shaken as she felt.

Best to address it. "Saved by the bell." Even though she was rattled—*I almost kissed this man*—she forced a smile.

"Are you eating at the lodge tonight? Because we're having Yule log. I'll make sure she gets the slice with the most frosting."

"I'll let her know." He got up so quickly his knees banged the table, and their drinks sloshed. "I have to get Jessa." He watched her for a moment. "But I've really enjoyed talking with you, Margot."

This is it. The last time she'd see him.

Her body felt heavy, and she couldn't even get up. Instead, she sat there with a stupid expression. A lonely woman who'd gotten too attached to a total stranger.

Words darted around her mind like fish in an aquarium.

I like you.

Can I go to dinner with you and your daughter?

We should keep in touch.

But they were all futile and dumb, and there was just no point.

So, she said the only thing she could. "Goodbye, Beau."

Chapter Six

AM I HAVING A HEART ATTACK?

With the heat cranked high, Beau's rental car was sweltering. His daughter was on her cell phone, filling her advisor in on the details of her lab results. But right then, with the windshield wipers matching the frantic rhythm of his heartbeat, he couldn't hear anything over the roar of blood in his ears.

I almost kissed her.

I wanted to do a hell of a lot more than that.

He didn't recognize himself. At all.

These feelings…they were so big, so overwhelming.

They made him frantic.

And I'm never frantic.

Beau was calm. He was the rational person in any crisis. When Walker had stopped breathing at eighteen months, his ex had screamed and panicked. He'd pulled to the side of the road, unbuckled his son, and tried to remove the mucous plug from his throat. When it didn't budge, he'd used his pinky to swipe it out. The one thing the textbooks said not to do, his gut had told him would save his son's life.

So, what had possessed him to try and kiss a woman he'd met *yesterday?* Who'd recently come out of a terrible divorce?

In the lobby of a hotel?

Thankfully, he hadn't done it. Because honestly, if he'd finally gotten a taste of her, he didn't think it would've stopped there.

After his ex left, he'd gone a little wild, trying to make up for what he'd missed the last seven years of his life. Sex had been transactional for Courtney. She'd barter it for a new car, a girls' weekend in LA, or a bathroom remodel. He'd rather use his fist, so they'd stopped touching each other long before they'd split.

At first, he'd been voracious. But after a series of hookups, he realized he just wasn't cut out for it. If he wasn't into a woman, he became too conscious of the way she smelled, the texture of her hair, and the noises she made. It threw him out of the moment, forcing him to concentrate to reach the finish line.

He'd always assumed he wasn't wired for romance. But then, he'd met Margot, and he'd been walloped with a crazy attraction. Just one look at her in the lobby that first morning had sent his pulse skyrocketing. Talking to her in the restaurant the night before had rendered him tongue-tied.

And now that he'd spent time with her, his emotions had reached a level he wasn't comfortable with.

He was an engineer. He understood how things worked.

He didn't understand this preoccupation with someone he'd never see again.

At the traffic light, he could either go left toward the lodge or right onto Main Street. When Jessa had called to say she was ready for dinner, she'd asked if Margot could join them. He'd been too rattled to ask. He'd needed to think. Figure out if it was a good idea.

But now, he knew it wasn't.

This is my time with my daughter.

Checking his rearview mirrors, he got into the right lane.

"Turn left, Dad," she whispered and pointed in the other direction.

"Change in plans."

She eyed him curiously, but she was on a call, so she didn't press him.

Which was good because if she did, he'd cave. And if he went back to the lodge, he'd probably go after Margot like a heat-seeking missile. His daughter would chase after him, calling, "Dad? *Dad?* What are you *doing?*"

But he wouldn't hear because he'd be tracking his woman.

Are you fucking serious?

She's not your woman.

Realistically, the only thing they had in common was they'd both been divorced. He didn't even know what he'd do if he had more time with her.

Well, he knew exactly what he wanted to do.

He'd kiss her so thoroughly she'd forget she even had an ex. He'd let her know with his hands and tongue she didn't deserve what that fucker had done to her. He'd peel off her leggings and flip her over, hike her ass in the air so he could watch her cheeks jiggle when he fucked her into an orgasm.

He needed to get his hands on her tits, maybe fuck them —*oh, yeah, definitely that*—and watch her tongue peek out to lick the head of his cock.

Jesus. You're not getting hard with your daughter in the car.

That's it. He'd block her from his mind. Think about work, a problem he could solve.

He pulled into the parking lot of a French bistro, found a spot, and killed the engine. As he waited for Jessa to finish with her advisor, he reached into the back seat for her Christmas present.

A moment later, she ended the call. "I thought we're having dinner at the lodge?"

"No, it's coming down pretty hard right now." Already, snow had piled up on the hood of his car. "I don't want you stuck at the lodge. We'll eat closer to campus." She didn't need to know about his near heart attack. "Do you want your present now or after dinner?"

She let out a long-suffering sigh. "It's like you don't even know me. Obviously, now." Digging into her backpack, she drew out a small wrapped gift. "Here's yours. You go first."

His daughter was many things, but a perfectionist wasn't one of them. Crisscrossed strips of tape held the jaggedly cut paper around the box. Inside, he found a blue and white hoodie. He unfolded it and read the logo. "'Whitney Dad.' Perfect. Thank you."

"There's more."

He reached back in and found a photo album. As he flipped through the pages, he realized it was a timeline of their lives together. His heart grew too big for his chest. He pointed to them dressed in matching onesies, each carrying a basket as they sought the hidden eggs. "Look at you."

She leaned across the console. "What?"

"You're laughing."

"Of course. It was so fun."

"I thought you hated that it was just me. That you wished it was Walker doing it with you."

"I mean, I would've loved having my brother play with me, but only if he wanted to. But I had you, and I loved that you did it with me."

"I'm glad to hear that. It's good to see how happy you were." There was another of him in bed as she and Walker brought him a breakfast tray for Father's Day.

"Best eggs you ever had, am I right?"

They both burst out laughing at the memory of the runny scrambled mess. He turned the page. "This one gets me every time." He'd taken the kids to the ocean in San Diego. It was Jessa's first time, and she didn't know what to make of it. So, she stood at the shoreline, lifting her shorts and dipping a toe into the bubbly water that washed over her feet. "Man, were you cute."

"I know, right?" She placed a hand on the book so he wouldn't turn the page. "I know it's not much of a gift, but I just wanted you to know how much I appreciate you. Mom was inconsistent, to say the least, and it kind of forced you into both roles, Mom *and* Dad."

"I wasn't forced into anything. I like spending time with you. More than I like working or going on dates or hanging out with friends. I *like* you. You're smart and funny. Creative. Thoughtful. Even if you weren't my daughter, I'd want to hang out with you."

"Well, that would just be weird." She rolled her eyes, but

he could see the sheen. And then, she lunged across the console and hugged him. "I love you, Dad."

"I love you, too, angel." More than she could ever know.

When she pulled away, she ran a thumb under her eyes to wipe away the moisture. "And I'm so glad you didn't listen to Mom and give up the mine."

"Yeah, well. It did *pan* out. Get it?"

"Ugh. What's worse than Dad jokes? Dad *gold mining* jokes that only thirty people in the universe would ever get." She smiled. "But it was never about money to you. It was about the ties to your family, the history. Well, and also, you're a total geek who loves rocks."

He flashed her a smile. "I can't argue with that."

She shifted to face him, lifting a knee onto the seat. "For me, though, watching you hold your ground taught me to believe in myself, to stay *true* to myself. You taught me passion. And I'm so sad Lorelei only had Mom. I know she wanted her career, but I can't help but wonder who she would've been without Mom pushing her into business decisions that weren't right for her."

"I wonder that, too. But because of what she's going through, maybe she'll make different choices." Now that she didn't have her band and the guidance of her mom.

"In any event…" She tapped the photo album. "I spent so much time thinking about what you wanted for Christmas, and then I realized what *I* wanted to get you, and that's to make sure you know how much I admire you. I'm so lucky to have you as my dad. There hasn't been a day in my life I haven't known you love me. You gave me the best childhood, and I don't ever want you to worry about the fact that you pretty much raised me by yourself."

"Thank you, sweetheart. This means the world to me." He reached out to hug his daughter, holding her close and breathing in the familiar scent of her lemon perfume. "I love you, Jessa girl. With all my heart."

When she pulled away, she flashed a grin. "Okay, my turn." She held her hand out, and he passed over the gift. She ran a hand over the smooth paper and fancy ribbon. "You did not wrap this present yourself."

"Of course not. Walker did it for me."

She rolled her eyes. "Seriously?" But she looked delighted as she ripped off the paper. When she opened the box, her eyes went wide. She held up the gold necklace with an oval bevel-set peridot. "Are you kidding me? This is stunning. I love it so much." Setting the box aside, she handed the jewelry to him and turned. Lifting her hair, she asked, "Can you put it on?"

"Of course."

"I can't believe you made this."

In hard-rock shaft mining, they often ran into seams containing secondary commercial minerals. When Beau was considering how to develop his land, he thought about finding a jeweler who could work on-site and sell only the minerals discovered on his mountain. Peridot was one of them. Out of curiosity, he'd worked with it himself and found he enjoyed making it. "There's another one in there."

In the second box, she found another handcrafted gift, but this bracelet was more rugged than the elegant necklace. The leather band had triangles of deep blue agate with a crystallized geode center framed in distressed gold. His daughter held it in her hand, jaw hanging open. "This is the most beautiful thing I've ever seen. Dad, I swear, you get better and better at this. You're so talented." She kissed his cheek. "I love that you did this for me. It makes me feel so special."

"I'm glad you like it." He watched her fasten it to her wrist. "Ready to eat?"

"Starving."

As they got out of the car, his daughter dashed into the restaurant to get out of the snow. But something caught his eye. About halfway down the street, he noticed a craft store.

An idea formed. There was someone else who needed to feel special.

He shouldn't do it. He really shouldn't do it.

But yeah, he was probably going to do it.

With the roads no longer safe, Beau had to drop his daughter off earlier than either of them would've liked. His tires had lost traction, causing him to slide a few times, but he'd made it back to the lodge safely.

After handing off his car to a valet, he remembered he needed a tree for his gift, so he'd left his bags of supplies with the concierge and traipsed out into the blizzard looking for just the right size—it had to fit on top of a nightstand. His hands were frozen, and more than once, he'd asked himself what the hell he was doing, but once he got to his room and began working on the project, he'd stopped overthinking it.

Because really, what could it hurt to give her a gift?

At least the storm had come early. It would pass through tonight, enabling him to make his midmorning flight. By the time she woke up and found her gift, he'd be gone, and this whole strange chapter would be behind him.

But if he could leave her with a smile…well, he'd like that.

It had taken him a couple of hours to get everything done, but now, with the tree and his bags, he stood outside Margot's door. He'd planned on leaving it all for her to find in the morning, but now that he stood in the hallway, it occurred to him someone could easily make off with it.

Some sleepy-eyed employee heading to work could come across the bags and easily think they were trash. No, he should knock.

He pressed his ear to the door to see if she was asleep and heard water running.

Yeah, okay, she's still up.

Look, just get it over with. Give her the gift and say, It was great meeting you. Best of luck. And then go back to your room.

Why are you making it a big deal?

It wasn't like they'd hug, so he wouldn't have to get a whiff of her peaches-and-cream shampoo. He could look anywhere but at her lush mouth. *This isn't about sex.* This is about doing something nice for a woman who's gone through hell.

Yes. Exactly.

It's nothing more than that.

Fuck it. Lifting the hand that held the bags, he knocked on the door. He was like a middle-school kid working up the nerve to ask out his crush.

"Yes?" Margot's voice was muffled.

"Hey. It's Beau."

After a moment of silence, he heard, "Give me just a sec."

Now, he felt like an asshole. She was getting ready for bed. Maybe she just finished washing her face. Or she'd just gotten out of the shower.

An image landed in his mind of her naked, dripping wet…a bead of water trickling down to her nipple. Him, licking it off.

Oh, no, you don't. No.

No.

You are not getting wood.

Fuck.

When he licked the sensitive peaks, her head would fall back, her thighs would press together, and she'd moan.

You're an asshole, you know that?

You're here to give her a gift. Not feature her in your own private porn movie.

The door flew open. "Hi." Her face looked scrubbed clean, and her smile lit a flame in his core, warming a spot he hadn't known had frozen over. "Did you have a good dinner with Jessa?"

"It was great. Exchanged presents." The gears in his brain locked. "Took her home early, though." His limbs felt like new parts he hadn't yet broken in. But she was waiting for him to say something. "Snow."

Her smile flattened. "Are you okay?"

"Fine." Embarrassed, his skin tingled as if he'd stepped into a hot shower after being in the snow.

"You didn't have a stroke?"

"A what?"

"You're not speaking in full sentences." She came out

into the hallway wearing a silky pink robe that hit the middle of her thighs.

Skin. All that smooth skin.

There it was. That whiff of her peach scent. His heart thundered, and he could imagine gliding his hands up her legs, under the thin robe, caressing the gusset of her panties. He'd like to get a handful of her plump ass, squeeze the cheeks as he hauled her up against his cock. He'd drop to his knees and tug on the elastic. How many licks would it take to make her come on his tongue?

Oh, man. He was a mess.

I'm never a mess.

Always in control. Level-headed.

This woman. She didn't even know what she did to him. Lowering his chin, he let out a laugh. "I feel pretty stupid."

"Stupid? Why?"

"I didn't want to bother you so late at night, but I also didn't want someone to see the bags in the hallway and think they were garbage."

She glanced down. "There's a tree."

"Yep."

"Is it for me?"

"Yeah. It's nothing much." He shrugged. "Just, you know, Merry Christmas."

She grinned as if she found him adorable. "Well, come in. Let's see what you got me." But just as she turned to go in, she stopped. "Do you need to go? You probably have to get up early to catch your flight."

"Not too early. I'm good." He picked up the tree. There was something about the sharp pine scent that woke him up, unscrambled his brains. "I'll just stay a minute." Following her, he took in the unmade bed, the dresser with the top drawer open, and the suitcase on a luggage stand. Seeing how she lived reminded him she'd lost everything, including the roof over her head.

Anger coursed through him, and he wanted to march over to her ex-husband's place and knock him senseless.

"It's a mess, I know. I was catching up on some work and figured I could clean up in the morning."

"Is that it?" He tipped his chin toward the suitcase.

"Is what it? Oh." She laughed. "Is that all I own in the world? No, of course not. There's a toaster in the closet."

He tried to give her the smile she wanted, but he couldn't do it.

"Oh, come on. You'd be surprised what happens when you get rid of your stuff. I couldn't even tell you what's in that storage room right now. I don't miss any of it."

"It's the point, though. How he could leave you like this and move on to something better."

"Is it better, though? I suppose as long as Petra doesn't get pregnant it probably is. Though honestly, I would die laughing if it happened. It won't, of course. In fact, he probably got a vasectomy before he ever slept with her." She gestured around the room. "This doesn't bother me because it isn't permanent. I may never own a home again or take fancy vacations, but I know I can pay my bills through my own creativity and resourcefulness." She touched his arm. "I'm doing okay. I promise." And then, she jumped onto her bed. "Now, let's see what you got me."

He'd nailed two planks of wood to the bottom, so when he set the tree on the nightstand it managed to stay upright.

She touched the pine needles. "This is so fun. I get my

very own Christmas tree." The bags rustled as she pulled out a strand of cranberry-colored beads. "This is pretty." She sat up on her heels and carefully wound it around the branches. Her robe gaped open, revealing the swell of her breasts.

He had to bite the inside of his mouth to keep from imagining sliding his hand inside and caressing her until her nipple beaded against his palm.

She dug back into the bag and pulled out some ornaments. "Wait." She studied the carvings. "Did you make this?"

He nodded.

"How? When? I don't understand…?"

"The storm…I had to take Jessa home early." He'd already told her that. "So, I had a little time."

"A little time? I make ornaments for a living. This would take me days." When she ran a finger over the grooves, he swore he could feel it on his cock.

Lust burned a path through him, and he had to shove his hand in his pocket to press down hard on his erection.

"Where did you get the supplies? The tools?"

"In town. There's a craft store down the street from the bistro." They'd even had a saw so he could take down the small tree.

"It's your last night with your daughter, and you went to a craft store?"

"She's stuck alone in a dorm for the next few weeks. Trust me, she was thrilled to buy some art supplies."

"Really?" She sounded wary. "What did she get?"

"You don't believe me?" He chuckled. "Fine. She got yarn, a sketchpad, charcoal, and some watercolors."

"Unbelievable." She ran her finger over the sparkly letter M he'd glued to the center of a wood round.

For some of the others, he'd bought Christmas cards from the sale rack, cut out a circle smaller than the wood, and used decoupage glue to plaster it on. He'd dipped the edges in gold glitter.

He'd only meant to make a few, but if he was going to give her a tree, it couldn't be sad and barren, so he'd wound up making a total of twenty ornaments.

She pulled the last gift from the bag. For the tree topper, he'd glued twigs in the shape of a star.

"I can't believe you did all this for me." Her cheeks went pink, and her eyes clouded with emotion.

"It's not a big deal."

"Yes, it is. Are you kidding? It's incredibly kind and generous. And thoughtful. It's your last night in town, and I just can't believe you did this." She got up and stood before him. "Thank you, Beau. I wish…" She shook her head. "Never mind. Do you need to go now, or do you have time to decorate the tree with me?"

"I'd stay up all night just to have every last minute with you." The words hung in the air like water vapor.

He wanted a cataclysmic event to crack open the earth right then and swallow him whole.

It was one thing to be preoccupied with her, but now he had no control over what came winging out of his mouth?

"Beau." No one had ever used that soft tone when saying his name. It was filled with a yearning that made his bones soften and yield.

And somehow, that soothed him. Her happiness made all the chaos in his body worthwhile.

"I love that you made all this for me. By far, it's the best gift I've ever received in my life." Her dreamy expression turned resolute. "But we can't trim the tree without hot cocoa and cookies." She reached for his hand. "Come on." At the door, she stopped abruptly. "Oh, my God." She burst out laughing. "I was about to go out there in my robe and bare feet. Like I think I'm at home or something. Hang on. Let me put on some pants."

As she slipped past him, he wanted to reach for her. One flick of his finger and that robe would drop to a puddle of silk at her feet. She'd be naked, her breasts high and full, her nipples tight from the slight chill. Her hourglass figure would be on display, the dip of her waist and flare of her hips.

He would kiss her with reverence, like the stunning goddess she was, and then he'd stroke, lick, and fuck her with abandon, just how the woman she was needed.

But he didn't do any of that. He watched her grab some clothes and dip into the bathroom, leaving the door ajar so she could continue to talk to him. "I can't tell whether you're just naturally talented or you did enough projects with your kids that you're familiar with a glue gun. How did you do the ones with patterns?"

"Those are Christmas cards. I used decoupage glue to adhere them."

"What a brilliant idea. Can I steal that one? They're really elegant." She came out in pajama bottoms and a sweatshirt, her feet tucked into shearling slippers. "All righty. Let's go."

Even this late at night, people sat in quiet groups in the

lobby, and carols still played on the speakers. The only thing new were the presents stacked beneath the tree.

He followed her through the kitchen door, and she flicked a switch that turned on the under-counter lights. "Can you grab a pot and a whisk, please? I'll get the milk and cocoa."

"Homemade? I'm used to the little packets."

"Oh, for sure. It's the only way."

He didn't know where anything was in this enormous industrial kitchen—she'd already set out the ingredients when they'd made cookies—but they couldn't be too hard to find.

He couldn't stop thinking about what she'd said. *By far, it's the best gift I've ever received in my life.*

This woman had married, had two children, and those ornaments a kid could make were the best gift?

He already knew the kind of man her ex was—but what about the kids? Did they keep in touch with her? Did her daughter know how hard it was for Margot to be so far away while she planned a wedding? He had the sense she didn't include her mom the way Margot needed.

Had her ex ever made her feel special? Had he encouraged the kids to pamper her on Mother's Day and birthdays?

He knew how hard it was to build a business—knowing you needed to provide for your family and couldn't fail because their well-being rested squarely on your shoulders—and still be a good father and husband. Nothing he did could please his ex, but that didn't stop him from making sure his children celebrated her.

Margot came over to him with a box of cocoa powder, a

bag of sugar, and a gallon of milk. "With the kids, I liked to do as much homemade as I could." She headed back into the pantry. "Because it was my job to make the magic. I'm kind of like my aunt that way. I wanted to build the excitement by putting up decorations a month in advance. I wanted my kids to wake up in awe on their birthdays with streamers and balloons and signs." She poked her head out. "Do you know what I mean?"

"I do. I figured that out after the divorce. Before, holidays and birthdays were about dinner reservations and piles of presents. There wasn't any magic. But after, I created family traditions for my kids. Not having them full time was hard for me, so I probably overcompensated by making a big deal about their every achievement—not just birthdays and graduations, but even the smaller successes of getting a good grade on an essay or playing well in a volleyball tournament."

When Margot returned with vanilla, marshmallows, and chocolate bars, she got busy measuring and adding the ingredients to the pot. "Do you want the Moravian cookies or should we make something different?"

"The Moravians are fine." He grabbed the tongs sitting beside a big glass cookie jar and pulled out four of them. "What can I do to help?"

As she whisked, she said, "You can give me a marshmallow."

He opened the bag and plucked a few out. He was going to hand her one, but she had her mouth open like a baby bird. He popped it in, intending to make it as sexless an act as possible, but his pinky brushed her bottom lip. He watched her eyes go hot and sultry, and his body lit up. In that moment, he knew how responsive she'd be in bed.

But he wasn't about to turn this sweet moment into an X-rated one. "Did you and your kids exchange presents this year?"

"I suggested we skip it. None of us can really afford it —mostly, the shipping—so why not wait till we're in a better position? Instead, we'll do a video call, just the three of us. There's no better present for me anyhow." She handed him the whisk. While he took over, she broke the chocolate bar into chunks and added the pieces into the warming milk.

"You're so positive. I really like that."

"Well, thank you. I certainly wasn't like this a few months ago. My ex is a doom-and-gloom guy. No matter how I tried to spin the future, he'd always say things like, 'By the time I make money again, I'll be too old to enjoy it,' And you know what? I'm not like him. Never have been. I didn't know I was living under his dark cloud until I walked out from under it."

"I get that." He'd suffocated in his marriage. It was all about Courtney's needs and how he wasn't meeting them. She did nothing to make herself happy—just expected him to do it.

"And I'll tell you something. I don't for one second believe that where I am today has any bearing on what tomorrow will look like. I feel *good*. I'm ready to make the best out of every moment I'm gifted with." She added vanilla to the simmering cocoa.

Damn, but he liked this woman. He couldn't help tucking a lock of dark, silky hair behind her ear. She flashed him a sweet smile, and a yearning rose so big, so encompassing, it stole the breath right out of his lungs.

It hurt to want someone this badly. To know he'd found a woman like Margot—the first woman who'd incited any kind of romantic spark—only to know in the morning, he'd walk away.

"You talk a lot about Jessa and Walker, but not so much about your oldest. Is it a difficult relationship?"

"Ah, just complicated, really." As much as he wanted to tell her about Lorelei, he couldn't. He had to respect—and protect—his daughter's privacy.

She watched him, waiting for more.

But Margot wasn't asking *who* his daughter was. She wanted to know his relationship with her. "My ex misrepresented me for many years, so my daughter believed I was a piece of shit. Fortunately, the truth came out at the beginning of this year, so I got to spend the summer with her." That first phone call had blown him wide open.

"Dad? It's me. Lorelei. Mom lied. She lied about everything."

It had taken a while before his powerhouse daughter had relaxed enough to trust him. But finally, she had. "It was great." Before the people she loved betrayed her.

"I'm so glad she got to see the real you." She touched his arm. "Because you're a good dad. Jessa obviously adores you, and you have a great relationship with your son and grandson. Your oldest deserves to know you, too." She grabbed two red mugs with white Christmas trees circling them. "Jessa showed me the photo album she gave you."

He cocked his head. "When?"

"This was before I met you guys. I heard her asking the

concierge if we had any wrapping paper. She said she didn't have a car and couldn't get into town to buy some, but I happened to have some in my room, so I grabbed it for her. What a great gift. I got a strong sense of you as a dad from those pictures, and it was really sweet."

"Yeah. I have…" He swallowed. "Good kids." His thoughts scrambled again, and he didn't understand why he kept locking up around her. "They mean the world to me." He cleared his throat. "Good gift."

"Okay, I get you now." She broke into a huge grin. "I totally get it."

"What do you mean?"

"When you get emotional, you get all choked up."

He gave that some thought. Was that the scrambling— him getting emotional? "Maybe."

"It's a good thing. Now, the question is…why did you get that way when you dropped off my present?"

"I think you know the answer to that."

"No, I don't think I do. Besides, even if I could guess, I'd rather hear it from you."

"Because I like you."

"*Like* me, like me?" she teased.

He nodded, not playing around.

"Even though you said you're not 'cut out' for romantic feelings?"

"Yeah. That's what I thought." He gazed into her eyes. "I was wrong."

Chapter Seven

MARGOT DIDN'T WANT TO PUT THE LAST ORNAMENT ON the tree. Because once they finished, it was over. They'd had a great night, but it was late, and he needed to pack and get ready for his flight.

She held up the clear plastic icicle. "This is so pretty." He'd filled it with red glitter. He'd made others in gold, green, and pearlescent white, too. All together, he'd created three different styles of ornaments. It must've taken him hours to do all this.

Finding an empty branch, she went ahead and hung it. Then, she took a step back to take in their handiwork. It was so festive, his effort so kind and overwhelming, she couldn't believe he'd done this for her. "It's perfect." She inhaled the sharp pine scent. "If I close my eyes, I'm in my house in Greenwich, trimming the tree with my kids and singing along to rock 'n' roll Christmas carols." She smiled at him. "Thank you for giving me a little slice of home."

"You're welcome." He eyed the tree. "I should've bought lights."

"Yep. You're right." She gave an exaggerated sigh. "Forget it. Let's just toss the whole thing." And when he broke into that dimpled grin, her pulse kicked into overdrive. "Cut it out. It's perfect just as it is." Affection tumbled through her. She couldn't help but hurl herself at him, hugging him close and pressing her cheek against his warm, solid chest. "You're an incredible man." His soft cotton shirt smelled of laundry detergent, and underneath was something unique to him. Something that connected with her very essence.

His hand went to the back of her head, and he held her to him like she was precious. She never wanted to leave the safety of his arms.

Wait a second—was he shaking? She leaned back to look at him. "Are you all right?" He looked tortured, and she tried to pull away. "Oh, my God. I'm so sorry."

His hold tightened. "For what?"

"For making you uncomfortable. I got carried away."

"No, you didn't. I'm just not used to…this."

She tried to laugh it off. "Hugs from strange women?"

"Oh, no. *That* happens all the time." He cracked a grin. "No, I don't connect with a lot of people. I don't understand why I like you so much."

She laughed. "Yeah, me neither."

"I don't mean it like that."

"I know." She touched his arm. "I know what you meant. Believe me, I've known a lot of people in my life, and I've never felt anything like this either. Even with my ex. And he was a force of nature."

"What does that mean?"

She stepped away from him to gather the empty bags and tidy the room. "He worked hard, he partied hard. He was funny and loud and the life of the party." She dusted the glitter off the nightstand and into her hand. "He swept me off my feet. It was exciting and fun, but we never had this kind of crazy energy." Fluffing her pillows, she climbed onto the bed. She patted the mattress, and he stretched out beside her.

"And what were you like?" he asked.

"When I met him, I was living my dream of being an artist in New York City. That's the pretty side of it. The reality was I was scared, overwhelmed, and didn't know how in the world I was going to make a go of it."

"Did you have a job?"

"I had an internship at a gallery. It didn't pay much, but it showed me I was way out of my element. All those ideas in my head of hanging out with artists and being the toast of the town went right out the window."

"I'm sure it was intimidating."

"It was, and not just because it was so competitive. New York is a whole other level of creativity."

"How did you meet him?"

"He'd just moved into his first nice apartment, and he wanted 'real' art. He was what my daughter's friends call a 'finance bro,' and he knew exactly what he wanted in life. Wall Street, big money, big life."

"Was that the life you wanted?"

"Oh, God, no. I was an only child, so all I really wanted was a husband, a family… I wanted to make pancakes and go apple picking, and somewhere in all that, I'd be in my studio painting and selling my work. As the kids got older, I'd have showings." She said it lightly as if it didn't matter, but it did. It mattered so much. "I got to have the family and bake birthday cakes for my kids. The only thing I didn't get to do was my art. But I can do it now."

"You are. You're doing it." His belief in her was empowering.

She wondered if he knew the impact he had. "You know, your daughter told me women fall all over themselves to get to you." She shifted onto her side so she could face him. "She thinks it's because of your air of mystery."

"But she's wrong?"

"Oh, yeah. Now that I've come to know you, I can see the real reason."

He rolled onto his side, too, making a show of sinking into the pillows and getting comfortable. "Go on."

"It's the wildfire in your eyes. Jessa thinks every woman wants to be the one the rich, mysterious man chooses, but *I* think they want to be the one who finally gets you to break down the walls and let the beast out."

"Beast, huh?" He stuttered out a laugh. "I can guarantee that's not what they're seeing."

"Why do you say that?"

"Because you're the one who lit the match."

A flash fire tore across her skin, enflaming her. "Beau?"

"Yes."

"If we had one night together…"

Don't say it.

Just shut your mouth.

He brushed the hair out of her eyes.

"I wouldn't want you to restrain yourself." The words tumbled out.

His eyes flared. His cheeks turned scarlet. "What're you saying, Margot?"

Her name in his mouth was the sexiest, most erotic thing she'd ever heard. Rugged, gravelly, it gave her flashes of their bodies grinding against each other, his big, calloused hands cupping her breasts, pushing them together as he sucked on her nipples. This nice, polite man would be unhinged in bed.

With me.

Only me.

"Nothing." She flopped onto her back. "You're leaving, and I couldn't survive a hookup. Not after everything I've just gone through."

Closing his eyes, he clenched his jaw. When he opened them, he said, "I'd never want to hurt you."

"And it's not because I'd feel used. It's not like that."

He remained on his side, hiked up on an elbow. "What's it like then?"

"I'm living in a room at my aunt's lodge. I'm disconnected from my old life, and I haven't connected to a new one. I'm just so…"

"Lost?"

"Sometimes, when I'm lying in bed at night, I see myself as this satellite moving across the sky. It's one small part of the galaxy, but it's separate. It doesn't really belong anywhere."

"You belong with your children."

"I love my kids with everything in me, but I don't feel…" She didn't know how to explain it. "I gave them my whole heart and soul, and I thought I was weaving us together, that we'd forever be this one piece of fabric, but what I realized is that I was nothing more than their steward. My job was to guide them to adulthood."

"Just because you don't live under the same roof doesn't mean you're not still deeply connected."

"No, I know that. I'm not saying it well. I just mean they have their own lives now. Their own *inner* lives they don't share with me anymore. I was a cheerleader, a therapist, a chauffeur, a chef, a nurse…but I launched them, and now, they're off in the world making their own decisions and living life without me. They love me. They're loyal to me. But…"

"I get what you mean. Your daughter's getting married and starting her own branch of the family tree. Connected, but separate."

"Yes, exactly. And I want to belong so badly. I want to be so tightly woven with another human being that nothing can tear us apart. I thought I had it with my ex, but I was wrong. I was nothing more than an accessory, there to serve him through that period of his life." She gazed up at the ceiling, seeing his face when he told her he hoped she, too, found an exit ramp. "You don't discard your person."

"No, you don't." His tone was adamant.

She liked that he got so worked up over what happened to her. Not only did she need the confirmation that it was disgusting, but she didn't have a protector in her life. Not since her parents died in a car crash her sophomore year of college had anyone ever made her a priority. "I like you, Beau, and it sucks that you're leaving tomorrow. But maybe we should look at it differently. Maybe the whole point of meeting was to give each other hope. Now, we know this kind of attraction's possible." Her brain delivered nice words that her heart wasn't buying into. She sighed. "I think I've waited my whole life to feel this."

He went dead quiet.

Regret seized her. *Why did you say that?*

He's a guy. He doesn't need you romanticizing your day together. "Sorry. I spend too much time alone."

Reaching for her, he cupped her chin, forcing her to look at him. "You're wrong."

"I am?" *About what?*

"You think, now that I've met you, I'm going back to Calamity, and I'm somehow open to falling in love? Bullshit. I'm not going to find another you. There *is* no other you."

Her blood turned molten, and that intense look in his eyes drenched her body in pure aching need. "I don't like charming men," she whispered.

"Fuck that. I wouldn't know charm if it grew out of my ass." He moved in even closer, his blue eyes burning. "I've never felt this way for anyone else, which makes it unlikely I'll ever feel it again. It's *you*. Do you understand me? It's not like you've healed me or unblocked me. I've never felt romantic interest before because I hadn't met you." His thumb swept over her bottom lip.

He was right. *It's Beau. Only him.* He awakened every cell in her body and made them sing.

His gaze caressed her features. "You're so beautiful. When I look at you, I see someone my heart recognizes but my mind can't place. I can't think straight, and everything feels new and exciting. I don't know how to explain it other than there's a magnetic field between us, and every time I come near you, I feel the pull."

"I feel it, too."

He sucked in a harsh breath, and his fingers tightened on her chin. "Listen to me. If you don't want me to kiss you right now, I'm going to leave. Because I've tried to rein it in, but I've reached my limit. I can't be this close and not get my hands all over you. I need…" His nostrils flared. "More."

Desire stole her reason, her fight, and her ability to protect herself. Inexorably drawn to him, she sealed her mouth over his and kissed him softly, sweetly…testing. *Oh, God.* Just a taste of him turned her feral. "You can have as much of me as you want."

His hand slid up her cheek, his thumb stroking her neck. "Margot." His voice came out a pained whisper.

"I'm here." Hers gave permission.

With a growl, his mouth was back on hers. He licked the seam of her lips, and when their tongues touched, a lightning bolt struck her heart. He tilted his head, gaining full access to her mouth before deepening the kiss.

The swirl of his tongue was achingly soft, his mouth silky warm, and his hunger barely leashed. He leaned closer, his fingers sifting into her hair. "I don't know what's happening to me."

She didn't either. She was dizzy, floating, lost in sensations. It was so much more than lust. It was an intimacy, a desire to consume him, body and soul. Reaching under his shirt, she touched his back, finally, *finally* getting her hands on his smooth skin. He was so strong and muscular, so hot.

His skin pebbled, and he let out a sigh in her mouth. "I'm leaving tomorrow."

"I know."

"You don't do one-night stands."

"I know." She moved restlessly against him, one hand grabbing his ass and pulling him toward her.

"That's all this can ever be."

"And I'll take one night with you because it's better than going through my entire life without ever feeling this." God, she was *shaking*.

With a hand gripping the back of her neck, he rested his forehead on hers. "Then, I'm going to ask you nicely to take off those pajama bottoms."

She kissed him deeply, their tongues tangling, and she shifted closer, desperate for more contact. "Do you have to be nice about it?"

"Fuck, Margot." He rolled off the bed and kicked off his boots. He shot her a look that said, *Strip.* As soon as she shimmied out of her pajamas, he yanked the shirt over his head.

Yes. With nicely defined abs and a flat stomach, his body was gorgeous. And that V driving her gaze to the tent in his jeans… She could barely stand it.

He unbuttoned his Levi's and jerked them down, exposing his muscular thighs and a cock so hard it hit his stomach.

Never in her life had she gotten aroused at the sight of an erection. Kissing, foreplay, sure. But this man was so virile, so masculine…so utterly dear to her that she couldn't wait to get her hands on him.

And her mouth.

I want him in my mouth.

When he got back into bed, he straddled her, bracing his hands on either side of her head. His flushed features and the bunched biceps told her he was still holding back.

His dark hair tumbled forward, and she scraped it off his face. "You know what I want?"

"Tell me."

"If we only get this one night, then I want the real you. *All* of you." He watched her as if assessing her ability to handle him, and it only made her crave what he was suppressing even more. "You gonna give it to me, Beau?"

"Hell, yeah." Elbows locked, his chest on full display, he stroked his cock between her legs, parting her, and wetting it with her arousal.

Luscious sensation streamed through her. "Oh." She'd never made a sound like that in her life, all breathy and needy.

"You know what *I* want?" he asked.

"What?"

"You. Naked."

The muscles at the back of her neck squeezed. *Ugh. Can't we have sex with my shirt on?* He didn't need to see a body that hadn't touched a yoga studio or a gym in nearly eight years. All she did now was walk through the woods in nice weather. But she wouldn't kill the mood by telling him that. Instead, she pulled off her shirt and slipped under the blanket.

To her surprise, he rolled and got under it with her. Had she killed the mood with her self-consciousness? A guy like Beau probably had sexy, uninhibited women riding him like rodeo queens.

Still, the unadulterated desire in his eyes kept her from freezing up.

With a hand on her hip, he nuzzled her neck. His palm skimmed up her belly and covered her breast, giving it a lustful squeeze. With his body flush against hers, she could feel his hot erection at her hip, and she wanted it in her hand, her mouth, her core, so badly she forgot all about modesty. She only knew she needed more of him. All of him.

His tongue traced a path from her neck to her collarbone, and she gasped when it licked down to her nipple. Sucking her breast into his mouth, he flicked the sensitive bead over and over, stirring her up into a frenzy. She'd never felt so purely sexual in her life, and it was delicious.

When he continued his trail of kisses, alarms rang in her body, shattering the haze of seduction. She thought about her pooch and her not-so-firm bottom.

Until he licked a fiery path between her legs, and then, she stopped thinking at all. His broad shoulders pushed her thighs open, and his hands slid under her ass, lifting her, devouring her, making her writhe and thrust and grab fistfuls of his hair.

Electric heat coursed through her, and she never wanted it to stop. When his tongue found her clit, sensation exploded in her body. "Oh, my God." Lust spiraled and spun, twisting her in its hot grip. "Beau. *Beau.*" Soon, she was crying out, her hips smashed against his ravenous mouth.

As his tongue circled and flicked, he plucked her nipple, firing up the thread that connected her two pleasure centers. Desire spiked so abruptly, she exploded in a climax that ripped through her. Catapulting out of her body, she floated free and unencumbered in a state of perfect bliss.

As the contractions eased, and her skin cooled, her bottom lowered to the mattress. But she barely had a moment to catch her breath before he loomed over her, his mouth sealing over hers and kissing her with voracious hunger. His cock teased her entry, easing in just slightly, then pulling back out.

He lowered his face into the crook of her neck. "I don't have protection."

Her fingers scraped across his scalp. "I haven't had sex in over a year, and trust me, I got checked out eight months ago." She wrapped her legs around his hips and squeezed.

"I haven't had sex in a long time, and I'm clean, too."

She reached for his ass and urged him forward. He notched himself at her entrance and watched her intently as he slowly pushed inside. Pleasure suffused features.

It had been so long since she'd been filled she'd forgotten how good it felt. Even longer since a man *had* to have her. And not because he needed to get off, but because he needed *her*.

She hadn't realized how her divorce had hardened her until Beau softened her with his hunger.

As he drove into her, she clung to him. His breathing grew erratic, and he groaned deep in his throat. She was frantic to get closer, to feel him everywhere, but he was lost, out of his mind, so all she could do was hold on. She caressed his biceps as they bunched and flexed, thrilled by his strength, his power. His features darkened and his body went hot, his groans turning desperate, harsh, like he was barely hanging on, and she went wild with lust.

When he slid a hand under her bottom, tilting her hips at just the right angle, she cried out. It was all so intense— the smell of sex, the way he was losing control, his expression fraught with a mix of pleasure and pain—she was driven to heights beyond anything she'd ever experienced.

She came again—a second time.

That never happens.

It's him.

I want him so much.

And then, he slammed up against her, pounding into her in fast, hard thrusts. His head tipped back, and his cries turned frenzied, as he drove into her again and again. Finally, he let out a roar. "Fuck, fuck. *Fuck.*" Once his tremors subsided, his thrusts slowed, and he glided in and out as though relishing the feel of her.

When he collapsed onto his side, he wrapped an arm across her and held her close. "Margot?"

"Mm-hm."

"I don't want to leave you."

Oh. She stiffened. She knew he was leaving, but already? No snuggle time at all?

"But I have to take a little nap. Just…a minute, okay?"

She laughed. "Go ahead. Don't worry about it."

In a groggy voice, he said, "You snatched the soul right out of my body."

She didn't think she'd ever felt closer to anyone. Sifting her fingers through his hair, she was aware of his breath—the way it slowed, evened out—and the way his body slackened. And she knew the exact moment he'd fallen asleep.

This man was so precious to her.

He'd never know the parts of her he'd healed.

Chapter Eight

THE PRESS OF SOFT LIPS ON HER NECK AWAKENED HER.
She opened her eyes only to shut them again from the
brightness of the lamp. It all came rushing back. The gifts,
the sex.

Oh, what a night.

Beau kissed her mouth. "Sorry. I fell asleep."

She picked up her phone to check the time. "That's okay.
It was only twenty minutes."

"Twenty minutes I'll never get back." He stretched and
yawned. "But Jesus. I lost my fucking mind. That's never
happened before."

"That's because I'm an animal in the sack."

He chuckled. "What kind of animal? I blacked out, so I
couldn't tell."

"Hm. That's a good question." She called over her
shoulder, "Hey, Siri."

Her phone answered, "Uh huh?"

"What kind of animal makes its partner pass out from
sex?"

"That's not a thing," Beau said with amusement in his voice.

"Here's an article for you," her phone said. "'Fourteen Weird Facts About Animals.' Would you like to read about it?"

"Hell, yeah." She rolled over to click on the link and read the first fact. "Holy shit. Did you know giraffes drink each other's urine?"

"Margot? We just had mind-blowing sex. How are you talking to me about piss?"

But she'd already moved on to the second fact. "Wait, wait, wait. There's an Australian marsupial who has sex for fourteen hours straight." She cut him a look. "Can you do that?"

"I mean." He reached for his semi. "With you? I'm game to try."

At that moment, the lights went out, and the room went eerily silent. "Uh oh." But a few seconds later, everything came back on. "That was scary."

He didn't seem worried. "I'm sure the lodge has a generator."

"No, I meant for your flight. You need to get home."

"I've been watching the forecast, and the storm should've passed over by now. The roads'll be fine in the morning."

"Okay, good." She hadn't checked her messages in hours, and now, she saw she'd missed a few from her son. "Look. This is my son's unit dressed as Santas as they deliver toys to an orphanage."

"Which one's your son?"

"He's not in it. He's taking the picture."

He pulled himself up to a sitting position, stacking the

pillows behind him, then tipped his chin to her phone. "Show me one of him."

She clicked out of the text message and scrolled through pictures. "Here. This is Owen." She missed her sweet, quiet boy. "Isn't he handsome?" It was a high school picture of him wrestling. "This"—she tapped the screen—"was one of the hardest things I've ever had to watch. At the first meet, I walked into the gym and saw this boy wearing a head and neck brace. I asked what'd happened to him, and the mom next to me said he was a senior who'd gotten injured last season. I'm like *last year*? And he's still wearing a brace? How awful is this sport?"

"I was lucky. Walker refused to wear 'a spandex onesie.' How did your son like it?"

"It wasn't really for him." *Thank God.* "Did you play sports in school?"

"I did. My parents bought a house the summer before I started tenth grade. It's a tough age to be a new kid, so it seemed the fastest track to making friends was to join a team."

"What'd you play?"

"I showed up for track, but…" With a shake of his head, he grinned.

"What?"

"It was stupid."

She nudged him with her elbow. "What was stupid?"

"Running endlessly around a track. I felt like a hamster on a wheel. What was the point?"

"Um, to run faster than everyone else?"

"Exactly. Like I said, stupid. I tried a few other sports, but in the end, it was decided for me. The football coach said he needed a receiver. I had no idea what that was." He shrugged. "So, that's what I played."

She loved talking to him, all cozy and warm like this. "Did you like it?"

"Sure, I guess." He gave it some thought. "Actually, no. I didn't."

"Let me guess." She found him adorable. "You thought it was stupid."

"Yes, okay?" He chuckled. "I caught a ball. I ran fast."

"It's about athleticism, you goofball." Laughing, she set her cheek on him and wrapped an arm across his chest. "It's about outwitting and outplaying the other team."

"Look, both my parents were in academia. In my house, it was all about education and grades. I worked hard to get into a good college and didn't see the point of running up and down a field when I could be studying. Or at least out there taking a nice long hike."

"And looking at rocks."

"Yes. Looking at rocks was much more interesting than catching a ball." He gave her a pat. "Now, show me your daughter."

"Fine." She rolled onto her back and scrolled until she found a recent one. "All right. This isn't the best picture because she's surfing but look at her. Look how happy she is." Crouched low on her board, Emerson grinned as she rode a barrel.

"Oh, wow. She's good."

"She really is. I hate that I've missed out on this whole new adventure of hers. I used to be involved in everything, and now I only get pictures. It makes me realize how many steps I missed for her to get from one achievement to the next."

"It sucks that she lives so far."

"It does. But she's so happy there, I can't begrudge her this life." She kept swiping until she found another picture. "Here. You can see her better in this one. This is when we moved her into her dorm."

"You had the whole matching-with-her-roommate thing."

"Yeah, this was in our Greenwich days."

"Was it hard for you when she dropped out?"

"Only because we failed her. But now, knowing how happy she is? I think she's right where she needs to be. It was definitely harder on her dad. He really pushed the kids to get a good education. They could only apply to the top fifty schools. Otherwise, what was the point?"

"My school's ranked eighty-nine, and I did all right. But then, who cares what he thinks? He's lost all credibility at this point."

"Harsh, Mr. Gentry." She couldn't believe how comfortable she felt with him.

Can you imagine a life with this man?

Someone who listens, who asks questions, and *who goes down on me?*

He snuggled up against her. "Now, let me see a picture of him."

"My ex?" He might as well have doused her with a bucket of cold water. She had to scroll through a year's worth of photos to find one. "Here." The twist in her stomach had her barely glancing at the screen before turning it toward him.

He caught her reaction, not even looking at the picture. "Hey. I'm sorry."

"No, it's fine." Her reaction surprised her. "I just don't like him in bed with us."

"I get that. I shouldn't have asked."

"No. It was a perfectly normal question. I don't know why it upset me. It's not like I miss him or our life together. I wouldn't go back—not for anything. To be honest, it's an enormous relief to be free of someone who took up all the emotional space in our relationship. Still, it's hard to look at him after what he did. He's so…"

"Weak."

"Yes, weak. But also, selfish. Anyhow, this is the day he found out he got the consulting job. I hadn't seen him that happy in years, so I sent it to the kids. Kind of a, *Hey, your dad's going to be all right* kind of thing."

Beau studied the photo. "He's not as ugly as I'd hoped he'd be."

She laughed. "Why do you care what he looks like?"

"I want his outside to match his inside."

"But then, he'd never have been Petra's target." Now that she had someone to talk to about it, she asked the question that had bothered her all along. "Do you think they just happened to fall in love? Or do you think she set out to get him?"

"It's hard to answer that since I don't know either of them, but if we look at the facts, we have a former master of the universe. He's good-looking, in shape, and he's willing to work for free. I don't know a lot of people who'd do that."

"Only someone who's desperate."

"Exactly, and he's looking for an exit ramp. If she *is* on the prowl, she'll pick up on that."

She looked at her ex's giddy expression. It wasn't a good look. "So, she saw his vulnerabilities and took advantage of them, but what do you think Petra wanted from a middle-aged has-been? He said it was his resume. She's trying to trade lithium, and she needed someone with his background to attract venture capital money."

"Okay, but all of that was a long time ago. Wouldn't she want to find someone who hasn't been out of the workplace for that long?"

"Yes. For sure. So, what're you saying?"

"I don't know. I'm just looking at the facts. How old is she?"

"Thirty-eight."

"Does she have kids?"

"No, but you're heading down the wrong track. My ex would do anything to get his Managing Director title back...except have a second family."

"That seems pretty random."

"Where we lived, it was almost a joke how many older, successful men dumped their wives and remarried younger women. In almost every case, the guy would swear up and down he wouldn't have kids again. And what do you think happens? Their new bride winds up pregnant. At every school event, my ex used to howl with laughter at all the white-haired men holding their babies. Trust me, if that's Petra's game, she's going to be sorely disappointed."

"If she sets out to seduce him, we'll see how long he holds out. Of course, this theory's coming from a jaded man whose wife made sex a transaction, but if she was wild in bed, maybe he'd give in. You'd be surprised what men will do for great head."

"Especially after they haven't had any in a long time." *Years.* "And trust me, I was never wild in bed."

"That's his fault."

"Oh, I don't know about that." She didn't want to think about the number of times her ex just needed to get off so he could fall asleep, leaving her wide awake, lonely, and sad. He'd always wanted her to be more into it, but she'd needed more from him, too. Like foreplay. "I'm definitely no Petra."

"Fuck Petra, and fuck your ex."

There he went, getting all protective again. She loved it.

"The problem was never you. If that fucker ever made you doubt yourself, he's a bigger loser than I thought. In bed, it's all about responsiveness. Did he ever take the time to find out what makes you hot? Did he hold off so he could get you there first?"

"Maybe in the beginning, he did. But not for the last twenty years." *Twenty years.* How embarrassing that she'd settled for so little. Though, to be fair, she didn't even know how good intimacy could be until she'd met Beau. "You're getting awfully riled up about sex with my ex."

"Yeah, because I saw you cover your body."

She winced, wishing she hadn't been so obvious. "Well, I'm not twenty anymore. I'm not even thirty-eight."

"Trust me, it's not about age or weight. It's chemistry, attraction. I've never wanted anyone the way I want you."

"And you showed me that." *Which is why I lost my inhibitions.* "That was pretty clever, Mr. Lady-Killer."

"It wasn't clever at all. I wanted to be with you. It's not going to be good for either of us if you're self-conscious. I needed to show you how beautiful you are. How much I want you."

She reached for his hand. "You're perfect. You know that? Absolutely perfect."

"I'm not, but I sure want to be for you."

She couldn't believe he'd just said that. But just as her spirits soared with happiness to have this amazing man, reality punched a hole, making her plummet.

Because in a few hours, he'll be on a plane. And she'd never see him again.

She shook it off because this time with him was too good, and she was determined to stay in the moment. "Your turn. Show me your kids."

He leaned over the bed, reaching for his jeans. "How come you never say his name?" He pulled his phone out of the pocket, then settled back in against the pillows and punched in his code.

She'd never thought about it before. It certainly wasn't intentional. "If I don't, it's because he doesn't deserve it."

"That's fair."

"And I don't want to look at him because he's my past. Right now, I'm building a future. It's not that I have regrets —I loved being a mom and I loved giving my whole self to my family—but I neglected my needs for a very long time, and now, it's my turn. I'm excited about the adventure— well, of course, I'm scared, too. Who isn't anxious about the unknown? But I want—I *need*—to focus on all the good things that are coming my way."

"I like that."

"My ex made a choice, and now we're on very different paths. Petra's everything I wasn't. She's aggressive, driven, and cold. He used to come home from work and tell me stories about her life, how she was abandoned by both her parents. Her dad left the family, and her mom couldn't handle being a single mother, so she was raised by her aunt. He'd talk about how ruthless she was in her relationships. My ex wants money and success, and I want love and friendship and to live off my art. And if he hadn't left me, I'd never get any of those things."

"Well, this is highly disappointing." Mischief gleamed in his eyes. "Sounds like, when you go to your daughter's wedding, you won't be sneaking into his hotel room and putting Nair in his shampoo."

She laughed. "No. I think the choice he made will be punishment enough."

"Do you have a picture of her?"

"Of Petra? Not on my phone, but I can show you their website." She typed the company name into the search engine, and when she got there, she clicked the Management Team button. Petra's face popped up. Slender with short blond hair, she wore a beige sleeveless silk shell that accentuated her curves.

"Yeah, okay." He barely even looked.

"Not your type, huh?"

"Not at all. See how she's got her arms folded under her tits? She's saying I'm a professional in the board room, but I'll blow you under the table."

She burst out laughing. "*Beau.*"

"Do you disagree?"

"No, you're right. That's exactly what she's saying."

He leaned closer, setting his chin on her shoulder. "You're way more beautiful than her."

"He didn't leave me for a hotter woman. He left me for his own survival. Okay, your turn. Can I see Walker?"

"Sure, but just so we're clear. Your body drives me wild, and you have great fucking tits. But that's not what attracted me to you. It was your smile. Your kindness. You're…special, Margot. Trust me on that, okay?"

She thought she'd lost her ability to do that, but with him—at least in this moment—she believed him. "Okay. And just so we're clear, for an engineer, you have a pretty bangin' body."

He grinned.

"And that double-dimpled smile of yours has the power to make women swoon."

"It's my secret weapon."

"Oh, really? So, you're aware of your superpower and wield it when necessary?"

"No." He scowled. "You think anyone gives a shit about dimples in the mining industry?" He scrolled through his phone. "Here's Walker on his last birthday."

"Okay, that's interesting." Where Beau's hair was straight, dark, and brushed his collar, Walker's was neatly trimmed, wavy, and blond. "If I ran into him in the lobby, I wouldn't think he was your son."

"He's got his mom's coloring."

"He's handsome. Can I see Courtney?"

His mood darkened. "I don't have any of her."

"Not one?"

"Nope."

"Hm." She tossed the phone onto his lap. "I guess after what she did to you and your daughter, you wouldn't."

"Yeah, I'm still salty about it."

"I don't blame you. Okay, we'll forget about your ex. Show me the mine."

"No, hang on. I can find her on social media."

As he searched, she admired his profile, his strong features and kissable mouth. She loved the smooth skin of his broad shoulder and the sprinkling of fine hairs across his chest. The way he narrowed his eyes made him look like a movie star in an old western. She could picture him with his hat tugged down low, leaving the focus on those piercing blue eyes and his masculine jaw.

"She's got everything set to private, but here's an old one." He handed the phone over.

A blond-haired, slender woman stared right into the camera. "She's gorgeous."

"I'm sure she is, but I haven't seen her beauty in a very long time."

"You said she mismanaged your daughter's career. What does she do?"

"She's in the music industry." He quickly scrolled through more images. "Here, let me show you the mine."

"Wait." She leaned across his chest. "What's this?"

"That's the lodge we built."

"You own a whole-ass *lodge*, too?"

"Yeah, I've developed the land a bit. I'm trying to bridge it to town."

"What else do you have? Your own Grand Canyon?"

"Uh, no. That's not a bad idea, but we're sticking with a Wild West theme." He grinned.

"Poor, poor Courtney. She could've had her hand in all this."

"Nah, it's not her style. She's more Fashion Week than

Gold Prospector. You'd love it, though. The lodge has costumed employees, and we went all-out with the décor. You feel like you're back in the eighteen hundreds, only it's all luxury. We've even got a place where tourists can pan for gold, and then this…" He skipped ahead until he found an unfinished building. "This is the shopping center. That's the newest addition."

"What will it sell?"

"Well, that's the question. We haven't hired a commercial realtor yet since we're still trying to figure that out."

"You're a busy man." Up until this moment, she'd had a spark of hope. Just one, tiny little burning ember that maybe, possibly, something could happen between them.

Because I have nothing going on. Anything's possible for me.

But not for Beau. He had a full life. And the moment he left Merry Falls, he'd get swallowed up in it, and he'd forget all about her. Sure, a memory might pop up here or there. But it'd be a passing thing.

For her, his scent would linger in the air like a candle. His ghost would flutter through her room as a constant reminder.

"I am." He set his phone on the nightstand. "I think Jessa was right, though. There's something missing." He swallowed. "I didn't understand what she meant until I met you."

"And you say you're not charming." He might not mean to be, but he'd sure charmed the pants off of her. "I like you, Beau Gentry." She ran her fingers through the fine black hairs on his chest. "And I'm gonna show you how much." She slid her hand lower until she gripped his cock.

Watching her, he sucked in a breath, his eyelids lowering to half-mast.

She kissed a path down his torso, caressing him until he went rock hard. When she landed between his legs, she swirled her tongue around the head. Everything about him was big and strong and so essentially masculine that lust crashed through her.

He cupped the back of her head as if she might pull away. *Oh, hell, no.* His response to her—the groans, the tight thrusts of his hips…made her thighs slippery.

Still, she could tell he was holding back, and she was done with him being careful. She released her grip on him. "We've been honest and real with each other from the moment we met. In a few hours, you'll be gone. This is all we have. I want all of you, Beau. Can you give that to me?"

"You might not like all of me, and I don't want to ruin this."

"I'm not precious. I have a voice. If I don't like something, I'll let you know. Just…be your whole self, okay?"

"You want all of me? Here you go." With a growl, he rammed his cock into her mouth. As his hips rocked, he studied her reaction, and while it was way more aggressive than anything she was used to, she loved the feral look in his eyes, loved the way he fisted her hair.

Loved the way she undid him.

It was exciting. Thrilling. Empowering.

Gripping his ass, she took him all the way down to the root.

"Fuck, Margot. Fuck. Yeah. Take it."

His tone went from careful to rough as he fucked her

mouth. This side of him turned her all the way on. She sucked him hard, dug her fingers into his tight ass, and let him thrust as deeply into her throat as he could go.

"Jesus. Fuck." His cock grew thicker, the vein under her tongue swelled, and then he was coming. His hand held her firmly against him, and he pumped in hard and powerful strokes. She had no choice but to swallow every last drop.

And when he pulled out, he caressed her cheek. "You." He closed his eyes. "Are." Elbow cocked, he rested his forearm across his forehead. "Everything."

Chapter Nine

Too often, Margot woke up with a stab of fear. The moment she opened her eyes, she'd find herself in a full-blown anxiety attack and then spend the next five minutes doing deep breathing.

Inhale for a count of seven.

Hold for four.

Exhale for one…two…three…four…five…six…seven.

When she finished, she'd remind herself about her ever-growing business, her healthy body and strong mind, and her ability to provide for herself. She'd picture her children, both of them living their best lives. And then, her heart would fill with gratitude for Aunt Lucy, the only person in the world she could count on.

This morning, though, she woke up *sore*. In places that made no sense.

Also, she felt…good. Happy.

She stretched her body out, toes curling, arms over her head, and felt the soft cotton sheets against her body—*whoa.*

I'm naked.

And then, it hit her.

Beau.

A sizzle ran down her spine as she remembered her glorious night. Her biggest fear about dating was exposing her body to a man who might be used to younger women. Or at least accustomed to the bodies he saw on social media.

But last night, instead of being self-conscious, she'd felt totally free and uninhibited.

Her arm lowered, searching for him, but landed on the mattress.

Where is he?

She sat up and looked around the room.

He was gone.

She threw off the covers and got out of bed, looking for a note or something. She knew him. He wouldn't just walk out the door without saying goodbye. Her small room didn't have many flat surfaces, though. The nightstand held the Christmas tree he'd given her, and her dresser had a jewelry box, a bag of yarn, and two boxes of clear glass globes.

She glanced inside the bathroom. Looking for what, though?

Do you think he'd write on the mirror in red lipstick?

Come on. You're being ridiculous.

This was the plan all along. How many times had she reminded herself it was one night? A *perfect* night.

She'd known they'd never see each other again. Obviously. She was okay with that.

But to leave without saying goodbye made her feel...

What?

I don't know.

Maybe like it hadn't meant as much to him as it had to

her? *But that's not fair*. He'd been nothing but honest about his feelings for her.

You need to stop it. He didn't do anything wrong.

Still, nothing she told herself eased the sickening feeling.

And this is why I don't do hookups. I get emotionally attached.

Rationally, she knew she was overreacting. But she was so much more than a rational human being. She had feelings and wounds, and right now, she felt stupid standing there naked, her body sore.

And cold. It was unusually chilly this morning.

I need a hot shower. Then, I'll brush my teeth, grab some breakfast, and get to work. Because her life was all about forward motion. She headed into the bathroom and turned on the faucet, testing until the water warmed.

She wanted hot. Scorching hot, but it wasn't getting beyond tepid.

Fine. Warm, it is.

As the water ran down her body, she reminded herself how much she hated goodbyes. It would've been so forced, chitchatting while he picked up his clothes and got dressed. He would've felt like he had to make false promises.

Maybe I can fly you out for a visit.

Let's keep in touch.

Ick. That would've ruined everything.

The lodge had a special deal with a new luxury toiletry brand, and Margot loved the smell of its products. She poured shampoo from the sleek black and gold container into her hand and lathered up her hair.

He had a big, full life, and he'd forget all about her. Sure, on the way out of town, he'd remember their hot sex and the fun times. Might get a little wood when he thought of the way he'd taken her from behind that last time.

But by the time he got to the airport and got to his gate, their time together would be replaced with work emails and family issues. His real life.

And that's okay.

It's fine.

As soon as she got dressed, she'd do the same thing.

When Margot felt confident, she walked with a swing in her hips like a boss bitch. This morning, though, as she headed down the hallway for breakfast, she felt sluggish, and all she wanted to do was crawl back into bed and feel sorry for herself.

But she wouldn't do that. Nobody had done anything wrong here. Beau hadn't "used" her. Just the opposite—he'd been nothing but good to her. If she was hurt that he didn't say goodbye, that was on her.

In any event, it was over. She'd never see him again.

And as far as the future, she could forget hookups. *I'm not cut out for them.*

But as soon as she hit the lobby, she stopped thinking about it at all. Something was wrong. People milled about in anxious clusters, and a line had formed at the check-in desk. Every luggage cart was loaded and lined up against the front door.

All at once, it all fell into place. The power outage last night, the chill this morning: the lodge was running off generators. She looked for a familiar face to ask what was going on, but everyone was busy handling guests.

She needed to find her aunt and see how she could pitch in. Foregoing her usual morning latte, she moved through the crowd, picking up bits and pieces of conversation.

This can't be happening.

The roads are closed. What's a rental car going to do for us?

We've already checked out. Where are we supposed to sleep?

She spotted her aunt near the concierge desk, but before she reached her, she'd picked up a microphone.

"May I have your attention?" Her aunt's voice came out of the lobby speakers. "Hello?" When the uproar barely subsided, her petite aunt shoved two fingers into her mouth and let loose an eardrum-shattering whistle.

The crowd quieted immediately.

"Good morning. As you already know, last night's blizzard shut down the airport and the roads. North Carolina's not set up for snowstorms of this magnitude, and our driveway's private, so we won't be getting help from the county."

"But tomorrow's Christmas," someone called.

"I know." Her aunt spoke with compassion. "And while I can't promise to get you home in time to open presents, I can assure you we're taking care of everything on our end as expeditiously as possible. If you've already checked out and find yourself with nowhere to sleep, don't worry. No one's checking in, so you can go back to your room. We've got generators and plenty of food and drinks, so the restaurant will continue to serve your meals. If you have any questions, my manager, Rodrigo, will be standing by." The man standing beside her raised his hand and waved. "Be kind to him and be patient. This isn't his fault. It's an act of nature.

Breakfast is being served in the restaurant and the coffee bar as usual. Okay, carry on."

Had Beau gotten out in time? When exactly had they closed the roads?

I can't be snowed-in with him.

Can you imagine?

Faced daily with the man who'd snuck out of her bedroom? Who'd rather chew off his own arm than say goodbye?

She knew she was being over-the-top, and it might've been funny except... She had to admit she felt humiliated. She'd gone all-in with him, shared everything, including her body. If the situation had been reversed, she would never have walked out without leaving a note or kissing him on the cheek and whispering, "Bye, handsome."

She didn't want to see his awkward smile or engage in phony conversation, all the while pretending she hadn't sucked him down her throat.

Was there even an ounce of hope he'd made it out before they shut down the roads?

Her question was answered when something caught her eye. She couldn't say whether it was the shape of him or just his stature—his height and broad shoulders certainly made him stand out—but there he was, sitting calmly in a leather club chair. He had his phone in both hands, elbows on his knees, as he stared right at her.

She froze. If she didn't owe her aunt everything, she'd run back to her room, lock the door, and dive under the covers. She was too flustered, too confused.

I don't need this in my life right now.

But she did owe her aunt. So, she had to ignore him.

I can't talk to him right now.

Besides, it would be busy at the lodge.

They didn't even have to cross paths.

Beau had been unreasonably happy. The moment he'd gotten the news his flight was canceled he'd run back to Margot's room. He'd knocked, but he heard the water running, so he'd let her shower in peace—instead of kicking down the door like he'd wanted.

He'd camped out in the lobby, handling work issues, checking in on his kids, and glancing up every few seconds in the hopes of catching her when she came to get her coffee.

So, when he finally saw her, he'd nearly jumped out of his chair.

Until he'd seen her expression, and the way she'd stiffened. What the fuck was that about?

So much for his plan to drag her back to her room and kiss her senseless.

She'd looked at him like he was the stalker who'd popped out of the stacks in the library.

No secret smile for what they'd done last night, and no promise of more.

He was gutted.

Sure, he wanted to spend Christmas with his son and grandson. Plus, the leak at the mine was only worsening. He needed to get home.

But another day with Margot was a gift.

What had gone wrong? Had he been too rough with her?

Dammit. She'd insisted he be real. She'd said she needed it.

And the more real he was, the wilder she'd become. He knew that because he'd gone down on her right after he'd come, and she'd lost her mind.

Did she regret it?

Did she feel demeaned? Hell, he'd shoved his cock down her throat.

Even though he'd given her what she'd asked for—his real self—she obviously hadn't liked it.

The idea that he'd hurt her—taken things too far—sickened him.

Well, there was only one thing to do. He'd have to apologize.

Around him, people fretted over travel plans, bemoaning missing Christmas with family. The lobby smelled of coffee and cinnamon, reminding him he hadn't eaten yet today. Maybe he should grab something from the coffee bar?

A text came in from his son.

Walker: Any idea when the airport will open?

Beau: No. But my assistant's talking to the nearest private airstrip.

The forecasters had accurately predicted the storm, but what they hadn't anticipated was that it would stall and dump eight more inches over the same region. At no point had there been hope of him getting out of here.

But he hadn't known that when he'd awakened with a start and checked his phone. He'd realized he'd have to race to get to the airport on time. As he'd scrambled to find his clothes and get dressed, he'd argued with himself over how to leave.

He couldn't imagine walking out the door without letting her know how amazing she was, what their time together had meant to him, so he'd tried writing a note. He couldn't find the right words, so he'd wound up crumpling a dozen pieces of paper and stuffing them in his pockets. Finally, he'd run out of time, and he'd left.

Could that be why she'd avoided him? Because he hadn't given her the courtesy of a goodbye? He tapped his pocket, still stuffed with balled-up notes. When he apologized, he'd hand them to her.

Walker: No worries. Colt doesn't know what day it is, so we'll wait till you get here to celebrate.

Beau: Sounds good. You hear anything from Lorelei?

Walker: Nothing. Anything you want me to do?

Beau wanted to hunt down the assholes who'd hurt her. He wanted to tear up the mountain, uproot trees, and roar from the summit. But there wasn't a single thing he could do for his daughter, other than let her know he was there for her.

Beau: Just leave the door unlocked in case she comes home.

Walker: I got you, Dad.

Setting the phone on the arm of the chair, he thought about his next step. He wanted to find Margot, but the lodge was in crisis mode, so now was not the time. When he'd asked Ms. Gibbins what he could do to help, she'd promised they were all set.

He glanced at the coffee bar, but he was too wound up to eat.

Forget it. He'd head back to his room and get some work done.

As hard as he tried, Beau couldn't concentrate when Margot's expression in the lobby kept flashing in his mind like a billboard in Times Square.

He kept analyzing it, trying to pinpoint the emotions, but the only thing he'd picked up on was embarrassment. Why, though? She had no reason to be ashamed. She'd been fucking glorious in her sensual abandon. Had he demeaned her somehow?

Dammit. He needed to know.

His laptop pinged with an email from the lodge.

Dear Friends,

We're sorry for the interruption to your holiday plans, but we want to reassure you that we will do everything in our power to make sure you're comfortable, fed, and warm.

Rest assured, the restaurant, the bar, and the coffee bar

will remain open for extended hours to accommodate everyone.

Below is a list of activities to keep us all entertained while snowed in:

Gingerbread House making contest: 2 PM today in the restaurant

Santa and Mrs. Claus will be in the lobby from 4-6 PM with cocoa, cookies, and snuggles.

Christmas Carols in the lobby at 6 PM in front of the hearth

Karaoke: 8 PM in the bar

Please check in with the concierge if you need toiletries or help with travel plans.

Warmly,
Lucy Gibbins
Proprietor

He reread the list of activities. Any other time, he'd ignore them. But today, he knew without a doubt Margot would be helping. So, he powered down his laptop and headed to the restaurant.

With nothing else to do, diners lingered over lunch, so they'd sectioned off an area for the gingerbread house-making contest. He scanned the faces but didn't see her. Normally, they went for cozy ambiance in this historic building, but now, for the event, it was bright and festive. Mistletoe dangled from the low wood beams and wreaths hung on the walls. A set of three Christmas trees clustered in a corner, ranging in size from massive to petite. The limbs were heavy with ornaments and garlands.

Where is she?

One long banquet table held ingredients, and people were already gathering their supplies. Some had already claimed a table.

The kitchen door swung open, and Margot strode out with a round silver tray loaded with bowls of icing. His heart thundered, and a voice in his head said, *Mine.*

What?

What the ever-loving fuck was that?

He didn't get voices in his head.

Yes, she was beautiful with her shiny, dark hair and the hint of mischief in her warm hazel eyes. He loved her curves. Jesus, he could feel them in his hands—just the memory kicked up a hum of desire. And yes, absolutely, there was something beneath the surface that called to him. That connected with him.

But that doesn't make her mine.

If they lived in the same town, maybe they could date. But come on, she was eight months out of a devastating divorce. Was she even ready for that?

Sure, they got along great. *Because this isn't the real world.* It was an escape. And she didn't need the hardship of adjusting to a new relationship when she'd barely escaped the pain of the last one.

Get your head on straight and go make it right with her. Somehow, he'd hurt her, and he needed to hear her out, understand what he'd done wrong, so he could apologize.

He headed over, watching her set the tray down and

unload the bowls. By the time he'd reached her, she was just pulling out a chair at an empty table, ready to sit.

The moment she caught sight of him, her smile wavered. She looked like she wanted to flee, but then, her shoulders pushed back, and her features hardened with resolve.

"I guess it's just the two of us." He didn't pull out a chair, though. If he truly made her uncomfortable, he wouldn't stay.

That challenging look in her eyes—so different from the warm, welcoming one he was used to—scrambled his thoughts. He wanted to apologize, but he couldn't do that until he knew what he'd done. It wouldn't be sincere.

What do I say?

Last night was the best of my life. The last twenty-four hours have...well, awakened me. Yes, that was it exactly. He'd never felt so alive.

But if he'd offended her, if he'd hurt her, then it would be a callous thing to say.

It's not about me.

Where should he start?

He didn't know. So, he reached into his pocket and grabbed the handful of crumpled notes. He dropped them on the table. "I—"

"Mind if we join you?" Arms loaded with supplies, an older gentleman pulled out a chair, not waiting for a response. "Charlie and I—he's my twin brother—stay here every Christmas. We live right in town. Well, in the woods, but not far. I'd say a brisk twenty-minute hike. But what are two old men going to do for the holidays by themselves? So, we stay here. Ms. Lucy's always got things going on. She's a fine woman."

"She really is." Each table held bags of candy, so Margot began opening them and dumping the contents into bowls. "I'm Margot." She reached out a hand.

"I'm Bill, and this is Charlie." The white-haired man shook hers and then reached across the table to Beau.

Forced to tear his gaze off the ignored crumpled notes, he introduced himself to both men. Charlie, who looked slightly more rumpled than his brother, took a handful of jellybeans and popped them into his mouth.

When more people joined their table, Beau quickly claimed the only remaining seat. If he'd sat down sooner, he could've been next to Margot, but he still wasn't certain what she was thinking, so it was probably best to give her space.

Numbly, he sat there watching everyone join in the construction of the house. Margot started gluing the gingerbread walls together with royal icing.

While she gave off no hostile vibes, she was clearly ignoring him.

Texting might be a better way to handle this, but he'd never gotten her number.

While he sat back and watched, the group laughed and talked about their holiday plans, offering suggestions on how to design the house.

"You want a jellybean?" Charlie asked.

"Sure." Beau held out his palm, and the older man shared a few pieces of the sticky candy. "Thanks." Well, he couldn't just sit there. He had to contribute something, so he took one of the empty plastic freezer bags and snipped off an end. Then, he filled it with the icing and piped a ribbon of snow dripping off the eaves.

"Oh, I love that," someone said.

"Look, now we're not basic anymore," another guy said, and everyone laughed.

Mostly, he felt like he was outside a bubble looking in. He needed to talk to Margot, find out what she was thinking. It was killing him to think he'd hurt her.

He'd thought they were happy. They'd seemed so in sync. He'd never felt that way with anyone, but did that mean he'd lost sight of her needs?

Fuck.

If he could go back, he'd pay less attention to his own pleasure and more to hers.

As she sat back down, the sleeve of her sweater brushed over the crumpled notes. He tensed, waiting for her to notice them.

One fell off the table, but she was busy gluing the gumdrops and leading the charge. He got up and put it back, but she didn't notice.

He'd just have to wait until the event ended. In the meantime, he'd do his part to make their house stand out. Going back to the supply table, he found some ice cream cones and then picked through the M&M candies, grabbing as many green ones as he could find. After he got back to the table, he glued the round candies to the cone to make it look like a tree.

"Can I have some of those?" Charlie pointed to the pile.

"Go get your own," his brother said, laughing. "Let him make the trees."

"No, no. It's fine." Beau pushed some over and then got up. "I can get more."

But when he returned to the table, he found Margot was gone.

And she'd left the notes behind.

At six fifteen, the guests gathered around the fireplace in the lobby to sing Christmas carols. From his vantage point in a club chair, Beau could clearly see a bouquet of flowers behind the check-in counter. They were the ones he'd bought yesterday.

Impulsively, he'd gone into a flower shop next to the bistro last night. He'd asked the concierge to deliver them to Margot today, on Christmas Eve. It looked like, in the chaos, they'd forgotten to give them to her.

He'd meant to shower her with gifts, turn a lonely Christmas into something better. Instead, he'd done the opposite.

He glanced to the corner of the lobby where Santa was finishing up with the kids. It was Margot, of course. He'd recognized her immediately—her smile never failed to light him up like the Fourth of July. But it was also the way she listened to the kids with such genuine interest, as if she had the power to deliver their dreams.

Talk to me, Margot. Let me know what you're thinking.

But she was busy. All he knew was that she hadn't read his notes, and she hadn't gotten his flowers.

Which meant she was still hurting.

And he just couldn't stand it.

Chapter Ten

THE SILVER LINING IN THIS HOLIDAY DISASTER WAS that Margot finally got a chance to truly help her aunt out.

The man they usually hired to play Santa obviously couldn't make it to the lodge, so Margot had stepped in. She'd strapped a pillow around her waist, shrugged on the heavy, itchy costume, and sat in that throne-like chair for three hours.

She'd loved listening to the children and was surprised by many of their requests.

"*I want…I want…I want… Can I have some peanuts, please?*"

"*I want tools and underwears that don't has no balloons on them…and I want my brudder to stop being mean.*"

"*I thought Santa had blue eyes.*" That one had her laughing out loud.

Mostly, it had taken her mind off Beau.

Now, karaoke was in full swing, and she was racing to fulfill drink and appetizer orders. With a tray loaded with espresso martinis, she wove through the tables, nearly stumbling when she saw Beau enter the dining room.

All he needed was a cowboy hat to complete the look of an outlaw striding into a saloon.

How crazy was it that in all the chaos of a restaurant crowded to capacity, she immediately noticed *him*? And when their gazes locked, she jolted so hard, the liquid sloshed out of the frothy drinks. *Dammit.*

She shook it off. She'd had a whole day to let her emotions settle, and she knew she'd overreacted. Beau's heart was good. If he left without saying goodbye, he had a reason. It was impossible to get in anyone's head, but maybe, in his engineering brain, he figured since they'd never see each other again, they'd said all there was to say.

And honestly, he was right.

She arrived at the table. "Here you go." With a smile, she set each drink down. "Enjoy." As she turned, she scanned the other tables to see if anyone needed anything— well, okay, and to see which table Beau had taken. But she didn't see him anywhere.

That's weird. *Where did he go?*

Not that it mattered. In fact, it was best if she avoided him. Spending more time together would be dangerous. Just coming out of a painful divorce, her heart was still tender and sore. And her feelings for Beau were obviously way too big. She couldn't handle another heartbreak.

A young woman waved her fingers to get Margot's attention, jerking her back to the moment, and she hurried over. After a song ended, the singer handed her microphone to Felix. "Let's give a big hand to Selena." The audience took a break from eating and chatting to clap for the young woman. "All right. Next up, we've got Beau Gentry. Ladies and gentlemen, let's give it up for our friend from Wyoming."

Beau?

He hates singing. As he headed up to the steps, Margot searched the tables for his daughter. But that didn't make sense. How would she have gotten here?

The whistles and applause drew her attention back to the stage. With his muscular frame and overlong dark hair, he looked formidable up there. That movie-star jaw was impressive, but it was when he broke into a shy grin, revealing twin dimples bracketing his mouth that the foot-stomping began. Beau's chin lowered, and he waved a hand in an *Oh, come on* gesture. He took the microphone. "Thank you."

She knew how much he hated performing, so she couldn't imagine why he'd put himself through this. Not if his daughter wasn't here.

He whispered something to Felix and then pulled out his phone. He didn't speak to the crowd, didn't announce his song. But as soon as the first notes started to play, it was recognizable to everyone in the room.

It was one of Lorelei Calloway's biggest hits, a song about regret. It was lively and fierce, and it was about wishing you'd done something differently—just not knowing what.

And from the very first note, his gaze was pinned on her.

Tell me what I did
Tell me how to fix it
Swear on my life

I'd do anything to make it right

She'd ignored him the entire day. Treated him like a stranger, and he didn't understand why.

Right then, she felt childish.

Worse, *damaged.*

Which meant she was clearly too messed up to carry on a mature relationship. She just wasn't ready. She'd talk to him, apologize for being such a drama queen, but that would be it. She wasn't going to have another night with him where she got even more attached, because then what would she do? Go back into her cave and cry her eyes out?

No, thank you.

She gave him a warm smile that let him know they were good and then turned away and went back to work.

The guests lingered, clearly not eager to spend Christmas Eve alone in their rooms. Finally, though, the restaurant had mostly emptied, allowing the servers to clean up and collect whatever cash tips were left for them.

From across the room, she could see Beau had left something on his table. She headed over to collect it for his server. Touching the chair he'd vacated ten minutes ago, regret nailed her hard in the center of her chest. She'd acted like an idiot. She wished she hadn't been so immature.

If only her first attempt at a relationship hadn't been with a great guy like Beau. If she was going to mess up, at least let it be with someone less amazing.

Except...she'd rather be alone than spend time with someone who wasn't as special as him.

Connections like that don't come around that often. They're special.

He's *special.*

Focusing on the table, she realized he hadn't left a tip. It was just a bunch of crumpled pieces of paper.

Probably the lyrics to the song he sang. Maybe he'd looked them up on his phone and written them down. *Oh, well.*

Moving on.

She dumped the scraps into a big black garbage bag and continued cleaning up the room.

Margot shut her bedroom door, kicked off her sneakers, and fell face-first onto the mattress. It had been one hell of a long day. She was exhausted but strangely wired.

Something crinkled in the pocket of her jeans, and she groaned into her pillow.

She couldn't believe she'd dug through the garbage to save Beau's pieces of paper. What kind of sap does that? *How pathetic am I?*

Closing her eyes, she pictured taking a hot bath, drinking some of the special tea she used to buy from Mariage des Freres, and pampering herself with luxury skincare products.

But she didn't have a bathtub, and she could no longer afford fancy tea or anything but the lodge's complimentary lotion. So, she'd settle for a quick shower and brushing her teeth.

She stood, stripping out of her jeans. Before tossing them into the hamper, she emptied the pockets. As she dumped the notes onto her nightstand, she noticed he'd scratched out sentences. She opened one.

I DON'T WANT TO LEAVE YOU, BUT—

Wait, is this... is this a note to me?

I DON'T KNOW WHAT IT IS ABOUT YOU—

IF I WALK OUT THAT DOOR, I KNOW I'LL NEVER SEE YOU AGAIN, AND MAYBE—

Maybe what? Oh, my God, finish your thought.

A gentle knock on her door had her snatching her robe off the bed. "Who is it?"

"It's Carla."

What on earth is she doing here this late at night? "Just a second." She tied the belt around her waist and opened the door. The front desk manager held a vase overflowing with deep red roses. "Is that for me?"

"Yeah. A guy dropped them off last night with instructions to be delivered today, but with all the craziness, I guess they were forgotten. I was just clocking out when I saw them." Handing them over, the young woman gave her a weary smile. "Have a good night."

"You, too. Thank you so much." She closed the door and breathed in the scent.

They'd come last night? So, not from Beau then. Who would send her flowers? She supposed one of her kids could've done it.

She set the vase on her desk and pulled out the card.

DEAR MARGOT,
MEETING YOU CHANGED ME.
BEAU

Adrenaline crashed her system. The flowers, the crumpled notes... She'd had it all wrong.

Tearing off the robe, she threw on a fresh T-shirt and pajama bottoms and shoved her feet into her slippers. And then, she was out the door. Only when she stood alone in the quiet hallway did she realize she didn't know his room number.

God, she was so frustrated with herself. She'd known how he felt about her. He'd made it abundantly clear. Still, thanks to her insecurities, she'd gone and wasted an entire day when she could've been with him.

She had to find him.

She took off to the check-in desk, got the information from the night manager, and then, she raced up the grand staircase. She had to get to him, had to apologize, explain... She just had to be with him.

Outside his door, she took a moment to catch her breath. Exhausted from the long day, smelling like the candy cane she'd found in her hair earlier that evening from playing Santa, she must look a mess. But she didn't care. More importantly, *he* wouldn't care.

She knocked. When he didn't immediately answer, she wanted to shout his name. But she couldn't disturb the other guests, so she knocked again. Harder this time. "Beau," she whispered. "*Beau.*" *Oh, dammit.* Maybe he was a deep sleeper. Maybe he was—

The door flew open. "Margot?"

When she threw herself at him, he let out an "Oof." But he caught her, his arms belting around her waist, his face tucking into her neck.

"I'm sorry. I totally overreacted."

"To what, though? I don't know what I did wrong." He tugged her into his room and shut the door. "It's been killing me all day because I had no idea what I'd done to upset you. What did I do? How did I hurt you?"

Shame burned a path from the back of her neck to the soles of her feet. "I woke up, and you were gone. And I just..." Her cheeks went hot.

"You thought I didn't care. You thought I was just fucking around on my holiday—using you?"

"It was all in my head. I know that. I know *you*. That sounds ridiculous to say—"

"No, it doesn't. We might not have known each other long, but..." With a shrug, he let out a huff of breath like he couldn't explain it, it didn't make sense, but *here we are*.

"I know. I *know*. You didn't do anything wrong. It was all my stupid insecurities. But I saw the notes you left on the table, and I thought they were just the lyrics to the song, so I threw them out. But I panicked because I wanted to hold on to a piece of you and wound up digging them out of the trash. I read them. *Beau*."

"It's my fault. I'm an asshole. I take too long to make decisions. I didn't know if I should wake you—"

"Wake me. Definitely wake me. I can always fall back asleep, but I can't get back the moments I lose with you."

He scraped both hands through her hair, pushing it off her face, and he looked at her like she was the most precious thing in the world. "You're here."

"I'm so sorry for ignoring you all day."

"It's okay." Cupping her ass, he lifted her and backed her against the wall. "I fucked up, too. You gave me all of you, every inch, and I walked out as if I didn't appreciate the spectacular gift that's you."

Spectacular gift?

It all came into sharp focus, what she'd done wrong. She'd married a man who loved her willingness to go along on his ride. She'd been the perfect companion, providing a comfortable home, well-behaved children, and well-planned travel. Thinking it was her role as a wife and a stay-at-home mother, she'd met his every need so he could achieve his dream of conquering the world.

But she'd never been his gift. She'd never been special just for being herself.

Yeah, because you never showed him. She'd only given him the parts she thought would make him happy.

With Beau, she'd been her true self. And he found her *spectacular.*

What a terrible, terrible mistake she'd made. She cupped the back of his neck and drew him to her mouth. She kissed him with a desire so overwhelming it didn't fit inside her body.

With the flint of his hunger, desire ignited into lust.

No one had ever kissed her the way he did, like he was desperate, like he needed to reach deeper, to touch the places no one else had ever gone.

No one had ever treasured her.

As soon as he lowered her feet to the floor, he stripped off his jeans and T-shirt and got on his knees to pull down her pajama bottoms. He kissed her stomach, her inner thighs, and then, he lifted each foot, one at a time, and tossed the pants aside.

Her body trembled, and her legs barely supported her, but he was rising again, gripping her bottom, and lifting her, urging her legs to wrap around his waist. Feeding her deep, hungry kisses, he eased his hard cock inside her.

Every inch of her body tingled and went hot, the feeling so dazzling she could barely catch her breath. He fit her so perfectly, filling her completely, and the friction of his thrusts had her back arching as she cried out.

With his hands on her ass, he drove into her relentlessly, and when his breathing turned ragged, when his hands started trembling, he tilted her hips, allowing his cock to stimulate the sensitive patch that set her on fire.

He lowered his head into her neck and growled, "Get there. Fucking get there."

A delicious sense of calm settled over her right when desire hit its peak, the clash so volatile that her climax burst from deep inside her core. Fiery sparks rained down on her, and she planted her hips tight against his and ground against him.

He drove into her again and again. "I'm going to come so fucking hard." His hips punched, slamming his cock up into her, and he shouted with his release. His frantic thrusts slowed, and he moaned like he was savoring every last sensation.

Staying deep inside her, he swayed. "Today was hell. I missed you."

"I could've had a whole extra day with you. I'm just so mad at myself."

"Don't be. We're together right now." Slowly, he set her on her feet. "Stay the night?"

"Of course." She was right where she needed to be.

"You've been working all day." He headed to the minifridge. "Have you eaten anything? I've got food."

"I'm good but thank you. The only thing I need is a quick shower, and then we can go to bed. I just want to be with you." She grabbed her pajama bottoms and headed for the bathroom.

"Margot." The urgency in his voice stopped her. He stood there, starkly vulnerable. "It's never hurt to leave someone before. I needed time to process it, to make sense of the mess of emotions. All I knew was I dreaded going back to the life I had before you. I have everything a man could want—great kids, a comfortable home. I'd even realized my dream of finding my family's legacy and turning it into a gold mine."

"You have a full life."

"When Jessa tried to tell me I was missing out on something vital, I didn't get it. But then, I met you, and I discovered a whole other dimension." There was a plea in his eyes. "I didn't know what my life was missing until you filled up all the empty spaces."

All day, she'd experienced chaos, fear, and anxiety. But when she was with him, she had none of that. He cleared it all away with his sincerity. And it just lit a fuse deep inside her, warming her, infusing her with a joy she'd never experienced.

"I hadn't figured any of that out this morning." He lifted his hands in a show of helplessness. "I didn't have the words yet, so I left."

"Neither of us handled it well." Eight months wasn't enough to heal from the kind of betrayal she'd endured. She knew that now. She'd be more aware of her reactions.

"I wish I'd left a note."

Me, too. But she'd already lost a day with him. All she could do now was make up for lost time. "Well, as much as I would've loved to read it, I'm hearing it now, and that's what matters. And after my shower, I think I'll write *you* a note..." As she headed into the bathroom, she cast a playful glance over her shoulder. "With the tip of my tongue."

Ooh, she loved the flash of heat in his eyes.

She turned on the faucet, finished stripping out of her clothes, and stepped inside the tub. She closed her eyes as the warm water coursed down her skin.

I'd never met anyone it hurt to leave before.

I didn't know what my life was missing until you filled up all the empty spaces.

Just when she'd found some stability, this man had come into her life and shaken it all up. She was such a wild mix of emotions because she'd never been anyone's *spectacular gift* before. And she wanted it.

But she didn't get to keep him. So, along with the happiness that streamed through her was an ugly twist of self-pity. Because she was just so damn alone.

She wanted to be the center of someone's world.

With Beau, she could very well see that.

The sliding door rumbled on its track, and his arms wrapped around her waist. He brushed aside the wet hair on her shoulder and kissed her. "I couldn't wait." He held her tightly against him. "I've missed you all day."

The fuse he'd lit sparked and ignited, making her hot

and needy. Tipping her head back, she brought his hands to her breasts. She loved the way his fingers curled, gripped, then pushed them together and squeezed. She thrilled at the lusty groan in her ear.

He sealed their bodies together, his hard cock wedging between her ass cheeks. "You make me crazy."

But instead of bending her over and sliding inside like she expected him to do, he stepped away. He surprised her by lathering his hands with the bar of almond-scented soap and smoothing them across her shoulders.

Because he knows I worked my ass off all day and want to clean up.

He puts my needs before his.

Both hands slid down her spine, rounding her bottom. He knelt, caressing her thighs, her calves, and then lifting each foot to soap it up. She smiled when he got between her toes. *He's adorable.*

But when he stood up, he said, "Missed a spot." And then, he was all hot man. He plumped her breasts, pushing them together and pinching her nipples, making her restless and hungry for him.

That was it. She couldn't take it anymore. She turned to face him and looped her arms around her neck. He kissed her hungrily, greedily. She reached between them, pumping his hard, hot erection with soapy hands. "You make me feel like the sexiest woman in the world."

"Because you are."

She shook her head. "Only with you." She ran her hands all over his chest, loving the way his nipples hardened and his muscles contracted. "No one's ever touched me the way you do. Like you can't get enough."

"I can't." He turned her toward the spray, his big hands wiping the lather off her body. Once she was clean, he walked her to the other side of the tub. "Hands against the wall."

She'd never heard that commanding tone from him before, and it sent a flash of heat through her. Bracing her palms on the cool tile, she popped her booty and lowered her head, waiting. When he didn't immediately touch her, she glanced over her shoulder to find him staring.

All the joy was snatched out of her when she saw his focus on her ass. But then, she stepped out of her own head long enough to realize he was stroking himself, eyes half-lidded.

His gaze roamed up her back and collided with hers. "Look at me." He held up a trembling hand. "I'm shaking."

"Then do it." She faced the wall. "Take what you want."

In one swift move, he was up against her, his big, hot hands covering her breasts and squeezing. "I want to fuck these." It was a growl in her ear.

Excitement rose to a pitch that was almost painful, and she shuddered. "Yes."

He twisted the lever, shutting off the stream of hot water. Stepping out of the tub, he reached for a plush white towel and wrapped her up in it. Then, he lifted her and grabbed the tube of lotion on his way out.

"Beau." She laughed as he carried her to the bed. "I can walk."

He laid her gently on the mattress. "Yeah, but this way, I get to unwrap you like a present." Slowly, he peeled off the towel, his eyes burning with lust. He held the edge of the soft cotton and said, "Lift."

Her hips rose, and he whisked it out from under her. He gripped his hard cock and gave it a few strokes while looking at her naked body. "Toss me the lotion."

Instead, she pulled him closer, pushing his hand away and drawing him to her mouth. When she licked the tip, his eyes flared. As her tongue swirled and flicked, his body went taut with tension, and his cheeks flushed. And then, when she had his whole cock glistening, she pulled him deep into her mouth. She held him there, sucking and painting patterns with her tongue.

A sheen of perspiration on his skin and the desperate look in his eyes had her releasing him. "I think you're ready."

Climbing onto the bed, he pushed her onto her back and straddled her. He traced her lips with his erection, letting her taste his arousal. "Open." Expression fevered, he pushed inside and watched his length disappear into her mouth. "There's nothing sexier than your lips stretched around my cock."

Desire surged hard and fast, and she squirmed beneath him. She couldn't talk with him stuffed inside her, so she moaned.

His wolfish grin told her how much he liked that. "Now, push those tits together."

She didn't think she'd ever complied so quickly. When she had them pressed tightly, he eased his cock into her cleavage.

"Yeah." Bracing his hands on either side of her head, he slowly pumped, watching as she licked the tip with each pass. "Fuck, yeah." He quickened his pace, his brow glistening with perspiration. "Look at you." With fierce concentration, he slid into her mouth, letting her slick him up. "That's good, sweetheart. Really good." He pulled out, pitched his hips back, and then thrust between her tits again.

When he talked with that growl, when his eyes burned for her, she lost her mind. Drenched in need, she rubbed her thighs together and pinched her nipples between her fingers.

Her response only made him pump faster, and his breathing grow more erratic. His hips rocking, pistoning, he kept his gaze on her jiggling breasts. A sound tore out of his throat, half groan, half growl. "I'm gonna come. I'm coming. I'm—" He sat back on his heels, fisted his cock, and then shot his come all over her chest. His features, contorted with ecstasy, slowly eased until they went lax.

When he finished, he shifted down the bed, lifted her thighs onto his shoulders and licked into her. He wasted no time working her into a frenzy, making her hips twist and lift off the mattress. Heat and sexual tension coursed through her, making her pant and gasp. She grasped handfuls of the comforter, her back arching off the mattress.

She was already so close it only took a few minutes before she slammed up to his mouth and cried out with the most intense release of her life. She lost all conscious thought, her body in freefall.

Good God, she *soared*.

Nothing had ever felt as good as being with this man. She felt feminine, desirable, and purely sexual. While she reveled in the delicious aftershocks, he went to the bathroom and came back with a warm washcloth. After cleaning her, he covered them both with the fluffy down comforter and gathered her in his arms.

She curled up against him, slung a leg across his thighs,

and ran her fingers through his chest hairs. Peering at the nightstand clock, she saw it was just after midnight. "Merry Christmas."

He turned to see for himself. "Merry Christmas, sweetheart." He caressed her forearm. "Wish I had more gifts for you."

"You've given me the best I could ever ask for."

"Oh, yeah?" He sounded sleepy, sated...perfectly content. "The ornaments?"

"Nope. Confidence." She snuggled even closer. "I knew I lost my ability to trust, but I didn't know my ex's betrayal stole my self-esteem until you came along and made me feel beautiful and sexy and..." She gave it some thought. "Worthwhile. I always asked my ex and kids how their days went, but they never asked about mine. Over time, it made me feel like what I was doing wasn't nearly as important. But you listen, you ask questions, you make me feel like everything I say is meaningful."

"Well, it's their loss. It's not about what they find interesting. It's about staying close to each other. I know this from my kids. If I don't check in with them, we drift apart. If I ask about their day—listen to the stories about the driver who zipped into the parking spot they'd waited ten minutes for, or about the kid who came to class hungover and shit his pants—"

"Wait, that happened?"

"Oh, yeah. Happened in Jessa's master's program in September. Anyhow, the more stories I listen to, the more they tell, and the more I know about their lives. I want to be close to them, so I ask questions."

"You're so right. My ex didn't know me at all." *And that's why he could walk away so easily.*

"Honestly, I have a hard time understanding how your ex didn't fall at your feet in appreciation of you."

"In some ways, he did. He was always good about thanking me for dinner or telling me I looked beautiful. He didn't take what I did for granted, but he didn't ask me a lot of questions. He didn't want to know me the way you do. And now that I know what it's like, I can't think of anything a person needs more. Just someone who wants to know every little thing."

She realized something else. "If my ex knew I was angry, he'd avoid me. Or he might say he was sorry, but he never wanted to get to the bottom of it the way you do. And I really like that. It means you don't want problems to go away. You want to make things better."

"Thank you. I'm glad you feel that way." He kissed the top of her head.

"I told you my best gift. What's yours?"

"That's easy. It was from my parents, and it came when things were the worst with my ex. I was thinking about selling the land and giving up on the mine, and for Christmas, they got me photographs of Sam and Joseph Gentry."

"No way. Where did they find them?"

"The lore only talked about a location and six prospectors. There's no mention of names, so my dad did a lot of research to track them down. I keep them in my office, and every time things got tough, I'd look at them and know I was on the right track."

"Your dad was awesome."

"Yeah. He really was." His soft smile radiated love for his parents.

"Okay, what was your worst gift?"

He laughed. "Anything my ex got me."

"What kinds of things did she buy?"

"A fancy watch. A shearling coat. Cashmere sweaters."

"Ugh. What a bitch."

He chuckled. "It was her motives. She wanted me to look well-heeled."

His fingers threaded through her hair, and she found herself slowly drifting off.

"Thank you for coming back to me," he whispered.

Yes, he was leaving, but at least she had one more day with him.

And she'd enjoy every second of it.

Chapter Eleven

IS THIS WHAT IT FEELS LIKE?

Over the years, Beau would notice married couples laughing, enjoying date nights, and wonder if it was real. The in-jokes, the knowing glances, the touches filled with private messages...he'd never understood it. He and Courtney couldn't stand each other, but she'd always played it up in public, so from the outside, it looked like they were having a great time.

Could people stay close after so many years of kids, job losses, moves...all the shit that made a life?

Now, he got it. Because he had it with Margot. And it did something to him, cracked open a fault line he didn't know he had, making him see how deeply he craved this kind of companionship.

As they headed downstairs for breakfast, his sense of contentment was only heightened by the lodge's scents of pine, cinnamon, and warm bread. After spending most of his childhood in an RV, he'd viewed his cabin in Calamity as his first real home.

But in this moment, he understood that home wasn't four walls or a zip code. *It's* who *you're with and not where you are.* And Beau was his best self, his truest self, with Margot.

What a fucking revelation. Happiness ran like a stream under his skin, and he brought Margot's hand to his mouth for a kiss.

This morning, the staff wore elf costumes as they greeted each guest with a cheerful "Merry Christmas" and a small wrapped gift.

"Your aunt's giving everyone a present?"

"Yeah. She loves making her guests feel like family—especially over the holidays. She says if they choose to spend it here, she's going to make it special."

"Well, it works." They headed across the lobby. "What can we do? Does she need our help?"

She stopped walking and gazed up at him with a beaming smile.

"What?"

"You said 'our.' You asked if she needs *our* help."

"Right." He didn't get it.

"You could've gone straight into the restaurant and filled your plate full of food. You could've been thinking about boning me. Instead, you knew I'd want to help her, and you were right there with me. That's just really nice."

"Well, thanks, but we should get one thing clear. I *am* thinking about boning you. But if your aunt needs something, I can put it off for a few minutes."

She burst out laughing, and she just looked so sparkly and full of life that he couldn't help himself from kissing her on the mouth right there in the lobby. And this sense of dissolving into another human being was so foreign to him and yet… It was everything he'd ever been missing in his life.

She tipped her head back to gaze up at him. "What was that for?"

"You make me happy."

"I know. It's crazy, right?" She sighed. "Come on. Let's get breakfast. You're going to need lots of carbs if we're going to spend the day in bed."

"Oh, is that the plan?"

"Is there anything you'd rather do?"

"Not a single thing."

"Thank you for asking." She reached for his hand. "But I texted my aunt while you were in the shower. She doesn't need anything. Let's just eat. You won't believe the spread she puts out for Christmas."

He combed his fingers through her hair, and when he got to the end, he twisted it. "You got it."

The restaurant was bright and filled with lively conversation, laughter, and the clatter of dishes. Joining the line for the buffet, they grabbed shiny white plates with the green and gold Merry Falls Lodge logo. He lifted the lid on the first warming dish to find brown rectangles that smelled like sausage. "What the hell is that?"

"That's livermush."

"*Liver?* For breakfast?"

"Yep. It's pig liver, cornmeal, and spices. It's a staple around here. Most people stick it in a biscuit, like a sandwich."

"Pass." And yet, he noticed everyone was spearing a patty and dropping it onto their plates. *Must be good.*

She laughed. "Yeah, it's not for everyone. I'm starving." She gazed up at him, all warm and soft and sated. "Are you?"

Damn. Look at her. With that long hair, clean and shiny from a shower, those pink lips still swollen from fastening around his cock, she was feminine, bold, and everything he'd never known he wanted. "There's nothing here I want to feast on more than you."

Heat filled her eyes, and her tongue swept her bottom lip. "You still thinking about boning me?" she whispered.

"How long will they serve breakfast?" he asked.

"My aunt runs the place. We can eat whenever we want." She set her plate down on the nearest table and grabbed his hand.

Was she serious? *Hell, yeah.*

They hurried out of the restaurant, practically racing across the lobby, and he was laughing so hard his cheeks hurt.

Had he ever been this happy? This free?

He knew he hadn't. His entire life, he'd been driven. To get into college, to find the prospector's cabin, to provide for his family, to make sure his kids felt loved…

But not once had he considered his own happiness.

Until he found it in Margot Rhodes.

And he needed to fuck her right then like he'd never needed anything.

They'd just hit the staircase when he heard, "Mr. Gentry?"

Breathless, they lurched to a stop. "Yes?"

The desk manager's elf hat drooped over her right eye, and she brushed it aside. "Your car's waiting, sir."

He didn't understand. "You mean my rental?" *Waiting for what?*

"No. We're taking care of that. Your ride to the airport."

He cut a look out the front windows as if he could see the roads, the airports, and the ability to get home.

"The main roads are cleared, and your assistant was able to get you a flight out of the airstrip. She tried to get a hold of you."

He patted his pocket, realizing he'd left his phone in his room. "Okay, thank you. I'll uh…" He pointed up the stairs.

"No rush, sir. The driver will wait." With a smile, she returned behind the desk.

He looked at Margot as if she could fix the problem. But of course, she couldn't.

Their time had run out.

"You should pack," she said quietly.

In his mind, he organized his next steps. Going into his room, shoving his toiletries into his bag, zipping up his suitcase, and walking out the door.

Leaving her.

Forever.

But that was unthinkable. "I don't have to go right now. It's Christmas Day. I'll go tomorrow."

"What does one more day get us? No matter how long you put off your flight, you're still going home. You have a business and a family, and…and I have a business to run. I can't take time off. I don't get a salary and benefits, so there are no vacation days for me. Besides, your grandson's waiting for you."

"I don't want to leave you."

"Well, Beau, I don't want you to leave me, either." She rallied with a forced grin. "But you have no choice. So, let's not make this harder, okay? I don't think I could bear it. Please, just go."

He weighed his selfish desire for more time with her against the eight months of pain she'd just endured and realized she was right. The more time they spent together, the deeper the bond would grow.

With a hitch in her breath, she put her hand on his arm. "Goodbye, Beau. I've loved every minute with you." And then, she turned and disappeared into the crowded, festive lobby.

Beau had never felt more lost.

At his core, he had a reliable compass that had never failed him. So, it made sense, when he headed up the stairs, that it went haywire. Because everything was wrong. His gut pulled tight with the knowledge he was moving in the wrong direction.

Turn around. Go to her.

Except...the last thing he wanted to do was make things harder for her.

And so, he had to go. He had no choice.

Once in the car, Beau called his daughter. Even though the heat was blasting, he felt a chill deep in his bones. Tires shushed on the slushy road.

"Merry Christmas, Dad."

"Merry Christmas. Did the power come back on?"

"*Finally.* For real, I was frozen like a popsicle. I had on my parka, my robe, my blanket, and my roommate's quilt. But the power kicked in around six in the morning."

"Good, good." What was Margot doing now? He tried to picture her at a table, digging into a freshly made waffle, chatting up the others at her table as she always did, but he couldn't.

If she felt anything like he did, she'd gone back to her room. She was hurting. Missing him.

Fuck.

"You all right?" His daughter's voice broke through his thoughts.

"Yeah, sure. Why?"

"You don't sound good. You know Colt's only two, right? He doesn't know what day it is."

"No, I know. I'm all right. I'm headed to the airport."

"Wait, what?" He could hear her throwing the covers back and scrambling out of bed. "Dad. It's a winter wonderland out there. How are you driving?"

"I'm not. My assistant booked me a ride and got me on a private jet."

"It doesn't look safe out there at all."

"The lodge cleared their driveway first thing this morning, and the main roads look good."

"Oh, okay. Are you stopping here first?"

"Yeah, of course. If the campus is cleared."

"It's not." Her voice fell. "I'm looking out the window right now."

That made sense. The university was closed for the holiday break, so plowing wouldn't be a priority.

"How far away are you?" she asked. "I'll get dressed and walk out to see you."

"Jessa, no. Don't do that. Hang on." He lowered his phone to speak to the driver. "Change of plans. We can head straight to the airport."

The man nodded in the rearview mirror.

"Wait, Dad. Are you sure? I want to hug you goodbye."

"I do, too." Snow piled high on either side of the road, making it feel like a tunnel. "But it's okay. We got to spend some good time together."

"Why do you sound so sad?"

He didn't know what to say. *I'm going to miss Margot* sounded pretty foolish. And what would she tell him anyway? *You knew her for two days. Once you get back to work and your life in Calamity, you'll forget all about her.*

That's what anyone would tell him.

But it wouldn't be true.

He'd never forget her because she'd changed him. He was alive, all his senses awakened, and there wasn't a chance he could go back to his routine. "I spent a lot of time with Margot." He paused, unsure how much to tell her. "And it wasn't easy saying goodbye."

"Okay, wow. I'm shook. I'm literally *shook.* Not that you like her because, swear to God, Dad, you've never looked at anyone the way you look at her. But the fact that you spent time with her… Like, *that's* what you've been doing? Way to *go.*"

"It's over now."

"Hm, there's something weird in your voice. What's going on, Dad?"

"Nothing. Let's stop talking about it. It's done. I'm moving on."

"Are you sure about that? You've known a lot of people in your life. Did anyone ever make you feel the way she does?"

"No." Irritation spread like a rash across his skin. "What's your point? You think I should walk away from the mine? From Walker and Colt? You think I should move to North Carolina?"

"Of course not. That would be silly."

He grew uneasy. That wasn't what he wanted to hear. He wanted his daughter to pluck a solution out of thin air.

And then, she said, "I think Margot should move to Calamity."

Something inside his chest popped open, and possibility flooded him. "She's not going to do that." He only said it to staunch the flow. The idea was absurd. He shouldn't even entertain it. "She's got no savings, no income. She can't afford her own place. Besides, she can't just pick up and move in with some guy she's known for two days."

Can she?

Would she?

"Okay, let me think."

"There's nothing to think about. It's not going to happen." He should never have told her about it. *This is a problem that doesn't have a solution.* "Look, everything's fine. I had a great time with her, but now it's time to get back to reality. I'll call you when I'm home."

"Now, hold on a second. Let's give this some thought."

Yes, let's do that. Please. "It's a waste of time." He didn't need false hope.

"I don't know her whole story, but she's living in a room at the lodge, right?"

"Yes."

"So, that sounds like a temporary situation."

"It is."

"Which means she needs money."

She was going somewhere with this, and normally, he might keep up with her. "That's right." But right then, he had too much noise in his head.

"And you have a mall that's sitting there empty."

He grew impatient for her to make the connections. "She's an artist, not a commercial realtor."

"No, but you need a manager to run it."

Blood pounded in his ears. "I don't want her as an employee." *I want her as a wife.*

Where the hell did that thought come from?

He barely knew her.

Marrying her—yes, that was ridiculous. But knowing himself well enough to know she was the right woman for him? *Absolutely.*

"Dad, seriously, now that you finally found her, are you really going to let her go?"

"No." With his hand on the driver's seat, he pulled himself forward. *Make that a hell, no.* He caught the driver's eye in the mirror. "Turn the car around."

The moment Beau entered the lobby, he spotted her in the coffee bar with her laptop, latte, and an untouched scone. Her wrists were perched on the edge of the table, but her fingers didn't move on the keypad.

She looked unbearably sad.

I can fix that. He hadn't moved that fast since high school football.

She glanced up as he approached. "Beau." Her chair scraped back so quickly, it nearly tipped over. "Did something happen? Is Jessa all right?"

"No, she's fine. But I want you to come with me."

"Come with you where?"

"To Calamity."

"What? You mean like on vacation?" She looked almost frantic with concern. "For New Year's?"

"No. I mean move there."

"You know I can't do that." But her voice wobbled, and she didn't sound convinced.

He needed to calm down and make his pitch. "You can run your business anywhere, right?"

She barely nodded.

"Well, I have to hire someone to manage the mall. Why not you?"

"Because I don't know the first thing about leasing?"

"The realtor will handle that. But you can come up with the concept and help us figure out what kinds of stores will work so far out of town. Look." He reached for her hands and kissed her knuckles. "I just found you, Margot, and I'm not letting you go. And if that means I have to move into the lodge and run the mine from here, I'll do that. All I know is I'm not getting on that plane without you. Do you feel the same way?"

"Yes." The word came out in a whisper. "But—"

"There are no buts. We're past the age of caring what anyone thinks. We've tried living by the rule book, and what did it get us? My wife walked out with my kids, and your husband left you penniless. It's our turn now. We get to be happy."

"Where will I live? I…" She glanced at the coffee bar where her aunt was talking to the barista. "I had a plan."

"Are you willing to make a new one? To be with me?"

"You can't pay me *and* be my boyfriend."

"I'm not. I'm trading one of the spaces in the mall for a job as its manager. It can be your studio. And if you don't want to live with me, you can have a room in the lodge. It's nine minutes from my house, and that's a hell of a lot closer than Merry Falls, North Carolina." He studied her, needing to figure out if she would even consider his idea. "Do you want to do that?"

She was practically vibrating with energy. "But I live here."

"Not anymore you don't." Her aunt slammed the laptop shut and thrust it at her. "I need your room back." She gave her niece a meaningful look. "I'm kicking you out."

Margot burst out laughing. "You would never do that." She pulled her aunt into her arms. "I love you so much."

"It's your time, sweetheart." Ms. Gibbins patted her back. "Take it."

Margot released her and covered her mouth with a hand. "Are we really doing this?"

"Yeah, we are."

Holy shit. It's happening.

Margot's moving to Calamity.

"Now, pack up. We have a flight to catch."

. . .

Beau couldn't believe it. He'd never thought she'd go for it. Uproot her life and come to Wyoming?

But she's here.

She's doing it.

"When you said flight, I was thinking commercial." In the leather chair beside him, she kicked up her feet. "Complete with no legroom, the last seat next to the toilets, and a bag of pretzels."

Beau reached for her hand. "If we'd relied on the airlines, who knows how long we'd be stuck in North Carolina. I have to get back."

"Right. Christmas with Colt?"

"Yes, but also, issues with the mine."

"Is it bad?"

"It could be." It wasn't the financial hit he'd likely take as much as the possibility of losing everything. But he didn't need to think about that now, because he had Margot. Coming to Calamity. To live with him.

He needed to tell her about Lorelei. "Hang on a sec." He released her hand to grab his phone off the table.

Beau: Merry Christmas! Want a homecooked dinner? Your stocking's stuffed with presents…

He gave her a moment to respond, but it didn't say Read or Delivered. *Damn.*

Beau: I've got a question for you. Can you give me a quick call?

Still nothing. His daughter and her security team had

very strict guidelines to protect her closest friends and family, but after what happened in town with Colt a few months ago, she was even more insistent about hiding her identity. He needed to tell Margot, but he at least wanted to give his daughter the courtesy of a heads-up first. He'd give her a chance to respond.

He set his phone back down. "So, what're you thinking? Cold feet? Want to turn the plane around?" It happened so fast. She must have doubts.

"Right now, it doesn't feel real. I mean, one day, I'm living in my aunt's service quarters, and then I blink, and I'm on a private jet heading off to Wyoming with this incredibly handsome man I met two days ago but feel like I've known a whole lot longer. I'm excited. I'm terrified. And I'm waiting for the other shoe to drop."

"And what does that shoe look like?" He wanted to be sure he paid attention. For this to work, he needed to understand her concerns.

"It looks like us finding out we're not compatible after all. Like me waking up one morning and realizing I made a terrible mistake."

He threaded their fingers together. "We have the advantage of age and experience, don't you think? We've learned how to read people better. We *know*."

"Yeah." He loved the certainty in her eyes. "That's how it feels to me."

He kissed her. "There'll be hiccups, we'll make mistakes, but Margot, we're both going to work hard to keep us on the right track." He kissed her again, his senses firing up at the touch of her tongue. The slick heat of her mouth, the now-familiar scent of her shampoo, and the way she always clutched him when they were intimate… All of it gave him a profound sense of rightness. "I'm happy." He kissed her again, longer this time, pouring his heart and soul into her. He needed her to believe him. "I'm going to love you like you've never been loved before."

Chapter Twelve

Margot had experienced cold before. She'd grown up outside New York City and raised her kids in Connecticut. But the moment she stepped off the plane, her entire body seized up. Wyoming in December was *freezing*.

"Don't worry." Beau wrapped an arm around her and pulled her close. "This is the coldest month. It only gets better from here." He ushered her into the back of a black sedan.

"Welcome to Calamity," the driver said before heading out of the airstrip's parking lot.

"Thank you. I'm so excited to be here." Hot drinks sat in the twin cupholders. It was a kind gesture, and she didn't want to be rude, but she didn't drink black coffee.

Beau tasted his. He lifted it so the driver could see through the rearview mirror. "Perfect. Appreciate it."

"No problem," the driver said.

Beau tipped his chin to hers. "That should warm you up."

He knew her preferences, so she chanced a sip and found

it was the best vanilla chai latte she'd ever tasted. "How did you know?"

The driver smiled. "Mr. Gentry told me what to get you."

Impulsively, she leaned in and kissed Beau's cheek. "Pinch me." She grabbed his hand and forced his thumb and index finger together. "So, I can be sure I'm not making you up."

Grinning, he pinched her cheek. "You're cute, getting excited over a chai."

"I think you know it's not about the chai." When she cuddled up to him, he gripped her thigh in a claiming gesture, and it made her pulse go wild.

She couldn't believe she'd actually done it.

She'd moved across the country with a man she'd just met.

But what-ifs were swooping around her mind like bats in the dead of night.

What if the passion fizzles out?

What if I get up one morning to find I've awakened next to a stranger?

All those possibilities seemed more probable than things working out between them.

Damn you, Scott.

Look what you've done to me.

Her ex had changed her definition of the word love when he'd shown her self-preservation trumped it. He'd shown her that loyalty hinged on the conditions of one's life.

She'd known Beau for a few *days*. He could be bored of her in a week. He could fall in love with someone new next month.

Or… It could work. And if she didn't believe that, then she should turn the car around and run back into her room at the lodge.

Nope. Not going anywhere.

She kissed his cheek, breathing in his woody, pine scent. "You okay?"

"Perfect." She wasn't going to vomit her anxiety all over him. She needed to get it under control. *The only way to make sure the relationship fails is to sabotage it.*

Yes, her ex had screwed her over, and no, Beau's character hadn't been tested, but something in her gut pressed her to trust him, to give him—*them*—a chance, and so, she'd give it her all.

The snow-covered forest on either side of the highway was right out of a fairy tale. "This is beautiful." A horse-drawn sleigh cruised across the vast acreage of the bison preserve. "We're going to have so much fun." *If we make the time.* Her ex wasn't a great communicator, so she'd made a lot of assumptions. She wouldn't make that mistake with Beau. "I know we're both busy, but I hope we make the time to have some fun together. All I've done is work, you know? But now that I'm here, there's so much I want to do and see. I want to live again."

He gave her a warm smile. "I have a pretty good incentive to delegate even more now."

And just like that, the anxiety broke. *See? All you have to do is talk to him.* "I want to see moose. And wolves. Do you have grizzly bears here?" She was talking too fast.

"Of course. Right in my backyard."

"Seriously? That close?"

"That close."

She was just so scared. Her emotions were like an out-of-control firehose, spraying everywhere. But look, no matter how hard she tried to convince herself otherwise, she wasn't going to get rid of the fear that Beau might lose interest in her.

She would do her best to combat it, but maybe the best solution would be to talk about it. Be honest. "All right, I'm just going to say it. I'm scared, Beau. This is the craziest thing I've ever done."

He shifted toward her, as though he'd been anticipating this conversation. "I know. I get that, but I'm so damn glad you took the leap. My words won't matter, but I'll show you how sure I am. How hard I'll work for us. All I ask is that you keep talking to me, letting me know where you are, and what you're thinking. Give me a chance to fix things."

She nodded. Had she and her ex done that? No, they absolutely hadn't. The entire time he was unemployed, she was worried about his mental health. She would never have told him her fears and anxieties. It would only have exacerbated his own.

"I will. I promise you." Instead of listing all the ways they could fail, it was time to flip the script and think about ways to make it work. She settled deeper into his arms. "So, give me the lay of the land. Who watches Colt?"

"For now, he's got a nanny, but Walker's building a childcare facility at the mine. The commute can get tough in winter, and it's hard for our employees to balance work and home life."

"I love that."

"Yeah. It makes sense."

She tilted her head back to see him better. "What will he think of you bringing home a woman?"

"Well, we're mountain folk, and there's a long history of mail-order brides in these parts. He won't bat an eye."

She gently whacked his arm. "I'm nervous, okay?"

"Sweetheart, my son's going to love you."

"You don't know that. He might be protective. He might think I'm a gold digger."

"Considering we're professional gold diggers, he'll probably just give you a prospecting pick and a hard hat and send you down the shaft."

"Well, look at that. Your feet hit the ground in your hometown, and you turn into a regular stand-up comedian." She grinned. "Also, I like when you call me sweetheart."

"Yeah? We'll have to try out a few terms of endearment to see what sticks."

"Okay, honey buns."

They held each other's gaze before laughing and shaking their heads. "Not that one."

She perked up when she saw the sign for the Gentry Mine Lodge. He'd said she could stay there. "So, this place is about nine minutes from your house?" *How will I see him?* She didn't have a car, and she wouldn't be spending her money on one. Not yet.

"That's right, but given that it's the holidays, you're welcome to stay in the house with us. It's up to you, of course. But it might be more fun for us and the boys."

She loved that he called them his *boys*. "Where do you want me?"

"In my bed." He whispered in her ear, "I will always want you in my bed."

201

His words slid over her skin like a silk scarf. "Charmer."

He shrugged. "I say what I mean."

"Yeah, I know." *Now, I just have to trust it.* "I like everything about you, Beau Gentry. I like your brainy engineering side and the way you touch me. I like your sense of humor. I don't think I've ever been more compatible with anyone."

"Believe me, I feel the same. That's why you're coming home with me." He leaned forward to speak to the driver. "Excuse me, would you mind pulling over?"

"Here?" the driver asked. "The mall isn't open yet."

"I know. I just want to show her around."

The man looked confused but flicked on his indicator. When he parked, they released their seat belts and got out of the car. The chill seeped right underneath her parka.

"Come here." Beau snugged her up against him as he led her toward the one-story building tucked within a copse of trees.

Built of dark gray concrete and plate glass windows, the mall was part of a larger complex that included the lodge and the gold panning facility. Its setting in the woods made it peaceful and still. "Where are we exactly?"

He pointed up the highway. "The south entrance to Yellowstone is fifty miles up the road." And then, he gestured across the street. "That's Grand Teton National Park. Calamity's fifteen miles that way." He pulled a ring of keys out of his pocket. "I hope the isolation isn't going to bother you." Pulling the door open, he ushered them inside.

"It's not much warmer in here."

"We've only got the heat on high enough so the pipes don't freeze. And as for the cold, I don't really notice it anymore. People who live here love the outdoors. We keep warm with skiing and snowshoeing."

She looked around. "I don't do much of either."

"There's a lot to do here. I don't think you'll ever get bored. Wild Wolff Village's got an ice skating rink, and they go all out for the holidays. And I'll take you into town for a Calamity Joe's vanilla chai latte any time you want."

"You're really selling this place. Think I might get bored and move on?" She sounded like she was teasing, but really, it occurred to her that he was just as worried about them working out. She'd have to be mindful of that.

As they moved deeper into the space, her creative wheels started rolling. It didn't look like any mall she'd ever seen. The smooth, dark concrete gave it a modern feel while the trees with benches circling them reminded her of a park. She could see so much potential but maybe not what he had in mind. "You know you're not going to sell shoes here, right?"

"I didn't picture stores like that, no."

"What did you picture?"

"It'll have to be something that grabs the attention of tourists passing through."

She'd been to enough national parks to know how many opportunities tourists had to buy souvenirs. She doubted they'd stop at a random mall for that. But then, something occurred to her. "We should probably make the mall itself a draw."

"Meaning?"

"I'm not sure." She looked up at the long row of skylights overhead, and an image popped into her mind. "I can just imagine millions of blown glass spheres hanging down. Maybe in a deep, rich blue? The light would travel through them, infusing all this dark concrete with color. That'd be really pretty."

"It would. But how would that be a draw?"

"What if the entire mall was an art installation? You've got trees—which is so cool, by the way—so we could have little landscaped areas—like actual parks where people could sit and eat lunch? And if we go with the art theme, we could even put sculptures in them."

He broke into the most gorgeous smile she'd ever seen. "I like that."

"Commissioning an artist to make the spheres would cost too much, so we don't have to do that idea exactly, but we can come up with something."

"Look, I have no artistic vision at all. You have free rein to do whatever you want with this place."

"Okay, well, give me a budget, and we'll go from there. This will be fun."

"If nobody comes here, then I've lost a lot of money. So, spend what you need to make it an attraction. What kind of shops would work with that concept?"

"I don't know. What about artists?" The idea gained momentum, and she grew excited. "Each store could be a gallery. You could have a nature and wildlife photographer. Someone who makes Western-style rugs and pottery. You know? It would be like an indoor art festival except everyone would lease their space. I mean, if we did this right, people would come from all over the world."

"I like that idea. It seems pretty perfect to me. You'd be surrounded by artists and have your own studio. Isn't that what you've always wanted?"

"Yes." The thrill of it traveled through her. She hadn't

dreamed of her own space since college. But even more astonishing was that this man she'd known a matter of days was thinking of her. He hadn't even considered the mall. "Do you know how incredibly special you make me feel? We're talking about a business investment, and you're thinking about *me*, about making my dreams come true. I swear, Beau, you make me feel like the most important thing in the world."

He reached for her hand and gave it a squeeze. "Good."

The warmth in his eyes seeped straight through to her heart. Because he meant it. This man would give her all the freedom in the world to become her true self. And it was mind-boggling. "But is it the best idea for the mall?"

"It's a great idea to make it a destination. That's brilliant. You're hired."

"Cool. Thanks for telling me after I moved all the way out here."

As they walked the long hallway, he showed her the food court and the shops of varying sizes. He stopped in front of a corner space. "This one's my favorite because it has a bathroom. It's also the largest. You can have it, if you want."

Wait. Does he think he has to buy my happiness? "Beau?"

"Yeah?" He sounded a little worried.

"I'm not Courtney. I'm not going to walk out on you because the house is too remote or my studio is too small. In my twenty-seven-year marriage, I didn't do that once. I stayed and fought. At the same time, you're not my ex. I can't impose his motivations on your actions. So, if we're going to work out, we have to see each other through a fresh lens."

"You're right. And I know that because, when you didn't respond, that's exactly where my thoughts went."

"Respond to what?"

"About whether the isolation will bother you. But you've never been here before, so that's not something you can answer. And I also know if it did bother you, I'd move into town and commute to the mine. Because you're my person, Margot, and I'll do anything to make you happy." He dipped, caught her behind her knees, and lifted her into his arms.

She laughed as he carried her over the threshold into the empty room.

"If you want this space, it's yours. You can sell tacos or hang your art—or use it as an office—whatever you want. You've spent your whole life taking care of other people, and now it's your turn. I get to take care of you."

Her heart swelled, and love spilled into her, hot and fast. "What I feel for you? It's so big it almost hurts."

"Let me make it feel better." He gave her the sweetest kiss, his mouth indescribably soft and warm, his tongue licking in slow, sensual swirls. Even as he walked her into the bathroom, he kept kissing her. And then, he gently lowered her to her feet. Turning her to face the mirror over the sink, he shrugged her coat off her shoulders and let it drop to the floor. She recognized that look in his eyes, and it kicked up a need so powerful, she trembled from deep within.

As she pulled off her sweater, he knelt to untie her boots and carefully remove them. Then, he yanked down her panties along with her leggings. When he stood, he took in her body from behind, clad only in a bra.

Color swept across his cheeks, and the muscle in his jaw

tensed and popped. He peeled back the lace cups and pushed her breasts together, holding them high, her nipples on display. "These are mine." Quickly, he kicked off his boots and unzipped his jeans, lowering them. He reached around and slid his finger inside her. "Yeah. So wet." Watching her face in the mirror, he stroked her clit.

She went up in flames.

He bit her neck, and with his other hand unclasped her bra. "Take it off."

With the back of her head resting against his chest, she took her time lowering first the left strap, and then the right. Watching her every move, he rocked against her bottom. Molten desire coursed through her.

"I can't believe this is my life now." With a hand between her shoulder blades, he lowered her.

As he slid inside, she gripped the white porcelain sink, savoring the pure, streaming pleasure. "Yes. Oh, God, Beau."

He gripped her hips, as he slowly pulled out and then coasted back in. "You're so tight." He cupped a breast, gave it a squeeze, and when she ground her hips on him, he pinched her nipple.

Her back arched, pressing her sensitive peak into his hand. Pleasure flooded her, and she sucked in a breath. "Harder."

His hips punched, sending his cock deep inside of her. His hand mimicked the motion of his thrusts as it moved across her breasts, back and forth. "Mine."

She wasn't going to last long. "Yes." Having this big, muscular man fucking her in a bathroom, watching him barely hold on to his sanity, hearing his growls and moans, just undid her. It was better than any fantasy she'd ever had. "I'm all yours."

His eyes narrowed, and he rammed his cock inside her. "Say it again."

"I'm yours."

He fucked her so hard she could barely speak. "I need you to mean it. No playing around."

"No playing, Beau. I'm yours."

Releasing her hip, he reached between her legs and found her clit. He circled it relentlessly, driving her out of her mind. When she reached the tipping point, when all the sensations coalesced, she lowered her head, closed her eyes, and burst into an explosive orgasm that sent hot, streaming sensations rocketing through her. Her hips rammed back against him. "*Beau.*"

He jerked her hips back and powered into her. His groans filled the closed space, and she watched his body shudder and quake as he found his release inside her.

When he finally calmed down, he set his chin on her shoulder. "Look at you." He had a look of awe. "Swear to God, I will not let you down."

Chapter Thirteen

Up until this moment, it had been just the two of them. They'd existed in a bubble of total intimacy, and Margot had loved every second of it.

But the moment they entered his home, reality hit. Beau dropped to a knee, and his grandson came toddling over to him.

"Ga-ga." Drool shone on the little boy's lips, and his eyes sparkled with joy. "Dada, yook. It Ga-ga."

"I see." Wearing a Santa hat, Walker followed right behind his son. "Grampa's home."

Beau scooped Colt into his arms and hugged him. The little guy rested his cheek on his grandpa's big, broad shoulder, his hand patting him.

"Missed you," Beau murmured.

"Miss you, Ga-ga."

Beau opened his arm to his son, and the three of them stood in a clutch that tugged at her heart. Hitching his grandson on his hip, he stepped back to include her. "Walker, Colt, I'd like you to meet Margot."

She could tell Walker had no idea what to make of his dad bringing home a woman. Still, he was gracious enough to shake her hand and welcome her.

Colt wiggled in his grandpa's arms. "Pesents."

"Yep. You got it. Let's do Christmas." After he set Colt down, he turned to her, blocking her from the room. "Is that okay? Or do you need a minute to settle in?"

"No, I'm fine. He's waited long enough." She followed the guys into the living room where a fire crackled in the hearth and Christmas carols played quietly.

Her first thought: *What is Courtney's problem?*

The classic cabin was absolutely a dream. It was cozy, charming, and extremely well-maintained. The stained-glass windows in the foyer poured rich patches of light onto the glossy floor, and one entire wall was made up of built-in bookcases.

Overstuffed couches formed an L-shape in the living room, and framed photographs lined the mantle. Colt ran to the giant Christmas tree, the ornaments glittering, the strings of lights twinkling brightly. He squatted, then dragged out a huge box. "Mine."

"Yes, sir. That one's for you." Beau sat on the floor, legs crossed. "You need my help opening it?"

"No, no. Dat mine." But the boy's little fingers weren't nimble enough to tear the wrapping paper, so he grew frustrated. "Open, pease."

"You got it." Beau slid a finger under a crease and ripped it off. Then, with the box exposed, he tilted it so the boy could see.

Colt's eyes went wide at the colorful block construction set. "I pay?"

"Sure, you can play." Beau opened it and tipped the pieces out. Once Colt settled in, Beau reached for her hand, tugging her to sit down beside him. He tucked her in close and kissed her cheek. "I'm glad you're here."

She didn't know how lonely she'd been in her marriage until she'd found Beau. All those nights when her ex needed time to unwind, the family vacations when he was distracted by work, and the countless weekends when they'd had to conquer and divide in order to get their kids to their various events, she'd been a team player. She hadn't wanted to face her own feelings of neglect and isolation because it would disrupt the peacefulness of her homelife.

But Beau made her feel essential. Even in the midst of unwrapping presents, he thought of her.

It was so nice to be wanted this way. She just hoped it would last once real life intruded. The magic of the holidays made everything glitter.

Don't let your thoughts go there.

Stay in the moment.

"A 'nudder pesent?" Colt asked.

Walker rooted around underneath the tree. "Here you go." He handed one gift to Colt and another to her.

"Oh." She took it but knew he must've made a mistake. "This isn't for me."

"It's for you and Dad."

Ah. So, whatever he'd gotten for his dad could be used by her, too. "Clever boy."

Walker chuckled.

While Beau helped his grandson wrestle the next gift out of its wrapping paper, Walker came closer to her. "If you're wondering why so few presents, my dad doesn't like a bunch of meaningless 'crap.' He's always been that way. He liked to build stuff with us or take us on adventures. He filled our stockings but only gave us a handful of presents."

"Oh, man. I was just the opposite. When my kids came downstairs on Christmas morning, it looked like a toy store exploded." It had probably been too much. "Did that bum you out as a kid?"

"Not at all because he always got the thing we wanted most. Like a dirt bike or a trip to Alaska. We preferred holidays with Dad because he spent his time with us. We played games, had movie nights, went snowshoeing… Yeah." He smiled. "We liked it better here."

"Here you go." Beau handed Walker a gift. "It's from Margot and me."

"You guys, you're very sweet, but you don't have to keep pretending I'm part of this."

"Oh, but you are." Beau kissed her on the mouth, and she loved the way he couldn't keep his hands off her. "You very much are."

"So, Margot." Walker peeled off the paper. "Are you going to be my mommy?"

She burst out laughing. "Oh, my God. That's it. I'm out of here. How about some snacks? Hot chocolate, anyone?"

"Shocklet?" Colt jumped up, stepping on the wrapping paper at his feet. "Can I has some shocklet?"

"Ooh, I should've asked you first." She threw Walker an apologetic look.

"Hey, it's Christmas," he said. "Anything goes."

"Need some help?" Beau asked.

"Nope. I got it. You guys just enjoy." It was sweet how they wanted her to slot in so easily, but they needed time as a family, and she didn't mind at all. She just hoped they had the ingredients.

The kitchen was right out of a design magazine. It had antique white cabinets, copper pots and pans hanging from a rack over the stove, a huge forest-green Aga oven, and a little cove for eating with a green and white checked banquette.

On her way to the refrigerator, she pulled down a pot. Fortunately, she had no problem finding milk, cocoa powder, and sugar in the pantry. She even found semisweet chocolate chips in a drawer. Perfect. She just needed some vanilla… And found it in a spice cabinet.

With her ingredients gathered, she got to work, whisking the cocoa powder into the milk. While it heated, she texted her kids.

Mom: So, how did it go? Did you have a nice Christmas?

Right away, her phone pinged with a photo from Owen of the troops eating a meal. It looked like a senator and a few commanding officers were there, shaking hands. A text came in.

Owen: When I get home, will you promise to make this for me? I don't think I can live without it.

It was a close-up of an unappealing grayish meat, some soggy vegetables, and a slop of mashed potatoes with coagulated gravy.

Emerson: Ew. I just hawked up my quinoa salad.

Mom: Absolutely! Please ask the chef if he'll share the recipes.

Mom: Oh, and be careful with that roll. You don't want to chip your tooth.

Owen: I don't think you get how Special Operations work, Mom. It's not a roll. It's a weapon.

Mom: LOL. Looks like it.

Mom: I miss you guys.

Emerson: I'll see you in ten days! Yay!

Owen: Wish I could be there.

She had to believe things happened for a reason. If she'd had her kids with her this year, she would never have spent time with Beau. And as much as she loved her babies... *Well, it's my turn. I get to be happy now.*

But what about next year? She could imagine her kids gathered around the table with Beau's family, everyone laughing and sharing stories, talking over each other as they teased and joked around. Joy spread through her in a hot, tingly rush. She wanted that so badly.

An arm wrapped around her waist and warm lips pressed against her temple. "You all right?" He smelled so good.

She gazed up at him, warmed by the concern in his eyes. She might've lost everything from her past, but she was sure excited about her future. More than money in her savings account and a roof over her head, she craved companionship. She wanted to be loved. Deeply. Unconditionally. *Who didn't?*

She wanted a love that didn't get cast aside when times got tough.

Could she have that with him?

"I really am." She poured some vanilla into the pot. "Do you want to get mugs?"

"Sure." First, he took a sippy cup out of the dish drying rack. "Before it gets hot, let's fill up Colt's."

"Good idea." Once she poured, they carried the drinks out to the living room where the little boy was unwrapping some smaller gifts.

Walker held up a red felt stocking with the name Grandpa written in white script. His dad smiled as he traded it for the cocoa, and then, they all sat on the floor.

"You ready for your cocoa?" Beau asked the little cutie.

Colt nodded, then backed up toward his grandpa and plopped down in his lap. Beau patiently waited while he got his hands around the bright blue plastic cup, and then held on as he brought it to his mouth. He drank heartily. "Das good." Then licked his lips.

"Margot made it. Can you say thank you?"

Legs kicking up rhythmically, Colt shyly glanced at her. "Fank you."

"You're welcome."

"Go on and open your presents, Dad," Walker said.

Just as Beau turned the stocking upside down and shook it out, the door swung open, bringing in a gust of icy-cold air. A young woman stood in the foyer and dropped several large travel bags onto the floor.

"Lorelei?" In one graceful movement, Beau caught his grandson under one arm and got to his feet. "You're home." He rushed over and hugged her.

Concern in his eyes, Walker was up and moving, too. "You okay?"

The young woman pulled away, smiling. "I'm great. Better than great." She touched her dad's arm. "I'm sorry if I worried you. I know I went quiet there for a while, but I just needed some time to figure things out."

"It's all right." Beau held her gaze with fierce conviction. "You can take all the time you need. As long as you know we're here for you, that's all that matters."

"Pesents." Colt grew impatient, struggling to get free.

While brother and sister caught up, Margot quietly headed over and relieved Beau of his grandson. It was just a flash, but she didn't miss the gratitude in his eyes. The boy was a little stiff in the arms of a stranger, and she wanted to put him at ease, so she went back into the living room and found his sippy cup. "Here you go."

"Where've you been?" Walker asked in his quiet, serious voice.

"In a cabin. Not too far from here, actually. And honestly, it was the best thing that ever happened to me. I'm ready, you know? I'm back."

"You have no idea how happy I am to hear that." Beau hugged her again, more tightly this time.

Over his shoulder, Lorelei caught the wrapping paper and the stockings—two were empty, and two were still loaded. "What's going on? It's so late, I thought for sure I'd missed the fun part."

"No, Dad just got home," Walker said. "Come on. You can still catch up."

Lorelei started to follow him but then shook her head. "Hang on." She went back outside and dragged in three giant gift baskets wrapped in clear cellophane. "Merry Christmas." As she was handing them out, her gaze landed on Margot, and she startled. "Oh. I…"

"Lor, this is Margot. She's——" It was a momentary pause, and yet the anticipation seemed to hold everyone in its grip. But then, Beau's features split into a two-dimpled grin. "Mine."

Lorelei's eyebrows shot up, and Walker smiled.

"It's nice to meet you." Margot stepped forward, taking the young woman's hand. She couldn't help noticing how cold it was. She'd grab a hot drink to warm her up. "You're too polite to ask what your dad means, but we met in North Carolina, and your dad asked me to manage the mall for him."

His daughter's skeptical look had Beau laughing. "That was the least important part of it. All that matters is I fell hard for her and asked her to move in with me."

"You what?" Lorelei's eyebrows hit her hairline.

"I just don't see how we can spin this." Shaking her head, Margot handed off Colt and headed into the kitchen. She lit the fire under the pot and skimmed off the skin that had settled on top of the leftover cocoa.

In the living room, she heard Lorelei ask, "Have I landed in an alternate universe? Dad *fell hard for a woman and brought her home?*"

"Wait'll you get to know her," Beau said. "You'll understand."

"I don't even know what to say. I have no words."

"Good. Because this little guy's waited long enough." Paper crinkled, and then Walker said, "Here. This one's yours. It's from me and Colt."

Margot pulled a mug out of a cabinet and filled it, then came out to join them. "Here you go. This should warm you up."

Lorelei took the mug and sipped. "Oh, my God. This is insanely good. Almost as good as Coco's Chocolates. We totally have to take Colt there."

"How do you know about Coco's?" her brother asked. "Before the music festival, you didn't eat sugar."

"Yeah, well, the Singing Baker's pastries changed me. They were to die for."

A strange sensation came over Margot, like she was on a rocking boat. Her vision wavered.

Music?

Hadn't Beau said Lorelei and her mom were in the music industry? She looked more closely at the woman. Over Lorelei's face, she superimposed bright red lipstick. She slapped on a wig with straight, blond hair, and she exchanged the overalls for a sequined dress.

And she got—

Holy shit. It's Lorelei Calloway.

The world's biggest pop and country star.

That's Beau's daughter?

But...how did that make sense in a cozy cabin on the outskirts of Calamity?

It took a moment for the pieces to start falling into place.

He'd said Courtney had broken contracts. Right, so,

Courtney *Jarrett. Lorelei's mom's the woman who's been all over the media for breaking contracts.*

And then, it all came rushing in. Margot had been deep in her cave, so she'd missed most of it, but she'd seen the media reports of Lorelei's ex and best friend in a store in Montana or camping in Idaho. It had been big news since Lorelei hadn't been heard from, and no one knew if the band was still together.

The moment turned surreal, and Margot got a woozy feeling.

As the family opened presents and drank cocoa, Margot stared at the singer. Without makeup, she looked pale, and her darker roots were noticeably growing out.

The woman must've felt her staring because she looked up.

Margot had made her uncomfortable, but she just couldn't wrap her head around it. "You're Lorelei Calloway."

The singer's attention jerked to her dad, but Beau stood up and came over to her. "Yes."

"I don't understand. Why didn't you tell me?"

Lorelei got up. "Because my fame makes life difficult. A lot of people use my family to get to me."

Wait, wait, wait. Did Beau not trust her? Did he think she was here for his money? "I would never do that."

"No, I know," Lorelei said. "It's nothing personal. It's just how we manage it, you know? It's been a big problem, so the people closest to me talk about me as their sister, daughter, cousin, whatever, but not as the 'singer.'"

Not personal? This is my life. On a whim, I ran off with a man I just met. "Of course. I understand." Even if the motives made sense, she couldn't imagine why Beau would drop her into this situation—his family *Christmas*—without giving her a heads-up. "It's just a bit of a shock. Please, go on and finish opening presents."

The warmth that had filled her went stone-cold. She sat with them, laughed when appropriate, even helped Colt put together his blocks—Lord knew she had a lifetime of experience with that—but the queasy feeling of distrust didn't go away.

She couldn't shake it.

She'd leapt right in. Trusted a man she'd just met because she thought they had some magical connection.

And it turned out, she hardly knew him at all.

Later, after dinner, after stories and bath time for Colt, everyone hugged and said good night and retreated to their rooms.

For the first time since entering the cabin, she was alone with Beau. She'd had a chance to calm down since recognizing Lorelei—*but come on, what a shock!*—and understood why the family would be so tight-lipped about her. Nobody wanted to be hounded by fans and paparazzi, especially when Colt had been traumatized by them.

But the whole situation highlighted the fact she barely knew this man. She had a sense of his kindness, his generosity. They'd swapped stories about their lives, but it was nothing more than a sketch. Maybe twenty stories out of a million that occurred over a lifetime.

What have I done?

He didn't need to see her flipping out, so she headed

into the bathroom and took a shower, brushed her teeth, and changed into her pajama bottoms and T-shirt.

When she finished, she looked at herself in the mirror. *What do I do? Do I go out there and pretend everything's okay?*

No, they'd agreed to talk about their issues. *Just do it.* She came out to find him sitting on the edge of the mattress. Still rubbing lotion into her hands, she said, "That was quite a surprise."

"I can imagine. I'm sorry."

"I get it. The last thing any of us want is paparazzi following us, asking about Lorelei Calloway. I'm sure you've all seen the worst side of fame, but I mean, I just don't get why you wouldn't give me a heads-up about something this big. Did you think I'd go blabbing to my kids? Were you worried they'd tell their friends, and then the word would spread?"

"This isn't about trust. You think I'd bring you into my home with my son and grandson if I didn't completely trust you? I do." He got up. "You have to understand. I didn't have her in my life for fifteen years. She's finally back, and I don't want to give her any reason not to come here. I wanted to talk to her first, make sure she understood how important you are to me, but she didn't answer my texts."

Everything he said made sense. But it didn't take away her unease because she wasn't telling him the truth. *I don't know you. Not really. And I'm kind of freaking out about it.* "I understand."

What she needed was a good night's sleep. She was sure she'd feel better in the morning. Less…lost. She really wished she could spend this first night in the lodge. Because it was one thing for her aunt to take her in—at least, they were related—but here, she didn't belong. She was imposing on a family's holiday. "We should get some sleep." Head down, she moved around him to get to the other side of the bed.

Strong hands gripped her shoulders. "Sweetheart, my daughter's been through hell. I was trying to make her feel safe, but I also should've done that for you." He tipped her chin, directing her gaze to him.

"It's just..." She stuttered out a laugh. "I packed up my suitcase and ran out the door. We didn't think this through. We were impulsive." She backed away from him. "I'm never impulsive. Just ask my kids."

But he wouldn't let her get away. He lifted her into his arms and carried her to a leather recliner. Sitting down, he settled her on his lap and brushed the hair off her shoulder and out of her eyes. "You're right. We were impulsive. And what I didn't think through was how it would feel for you to be dropped into my world. I'm thinking about it now, and I imagine you feel like you don't belong. Like getting into my bed in my home with my clothes in those drawers and my children under this roof makes you feel like a guest."

"Yes," she whispered. He'd nailed it.

"There's only one absolute, and that's us. So, if you're not comfortable here, then we'll move. We'll get a place of our own. Because we come first."

"Your family needs you. And you just got Lorelei back."

"I raised my kids. Now, it's my turn, and I'm not willing to risk my relationship with you. Look, I can manage all the moving parts of my life if I know what they are. I need to know how you feel, what you're thinking, and what you need. *You* need to know you're my priority. I'll do whatever it takes to make you feel you belong here."

She softened in his arms. "I like that. And I'll let you know how I feel. Even if it's messy, and I haven't quite figured it out yet."

He nodded his agreement. "Nothing's set in stone. We have to create a space that fits the two of us."

She wrapped her arms around his neck and snuggled up to him. "You're a marvel. An absolute gift. I can't believe I found you."

"I think we've earned each other."

She cut him a look, wondering what he meant.

"If we'd met earlier, we might not have known how to treat each other. We had to go through hell to get to this moment where we appreciate—and know how to treat—each other. And sweetheart, hear me. I want this enough that I'll work hard for us, and I won't give up. No one has ever made me feel this good, and no one has ever fit me so perfectly."

"Yes. I agree."

"But also, we know going in, we've both got triggers. I think with your ex, you had to be in a good mood all the time. You had to be the cheerleader. With me, you don't have to do that. You can be yourself. You can show me all your moods because I'm not going anywhere. Do you understand that? I fucked up by not telling you about Lorelei. You're not just someone I'm dating. You gave me the gift of trusting me enough to come out here and live with me, and I didn't honor it by giving you full disclosure about what you're getting yourself into."

"You don't know what it's like to hear you say that.

That I can be my whole self instead of pretending I'm not terrified every minute of every day. You can't imagine how many times I had to remind my ex that I was in this, too. It wasn't just him who lost everything, who worried about our future, who couldn't sleep at night for the fear of winding up penniless. And he would just say it was on him to get us out of this situation, that I could never make the kind of money we needed to save us, and so I just shut my mouth and went back to being the voice of hope because…"

The truth came roaring up, crashing through the wall she'd erected, and she buried her face in his shirt.

"Hey. You can tell me anything. You know that, right? If we're really in this together, then every emotion in your beautiful heart is mine. Every tear you shed…it's mine. Give it all to me."

She hadn't told a single person. How could she? "I found a letter on his computer. It was hidden in a folder called 'Family.' It was to his older brother and it said, If you get this, it means I'm gone." Tears spilled down her cheek. "I couldn't tell him I saw it. I had no business being on his computer, but I knew something was up, and he wasn't talking to me. It was at the same time he'd had his will redone, and he'd written out a whole document on what I should do in the event of his passing. I was freaking out, so I checked his computer to look for clues."

"He's a selfish prick. You should never have to live with that kind of fear."

"I finally got him to talk about it, and he said it wasn't something he wanted to do, but he couldn't leave me destitute, so as a last resort, he had an escape hatch."

"Meaning, he'd off himself and leave you with a fat life insurance policy?"

She nodded.

"Jesus, Margot. No wonder you played cheerleader for seven years."

"It was awful, especially because I couldn't tell anyone. I had to keep that horrible secret."

"I can't imagine what he was going through. To lose everything, to not have hope you'd recover…I can't know what it's like to be in his shoes. But the burden you carried is unreasonable and unfair."

"Well, it's my fault for snooping. I swear, I'd never checked his computer or his phone before that. But when I found that letter, I was shaking like a leaf."

"You fucking amaze me."

"Me? What do you mean?" There was nothing unique about her experience. Despite how social media made it look, no one got through life unscathed. Everyone dealt with hardship.

"I've never admired and respected anyone more than you. And he's an asshole to let go of a woman who would stand by him through the worst of times. He had a true partner in you. You're fierce, loyal, and unstoppable, and I'm so damn lucky to have you. Mark my words. Karma's gonna bite him on the ass. Hard."

Every morning of his life, Beau stood at the counter and ate whatever fruit he could find in the basket, drank his coffee, and read the news on his phone.

Except this one. This morning, he sat in the banquette with Margot, peace spreading into every crevice of his body. Until her, he'd never really connected with anyone. Which meant in every relationship he had a vague sense of unease that he was saying the wrong things or being misunderstood.

She was talking about how much she liked his house, but he was having a hard time listening over the tsunami of emotion building inside him. The emotion had a name, but it was too soon to say it. Way too soon. Especially after last night when he'd clearly seen the effect of moving too quickly.

She'd packed up everything she owned and moved into someone else's life. If he said the words now, it might add more pressure. He had to be careful, give her a chance to adjust.

When he said those three words, he wanted her to believe him.

"My house was totally different," she said, oblivious to his turmoil. "I worked with an interior designer—oh, this was over twenty years ago—and I never updated or changed anything since. I thought I loved it. I thought it fit me, but I've never seen anything like this." She gestured around the room. "It gives the impression of a small and cozy cabin, but this place is actually huge."

"That's because we've added on over the years."

Hair still damp from a shower, Walker came into the kitchen, heading straight for the highchair where his son shoved fistfuls of mashed banana into his mouth. "When my mom left, it was just a five-room cabin. But over the years, as the mine started producing, my dad kept adding on. You can't tell, but he kept the integrity of the original structure."

Awareness dawned on Margot's lovely features. "You kept the prospector's cabin, didn't you? Sam and Joseph's place?"

Beau nodded, pleased she understood the significance. "I did. There wasn't much to keep, of course, but we fortified it, and it became the original bathroom."

"All right, I'm out of here." Walker unplugged his phone from the charger. "You sure you're good with childcare?" he asked his dad.

"Absolutely."

"I could be gone as long as two weeks, and with everything that's going on at the mine, I know the timing isn't good."

No, it wasn't. They'd probably be shutting down the new crosscut. The loss would suck, but the real issue was so much bigger. It was a wait-and-see situation. "If I need help, I'll find a babysitter."

Walker winced. "And this is why I need the childcare center at the office."

"I know you don't want me using a service, but Lorelei's here now, and my assistant's mom babysits. If I need help, I know who to call."

"Dad, Lorelei doesn't know how to change a toilet paper roll."

True. Not to mention, she seemed wired. She said she was writing new material, and they hadn't seen her since she'd gone to bed last night.

"Besides, it's the week between Christmas and New Year's." Walker paced back over to his son. "Which is why the nanny bailed on me."

Beau didn't want to get up—he wanted to stay in this

cocoon with Margot—but his son needed reassurance. So, he headed over and clapped him on the shoulder. "If you're uncomfortable about leaving him, you can talk to the developer and see if he can train you another time."

"I can't do that." Walker shook his head. "He's doing me a huge favor, and it's only because I pestered him for so long. No, I have to go." He glanced at his son.

Margot slid out of the booth, too. "I know you don't trust me yet, but I'm here, and I raised two children, so together, I think we've got this."

A weight dropped from his son's shoulders. "I know you've got your own work, so I don't want to impose on you."

Beau nudged him. "When someone offers to help, you say thank you."

Walker grinned. "Yeah, okay." He turned to Margot. "Thank you. I appreciate it." He gave Beau a hug, then reached a hand out to Margot. Quickly, he lowered it and leaned in for a hug instead. But before he could make contact, he jerked back. Bright pink spots bloomed on his cheeks.

Margot didn't laugh or make a joke, she just moved forward and hugged him, her hand patting his back. "We got this."

When they pulled apart, Walker went to the highchair and kissed his son's forehead. "I think you got more banana on your face than in your belly, but you sure are cute." Walker crouched. "I love you, little guy. See you soon." He headed out.

Beau and Margot slid back into the booth. He was so damn happy to be with her that he reached for her hand and kissed her palm. Feeling eyes on him, he glanced over to find his son in the doorway, watching with a smile. Caught, Beau could only shrug. His kids had never seen him in a good relationship. They'd never seen him show a woman affection.

"Where's Walker going?" Margot asked.

"Sweden. He's getting trained on a piece of hard-rock mining equipment we just bought. I know he didn't want to be separated from his son over the holidays, so I was going to do it, but if he's going to take over, then it's something he needs to do." But there was something he needed to clear up. "Thank you for offering, but you don't have to babysit."

"Well, honestly, I'm not sure what my role is here. You know? No matter what we talked about last night, I still feel like a guest. And I think the only way to find my place is to jump right in. If I live here, then I have to pitch in. If you draw lines and separate me out, then I *am* a guest."

That made sense, but it might be too much too soon. "Okay, but it's your first week, and I don't want you to fall behind with your work."

"I appreciate that." She stared at her toast. "I didn't think anything through. I didn't think what it would feel like to live in your house with your family. I don't own a car or a bed or anything. I mean, I can't live off you." She let out a breath. "I just need to figure things out."

Shit. She was already regretting it. "I wish we could fast forward to the place where you feel comfortable here and integrated into our lives."

"I guess it doesn't work like that."

"I do have an extra car if you'd like to use it. Since Jess is mostly on campus and can walk into town, she didn't take hers to school. It's just sitting in the garage."

She hesitated, and he could tell she struggled with accepting handouts. But in the end, she came around. "I don't know how else I'll get to the mall without asking for rides all the time, so yes. That'd be great. I'd appreciate it."

Even though that was one problem solved, he could see she remained uncomfortable. "You don't have to live here. I promised you a room at the lodge, and it's yours if you want it. Or, if you'd rather rent an apartment in Calamity, we can call a rental agent right now."

"No, that'll only create distance. I'm more the type to dive right in." Finally, she smiled. "It'll be okay. It's just a matter of time."

"As long as you know I want you with me in my bed, right here at the table...just sitting next to me at night reading. As far as what role you want to take in the household, it's entirely up to you. If you never did anything but paint and talk to me, I'd be happy. Because all I want is to have you by my side." He leaned in. "I want to spend the rest of my life with you."

"I want that, too. So much. I'm just scared. It would be so easy to fall right back into my old role as housewife, making meals and doing laundry. I wouldn't even think twice about it. But I have to make sure I don't do that. I have to build my business and stay true to myself." She leaned close enough for him to smell the strawberry jam on her breath. "But the truest part of me is meant to be with you."

"Damn." He picked up his mug just to have something to cover his dopey grin. "Okay, then."

She caught his wrist and lowered his hand so she could kiss him. It was sweet and gentle, but a rumble deep inside foretold the crush of desire heading his way, and with his grandson sitting right there, it wasn't a good idea.

"Go pay now, Ga-ga."

Beau kissed her one last time. "Yep. We'll go play, buddy." He got up and released Colt from the chair. "First, let's get you cleaned up. We've got a construction set to put together."

Margot stayed at the table, finishing the latte he'd made for her. "Your kids are so lucky to have you."

With Colt nestled between him and the sink, Beau turned on the faucet and waited until the water warmed. As he wiped his grandson's mouth and hands with a dishtowel, she said, "Just to say, there's one particularly good point in my asset column—"

"You have a deficit column?" He glanced at her over his shoulder.

"Well, to be fair, it's extremely short."

He chuckled, swiping while Colt twisted and ducked and fought against the wet cloth. "Go on."

"My superpower is finding the best value. So, the first thing I'm going to do as manager of the mall is find local artists willing to cut their commission for the exposure this unique opportunity provides."

Tossing the wet rag in the sink, he grabbed a dry one. "I'm just going to point out it's Christmas. And you haven't even been here twenty-four hours."

"As I said, I dive right in. Anyhow, my first stop is the Museum of Broken Hearts to meet with Callie Bowie—do you know her?"

"No, I don't."

"Well, she runs it. She's also an artist. I'm going to see if she knows anyone who can do the kind of glass work I'm looking for."

"You already know about the museum and who runs it?" He settled his grandson on his hip.

"Sure, I do."

"I see another superpower. She gets shit done."

"I know, right? It's a good one. There's also an art gallery in Wild Wolff Village, and a woman named Phinny runs a boutique for all kinds of artisans."

"Is this a plan for today? Or the next month?"

"Today."

He laughed. "Okay, my little begonia." He cut her a look, and they both shook their heads.

"I like sweetheart the best. It works for me."

"And yet...the world is full of possibilities." He brushed the hair out of Colt's eyes. "So, can me and this little guy come along? Or are you riding solo?"

"I'd love to have you. And not just for the company. You'll need to hear the costs of this project. You might not like it."

"You know you have no budget, right?"

"Well, that's just silly." After finishing her coffee, she slid out of the banquette. "Every project has a budget."

"Normally, I'd agree. But if your intention is to draw people to the mall to see an art installation, then we'd better give them one that's worthy of their time. Now, the question is, for this new direction we're taking, do we still need a realtor?"

"Let's hold off on making that decision. First, we need to see if this idea is viable. If it is, we'll need a lawyer, someone to negotiate leases and contracts." After she rinsed out her mug and set it in the dishwasher, she wrapped her arms around him and Colt, inhaling. "Mm. I missed the smell of baby shampoo." She lowered her face into his neck. "And you? I don't know what soap you use or if it's just your natural scent, but you drive me wild."

With his free hand, he cinched her waist. "I can't wait till nap time."

"Nap time? How old are you?" But she had a gleam in her eye that told him she understood what he meant.

"Old enough to know how to multitask when babysitting a toddler."

She grinned. "And I'm old enough to know there are other things to do than sleep."

Chapter Fourteen

THEY NEVER MADE IT TO NAP TIME. BEAU GOT A CALL from the office that required him to go in, leaving Margot alone in the house.

Well, not alone. Lorelei was still in her bedroom, but that only made it worse because Margot felt like she had to be quiet. She was literally tiptoeing around, yanking the kettle off the burner before it screamed, and making sure cabinet doors didn't slam.

Also, Beau had taken Colt to work with him, and that had been an awkward conversation. He knew she'd let her business slide over the past few days, so he'd insisted. But come on. It didn't make sense to take a two-year-old when he had serious work to do. Whatever. In time, they'd get the hang of living together, and it wouldn't be so fraught with tension.

She didn't want to snoop or anything—well, no, she totally did—but she needed to get the lay of the land, so after Beau left, she'd wandered. It was a very well-lived-in house with stacks of books on tables and nightstands and scented candles in the kitchen and family room.

She found Jessa's bedroom—that was obvious from the framed photos and sketches pinned to a corkboard. The space was crammed with clothes, books, instruments, sports equipment, and trinkets like snow globes, stuffed animals, and jewelry. It reminded her so much of Emerson that her heart contracted into a hard knot.

Did her kids miss having a bedroom with a lifetime of memorabilia? Except for some clothes and books, Owen had thrown most of his stuff away. Emerson had boxed hers—did she ever think about it? Or had she forgotten about most of it like Margot had?

As she continued through the house, she couldn't help imagining holidays here. She could picture Emerson and her husband—maybe with a few kids in tow—and Owen and his future wife sitting around the dining room table for Thanksgiving. She'd have that alone time with Owen first thing in the morning, right when he got back from his run, and she'd get to go shopping in town for baby clothes with Emerson.

She liked that idea. A whole lot.

All in all, the furniture was high quality and comfortable, and the bathrooms were luxurious with big shower stalls and gorgeous tiles. Yeah, she could be very happy here.

After her tour, she caught up with the business side of her work—mostly, printing out mailing labels and returning emails. She had a glitch on her site that called for technical support, but she was pretty much done for the day. At her aunt's house, she'd do her art next, but here, they hadn't figured out where she'd work. She'd brought her watercolors and brushes, but her aunt would have to ship the ornament supplies and canvases.

Until she was cast out of her marriage, she'd never taken the time to define her art. To get there, she'd needed to play, find inspiration, and find her voice. That had only come once she'd had nothing left.

With all those free hours at the lodge, she'd wound up drawing and painting, and she'd found herself opening up more and more. She needed to keep that momentum going. If she was going to live here, she needed a studio.

After pouring herself a fresh mug of tea, she took a second tour of the house, this time considering spaces that might not be used very often. *Does it have a basement, maybe?*

When she passed Lorelei's room, she heard the humming, strumming, and occasional outbursts that had been going on all day.

"Shit."

"Ugh, are you high? That doesn't work."

"La la la. You suck."

She hadn't seen her since last night, so she wondered when she'd last eaten. She knocked lightly. "Lorelei?"

The strumming stopped. "Yes?"

"Can I come in?"

"Yeah, sure."

When Margot opened the door, she found the singer sitting on the floor with a guitar on her lap and crumpled bits of notebook paper strewn around her. "Sorry to interrupt. I just wondered if you wanted something to eat?"

Lorelei glanced at her phone. "Oh, wow. I had no idea it was so late."

She came into the room. "You doing all right?"

"Oh, yeah." She plucked her guitar strings. "I'm on a tear. I've got so much material I can't even keep up with it."

Did she seem a little…too enthusiastic? "Well, that's good, right?"

"It's fantastic. With everything that's happened this year, I knew I couldn't go back to the style of music I used to write. So, then, it was like, how do I reinvent myself? But now, I think I've got my mojo back." She paused to ask, "I assume you know the whole story?"

"I know bits and pieces."

"Impossible not to. The best part of being in the woods was having spotty Wi-Fi. But I met this guy—"

"You've been out in public?"

"No." She smiled. "Crazy story. My manager booked the cabin, but I went to the wrong one. I had no idea until the owner showed up…" A pink blush spread across her cheeks. "Anyway, he had to reinvent himself, too, and it made me realize I just have to go for it. I have to own what happened to me and create a new path forward, and I can't do that when I'm hiding out and avoiding the press." She lifted her guitar. "So, I'm writing the next album."

While Margot was rooting for her, something seemed off. Like maybe she was forcing herself to move on, skim over the unshakable pain of betrayal. Setting her tea on top of the dresser, she came over and sat on the mattress. "You know, it's okay to hurt. It's okay to be lost. There's no timeline for healing."

Briefly, Lorelei's eyes closed. "I'm not the only woman in the world whose boyfriend cheated on her."

"No, but you had a triple whammy with your mom and best friend, too, so I think it's fair to say it's been an unusually tough year for you." She stood. "I know you don't know me well, but I've got a boneheaded ex, too. So, if you ever need to talk, I'm here for you. I'll let you get back to it." She headed to the door. "Let me know if you want something to eat."

"I should probably have something." But she didn't get up.

Margot sensed the singer didn't want her to leave. *Does she have anyone to talk to?* She'd share a little of her story and see if it helped. "You know, when I found out my ex had cheated, it pulled the rug right out from under me. The reality I thought I was living turned out to be a lie. And it took me a while to find my footing."

"How did you do it? Because I look at you, and I can't believe you've been through anything like this. You're so… stable." She laughed, gesturing to the crumpled notes. "I'm a hot mess."

"No, you're really not. You're working through it the best way you know how: through music. But it was pretty simple for me. I wanted to be happy again, and I was willing to do the hard work to get here." *Including taking a risk on a man I met less than a week ago.*

"I want to be happy, too." Lorelei's voice held the barest whisper of hope.

"What will it take for you to get there?"

"I want to know why they did it. I want to know how

they could be so two-faced. I feel like I can't move on until I find out."

"Well, there's really only one answer to that."

Lorelei stilled as if she was about to get the answer from the gods themselves.

"Because they wanted to. They wanted to be with each other more than they cared about their relationships with you." She knew that answer wouldn't help right now. But soon, it would. "Look, I've been there. I've been stuck in the rut of trying to figure out the unanswerable questions. Why did he cheat? Didn't he love me? How was I lacking? How was the other woman better for him? All I can tell you is it's an endless loop of misery. And like I said, I wanted to be happy. I wanted to love again. And the only way to get there was to figure out my side of the relationship since I'll never understand his."

"And did you? Figure that out?"

Margot nodded, very willing to share her story. "I was a stay-at-home mom, and while I loved every minute of it, I put myself last on the list of priorities. My needs were so unimportant, I didn't even acknowledge them. And come on, if I met all his needs, if I *prioritized* them, what message did he get?"

"That his needs mattered most."

"Exactly. If I'd said, 'No, you can't go golfing this weekend because I'm going to an artist retreat,' he would have seen me differently. He would've had to accommodate my needs. What he did is inexcusable, but I'm not going to spend my life being angry and bitter. If I work on me, I'll be a better person, and that means I'll have a better relationship and a better life."

"I really like that. Thanks for talking to me."

"You're welcome. Any time." She smiled warmly. *You know what? She's been all alone in a cabin. She needs someone to take care of her.* "How about I make you some lunch?"

"Oh, you don't have to cook for me."

"I don't mind at all. Come on out when you're ready." Grabbing her mug, Margot left the room. She headed to the kitchen, concerned about the wild look in Lorelei's eyes. It brought her back to those horrible days when she couldn't manage to take a full breath without it hurting.

She didn't know what the singer liked to eat, but she figured she couldn't go wrong with scrambled eggs and toast. She pulled out a carton of eggs and a block of cheddar cheese. "What else?" She eyed the spinach in the vegetable drawer and thought about Lorelei's pale pallor. She'd throw a little in and get some iron into her body.

By the time she'd plated the food, Lorelei had come in. Her hair was wet, her cheeks scrubbed clean, and her skin was pink. "I'm starving." She sat on a barstool at the island and dug in. "Yum. This is delicious. I haven't had real food since I left my dad's house."

"What did you eat in the cabin?"

The singer cringed. "You don't want to know."

"Don't tell me you put on your Daniel Boone cap and went out in the snow to forage berries and take down elk?"

Lorelei laughed. "Uh, no. I couldn't even tell the good berries from the bad ones."

"Well, if you need me to teach you a few cooking basics, I'd be happy to do that."

"Thank you." Sounding both relieved and grateful, she

went back to eating. "You know, I've never seen my dad look at anyone the way he does you."

"Oh." Warmth spread through her, and she brought the skillet to the sink. "Yeah. I know we just met, but honestly, he's the best thing that ever happened to me. It's just…magic."

Lorelei looked sick to her stomach. She set down her fork. "That's what scares me, though. I thought what Landon and I had was magical, and he'd been cheating for an entire year."

She shut off the faucet and went over to her. "Hey, this is not your fault. You're a creative, talented woman at the top of your career. If he couldn't handle it, if he fell for someone else, he could've broken up with you. He had choices, and the path he took tells you everything you need to know about his character. Not yours."

"I'm just so angry. And that's my next album, right there." She tried to laugh it off. "Rage, revenge, and a lot of fuck yous. Hey, I think I've got my title."

"You do what you need to do to get it all out of your body. Just know hate is often a mask for hurt, and I know for me, holding on to it kept me a victim. I only started to get better when I shifted to the truth of my feelings—that I was deeply hurt, I felt like a fool, I felt unlovable, and I was scared to death of what my life would look like without him. And guess what?"

"What?"

"My life is so much better now. If I'd stayed with him, I would never have found my voice as an artist, and I would never have found your dad. And he's…" She sighed. "That man is one of a kind, and I'm so damn lucky to have found him."

And she would remember that the next time she felt awkward about him taking his grandson to work or when she wasn't sure of her place here.

All the bumps in the road were worth it if, in the end, she got to love Beau Gentry.

Margot had her list of museum and gallery visits prepared by the time Beau got home. Though still distracted by work, he insisted on giving her a tour of the town and helping her find Callie and Phinny.

Their first stop was a very cute coffee shop called Calamity Joe's. Thanks to its Wild West theme and tasty pastries, it was incredibly popular. Margot got a vanilla chai latte, but they held off getting anything for Colt since they had an art gallery in Wild Wolff Village to visit. Apparently, it had the best cocoa and crepes, so they'd save that stop for last.

The Museum of Broken Hearts was just two blocks from the coffee shop, so they went there next. Beau stayed in the heated car with Colt.

"I'll just be a minute." She kissed him on the mouth. "Be right back."

By the time she'd unhitched her seat belt and stepped out into the cold afternoon, he had Colt on his lap, playing with the steering wheel. "Take your time. We're fine."

"Thank you." She could see in an instant she'd love this small town with its quirky locals and high-end shops. She'd never given much thought to outlaws and gold rush history, but Calamity was utterly charming.

She breezed right in, ready to ask if she could speak with Callie, but stopped when she found the most curious displays. Televisions hung high on the walls, and when she got up close to one, she saw they displayed a ticker tape of personal stories. She'd been so focused on the mall and her goal she hadn't stopped to consider what this museum was actually about.

It's about heartbreak.

In the center of the room was a tree with dangling bits of paper. Each was a handwritten note, so again, it was all personal stories. A table next to it held pencils so visitors could hang their own.

Oh, hell yes. She grabbed a pencil and wrote down hers.

I gave you everything, and you took it greedily.
And then, you left me.
Thank you for freeing me so I didn't waste another moment
with a weak, shitty man.

"Welcome to the Museum of Broken Hearts," a woman said.

Margot turned. "Oh, hi. I was just writing my story. Well, it's actually more like a thank you note." She laughed. "Sorry about that. I guess I didn't meet the brief."

"Don't be sorry at all. The purpose of the museum is to share our experiences so we feel less alone. Any way you want to express your heartbreak is perfectly fine."

"This is such an amazing idea. Because that was the

hardest part for me, knowing I couldn't share it with anyone."

"Or even if we do talk, people get tired of listening. A lot of times, our closest friends and family don't want to hear it anymore. But that's how we heal. We look at our breakup from every angle until we finally make peace."

"That's exactly right." She held up her note. "Ultimately, my story's more about healing myself, so my next relationship can be healthier."

"Sounds like you've done the work."

"I think I have." *God, I hope so.*

"Here, let me help you hang it." The woman slid a bit of string through the tiny hole and tied it off on a limb.

"Thank you." She reached out her hand. "I'm Margot Rhodes. Are you Callie Bell?"

"No, I'm Alicia, one of the docents here. Callie's home with her family. We have a skeleton staff over the holidays."

"Of course." Embarrassed, she shook her head. "I was so focused on my project I lost all sense of time." She didn't know what her rush was. She'd gotten into town yesterday. Literally, Christmas Day.

No, she did know.

She wanted to be useful. She didn't want to just slide into Beau's life. Nothing would make her feel worse about herself than to live off him.

I need to carve out a space for myself.

"How about I just leave a message?"

"Perfect. Let me grab a piece of paper, and you can leave your name and number."

"Awesome." She followed the woman to the reception desk and quickly wrote down her information. "Thanks very much." On her way to the exit, she took another look around.

Is that a Pop-Tart on the wall? She headed over to read the description.

Every day, Jorge ate two blueberry Pop-Tarts before work. I kept boxes of them for him in the pantry, so he'd never run out. When I had complications with my pregnancy, I had to stay in the hospital for three weeks, and Jorge never visited. I found out he was cheating on me with my best friend, and when I asked him how he could do that to me, he said he felt like I didn't care about him. I asked what he meant by that, and he said "You stopped buying me Pop-Tarts. Angela brought them over, and I just felt like that was a sign, you know? She cared."

What a dickhead. Unreal. But it was such a fascinating concept, donating a symbol of the failed relationship. It created fellowship. Hm, what would that be for her?

She knew right away. A wooden spoon. She'd made dinner for her ex every night because she'd wanted him to feel loved, to know he wasn't alone during that incredibly difficult time. But through those hard seven years, what had he done for her? He'd been generous before he lost his job, but after...it had all been about him. His fears, his misery, his inability to find a new job.

She'd left that spoon behind in the apartment. That was symbolic enough.

Well, Beau and Colt were waiting, so it was time to go.

"Oh, you're here," the docent said to someone.

"One of my Christmas presents is yoga," a woman said. "So, Fin's home with the kids while I take a class. Since it's just next door, I figured I'd drop off this donation. You're not going to believe it. Here, look."

"Hang on just one second. Someone's here to see you. Margot?" the docent called. "This is Callie. Callie, this is Margot Rhodes."

"Hi." Margot hurried back over, determined to take as little of this woman's time as possible. She held out her hand. "I'm Margot." She was surprised to find a young woman—maybe a few years older than her daughter. "I'm sorry to bother you over the holidays, but I'm working on a project I thought might be fun for you."

"Oh, no, that's fine. I'm enjoying the break. My house is Lego and puzzle pieces and crumpled wrapping paper, so I'm happy to get out for an hour. Tell me about the project, and how can I help."

Oh, she was really nice. "Are you familiar with the Gentry Mine?"

"Of course. The kids love panning for gold."

"Well, they've recently built a shopping mall, and I'm the manager. It's a bit off the beaten path, and we'd like to bring in more than just tourists passing by on their way to Yellowstone, so we're going to make the mall a destination in itself." She could see Callie wondering how this involved her, so she got to the point. "I'd like to commission unique art pieces."

"Okay." Callie perked up. "What kind of pieces are you looking for?"

"It's got skylights across the entire length of the building, and I think it would be amazing for the light to pass through glass globes hanging from steel rods. Like literally thousands of them for the entire ceiling."

"Ooh, I love that."

"Right? And instead of shops that sell shoes and pants, I thought the mall itself could be an art installation."

Callie shifted towards her fully. "Explain?"

"In each space, we'd have studios. So, the artists could work there *and* sell their pieces."

"I'm not sure we have enough professional artists in Jackson Hole to fill a mall."

"Not to mention, how many artists can afford to lease a space?" the docent added.

"You both bring up good points." But an idea came to her, and she wondered if it was viable. "What if instead of leasing them, we offer artist-in-residence opportunities? They'd get to live in Calamity for a year and have free studio space, *plus* the chance to sell their art to all the people who pass through here."

"I love this idea so much," Callie said "But how will you make money?"

Ha. Another good question. She had to think on her feet. "We could take a percentage of their sales."

"And if they don't have any?" Callie asked.

"I think we can be selective enough that we only invite artists whose work we think will do well here."

"There's a lot to consider, like housing—it's expensive in Calamity—but we can talk about it." Callie broke into a smile. "So, what can I do?"

"I'm new here, so I don't have connections, but I'd like to start by commissioning the glass globes. After that, it's up to you how involved you'd like to be."

"I am all over this. I'll tell you what. After the holidays, let's meet up. We can invite Phinny, too. She runs a boutique in town that sells locally produced products, so she's in touch with a ton of artists. Do you know her?"

"Not personally, no. But I've heard about her and was going to visit her shop next."

"Perfect." Callie turned to the docent. "You got her information?"

The woman waved the piece of paper.

Callie reached out a hand for a warm shake. "Let's talk the first week of January."

"I love it. Thank you so much. Happy holidays to you both." She couldn't wait to tell Beau, so she practically ran out the door. As soon as he saw her coming down the steps, he got out of his truck to put Colt into his car seat. Buckling in, she warmed her hands in front of the vents. She couldn't keep the grin off her face.

Once he got back in, he said, "Looks like it went well."

She took a moment to take in his cold-slapped cheeks, the shiny, dark hair that hit his collar, and those crystalline-blue eyes that still had the power to shock her.

But there was something off about him. "Are you okay?"

"Sure. Did you talk to Callie?"

"I did, and it went better than I expected. She's excited about the idea and wants to meet next week to talk about it."

"Great." He gave her a weak smile while pulling away from the curb. "That's good."

He tipped his head to see his grandson in the rearview mirror. "Ready to go?"

She put her hand on his thigh. "Hey. Talk to me. What's going on?"

"It's a work thing." He brushed it aside. "It'll be fine."

"Okay, so, either you think I'm too stupid to understand mining concepts or you're dumping me into the same box as your ex who didn't care about your work." But then, she remembered what Jessa said. "Or, option three, you're preoccupied and all up in your own head."

He smiled. "Ninety percent distracted and ten percent the Courtney factor."

"Since we've eliminated the stupid part, I hope you know you can talk to me about anything. I don't want you to shut me out of certain parts of your life. I want to hear the random thoughts that go through your head, and I want you to vent to me about work." She needed to make sure he heard her. "Don't shut me out."

"Okay." At the stop sign, he braked. Picking up her hand, he kissed it. "We dug a new crosscut that's producing water. We'll have to abandon it—which is bad—but it's seeping into the mine shaft, and that could be disastrous."

"Oh, no."

"For now, we're pumping and controlling it. But decisions have to be made, and each has a risk profile."

"Oh, I'm sorry. No wonder you've been so distracted."

"Yeah. We've got our engineers and geologists working on it, but now, we're flying in a hydrologist." He gazed out the windshield. "We'll lose money on the crosscut, but that's always a risk. Anytime you dig into the earth, you don't know what you're going to find. What we don't want is to lose the mine itself." He looked troubled, so she knew he wasn't done. "And that means I can't go to Emerson's wedding." He lifted his phone out of the cupholder. "Which is what I found out while you were in the museum." He set it back down. "I'm sorry."

"No, of course, I understand."

Wait a minute. That was what she'd said for twenty-seven years. When her ex was about to close his first big deal and had to miss her parent's thirtieth anniversary, she'd said, "I understand."

When he had to work from the hospital room after she had her first baby, she'd said, "I understand."

Every time he had to leave a family vacation, she'd said, "I understand."

She was done acting like her feelings were a burden to someone else.

"I'm disappointed, but I understand." Yes, she liked that better. It was the truth. Sure, he felt bad about it, and maybe hearing those words would make him feel worse. But her feelings mattered, too. And in that moment, if this relationship was going to work, to be healthy, she needed to have more than a physical space in his life. She needed to carve out an emotional one, too. "I don't want to go alone."

"I know. I feel like shit about it. Why don't we wait and see—"

"No. It's all right, I promise." She offered him a gentle smile. "It would've given me comfort to have you there, but I totally get why you can't. Look, my ex and I have two kids together. We're bound to see each other. It's better I get it over with anyway." Just saying the words out loud gave her relief.

"We go now?" Colt asked from the back seat.

Beau peered at him in the mirror. "Yep. We're going to the Village, okay?"

"Colt get hot shocklet?"

"Yeah, buddy. You get a hot chocolate."

Colt grinned and kicked out his legs, perfectly content.

Beau turned onto Highway 191, heading for the fancy ski resort. "Maybe I can get Walker to come back early."

She opened her mouth to say, "No, don't do that." Because she didn't want to disrupt their lives, disappoint his son... the usual self-sacrificing bullshit. But she switched courses. "Maybe check in with him, see how it's going. If he's learned everything he needs to know, he won't mind leaving early. If not, it's fine. I was going to go by myself anyway. Like I said, I'll be all right. But thank you for considering possibilities."

"I would do anything to make you happy."

She knew that. She really did.

Wild Wolff Village looked like a charming European mountain town complete with a grand mountain lodge, wrought-iron streetlamps, and an old-fashioned grandfather clock in the middle of the square. A trolley clanged as it came to a stop on the cobblestone street, horses pulling a festive carriage clip-clopped down the road, and hot chocolate and warm crepes scented the air.

"This place is magical."

Beau carried his grandson on a hip. "We'll come for New Year's Eve. They have a torchlight parade on the slope over there." He pointed to the mountain. "And if it's not too late, I can get us tickets to the fireworks display that we can watch from the rooftop of the lodge."

"I can't wait." She touched Colt's nose with her mitten-covered hand. "You ready for your cocoa?"

"Horsey."

Beau looked to Margot to make sure the change in plans worked for her. They'd talked about ice-skating, but she lived here now. She could skate any time she wanted. "How about we grab cocoas and then take a ride?"

"Perfect." Reaching for her hand, he led the way to the food kiosks, which were dressed up with big red bows and garlands of pine. As they waited for their drinks, a surge of absolute certainty hit her.

There'd be growing pains—that was inevitable in any new relationship.

They'd both suffered deep scars from past relationships —*who hadn't?*

But they were starting off on the right foot. They were being honest. They were communicating. And they had an intense bond worth fighting for.

Happiness flowing through her, she squeezed his hand and got up on her toes to whisper the words she couldn't keep in one second longer. "I love you."

Chapter Fifteen

Soft hands gliding across his skin, caressing...

The swish of silky hair over his thighs.

A bloom of arousal made Beau stir. Usually, he had a hard time sleeping through the night, so he kept his bedroom blackout-dark. That meant when he opened his eyes, he couldn't see the woman kissing a path down his chest. But her sweet, feminine scent filled his senses and made him go hard.

A wet tongue swirled around the head of his cock, sending an electric current through his nervous system. When her hot mouth sucked him deeply, his back arched off the bed. His fingers speared into her hair, and as she worked his cock, he had to muffle his cries so no one in the house could hear him.

Cupping the back of her head, he rocked his hips, thrusting his aching cock mercilessly until the pressure grew unbearable. He was going to come, and it was too soon. He pulled out of her slick mouth, reached under her arms, and hauled her up the bed. He flicked on the lamp so he could see her swollen mouth and disheveled hair. "Get on your hands and knees. I'm gonna fuck you from behind."

She let out a breathy gasp and did as he asked, leaning on her elbows and hiking her bottom for him. Fuck, but he loved the shape of her ass and that soft, smooth skin. He couldn't resist giving one cheek a smack. She moaned, pushing back and swaying her hips. As badly as his cock ached to be inside her, he needed to touch her. Everywhere.

She loves me.

This perfect, beautiful, smart, talented, kind woman loves *me.*

It was the last thing he'd expected her to say. Not since he'd been holding off, worried about scaring her with the intensity of his feelings.

But that's the difference between us. She's so fucking brave.

Pressing himself tight against her, he ran his hands up her back and around to her chest, filling his palms with her plump breasts.

"Fuck me, Beau. Do it now."

Not until she knew what she meant to him. He kissed the small of her back, pinched her nipples, and then reached between her legs to find her clit. She moaned, those sexy hips rocking back, chasing his cock.

As his finger swirled, she lowered her head, making the kind of erotic sounds that had him frantic to get inside her. He grabbed a fistful of hair and yanked her back. "I love you. You hear me?" And then, he pushed inside her. "I fucking love you."

Her inner walls clenched, and he began thrusting.

More. Harder. Faster.

It would never be enough. He would never get his fill of this woman. He loved everything about her.

She was moaning, matching his thrusts. "I need...I need..."

"Me." He slammed into her so hard, she nearly toppled over. "You need *me*. And you've got me for the rest of your life." Hands gripping her hips, he drove into her again and again. "With us, it's only going to get better. You get me?"

"Mmhm."

All his senses collided in an explosion that rocked him to his core. It was the sight of her long hair shimmying and her ass cheeks jiggling with the force of his thrusts, her scent surrounding him—that hint of peach from her hair, and the now-familiar essence of her that drove him wild. It was the feel of her smooth skin under his palm as he skimmed it up her back to trace her hourglass shape. And it was the sounds she made as she lost herself in desire, the rising urgency, the desperation for release.

"I love you, Beau." She could barely get out the words. Her tone was almost panicked.

He reached between her legs, found her sensitive nub, and felt the rush of need drench his fingers. Her back arched, and her hips shot back.

She ground against him. "*Beau*."

Jesus, she was hot, slick, wild. She was everything, and he couldn't lose her. She was it for him.

He didn't think he could last. And fortunately, he didn't need to. Because her body stiffened, and she cried out as tremors shook her body. He loved the way she lost herself so thoroughly to pleasure. Loved that he could bring her there, that together they were fire.

Little tremors rocked her, and she lowered her forehead to the mattress. He grabbed her hips, hiked up her ass, and pounded into her. He lost his tether to reality. Holding her tightly to him, he ground against her ass, coming hard, one spasm after another. He came until he had nothing left to give, and then he wrapped an arm around her and brought her with him on his collapse to the mattress.

He closed his eyes, breathing her in, loving her soft warmth tucked into him. "You. Me."

"You," she whispered. "Me."

Beau's phone vibrated on the nightstand. He jackknifed up and grabbed it, hoping it didn't awaken Margot. He'd worked her pretty damn hard all night. But Jesus, he was insatiable for her.

He thumbed the Accept button and whispered, "Yeah?" as he got out of bed and headed out of the room. Given the time, he figured it was Walker. His son wasn't used to being overseas, so he might forget the time difference.

"Beau."

He recognized the hydrologist's voice but not the dire tone. "What's going on?"

"The water broke through. You need to get over here."

"On my way." He disconnected and hurried back into his bedroom, flicking on the bathroom light and leaving the door ajar so he could find the clothes he'd tossed onto the floor. Once gathered, he locked himself inside and took a quick shower.

He'd held out the slightest hope of going to the wedding with Margot, but this killed it. And it sucked because she shouldn't have to see that asswipe by herself. But he had no choice. He was probably twelve hours away from losing the mine. He had to get over there and figure out a way to shore up the breach.

What do I do about Colt? I can't take him with me.

The shower door opened, and Margot stood there naked, squinting as her eyes adjusted to the light. "What's going on?"

"The pumps can't control the amount of water. We need another solution, or we lose the mine."

"Oh, no. That's terrible. I'm so sorry. What can I do?"

Hot water pummeled his body, and yet everything in him stilled. It was the strangest sensation.

Beau's mom had never been happy, so he'd always tread lightly around her. After she left, his dad played both roles, but he had a hard time juggling work and full-time parenting. Then, his dad met Annie, and they'd become a team. Inseparable. They hadn't left Beau out exactly, but he'd had no choice but to go along with whatever they were doing.

And, of course, his ex wasn't much of a partner at all. Like his mom, his dad, and even Annie, she had her own agenda, and nothing outside of it mattered. Not even her kids.

But with Margot, for the first time, he had someone he could count on. And really, that was all he'd ever wanted. To feel like he wasn't entirely alone. In this situation, his ex would've told him the whole reason he hired people was so he wouldn't have to get up in the middle of the night and deal with crises.

Margot was ready to enter battle by his side, and it was

just so fucking nice to have a teammate. "Nothing. But thank you for asking." He looked away so she wouldn't see how undone he'd become from such a simple question.

He shut off the faucet, and when he turned to step out of the shower stall, he found her waiting with a towel. With a look of concern, she wrapped it around him. "Thanks. Go on back to bed. You took yesterday off, so you have orders to fulfill today." After drying off, he quickly got dressed and brushed his teeth.

"Can I make you some coffee?" She sounded concerned, like she was trying to figure out how to help him.

He rinsed his toothbrush, and they left the bathroom. "No, thanks. I have to run." *Well, wait.* He *did* have a partner in her. *Why push her away?* "Actually, yeah. I'd like that. It's going to take me a few minutes to get Colt up and dressed."

She snatched her bra off the floor and put it on. "Colt? You're taking him?" It only took her a moment to put on her leggings and a sweatshirt.

"I have to." What else could he do? He headed down the dark hallway.

"Well, hang on. Are you just standing around an office, looking at computer screens and throwing out different ideas? Where's he going to be?"

"No, we'll have to go into the mine, visit the crosscut, and see for ourselves."

"That's no place for a two-year-old."

"I know that, but Lorelei can't even boil water. She doesn't *drive*. I'm not leaving her with an active toddler."

"Okay, but I'm here. I can watch him."

There it was again, that odd sensation that built into a

massive rush of emotion so strong it threatened to flood him.

Shit.

Fuck.

He stopped walking and pulled her into his arms.

She held him tightly, absorbing his overwhelming gratitude. "It's okay. I got this. You just go and take care of the mine."

She knew. She understood.

His emotional life had been so flat, the only real highs and lows had been attached to his children. But this... romantic love?

No. He finally got it. He understood.

This is wild love.

It seeped into every cell and molecule, infusing him with a hot, excited energy. He would do anything for this woman.

And now, with a partner...a teammate...a lover...there was nothing he couldn't handle.

"Thank you." He wanted to stay with her. Wanted more than anything to make her feel the same way—like she had someone to go through life with, too. And the best way to do that would be to go to the wedding with her. "I'll be back as soon as I can."

He would try. He'd do everything in his power to make it happen.

Margot was exhausted. It had been a long time since she'd had to deal with a toddler.

She'd had three days with him, so she knew the little boy

well. He loved food, but he didn't necessarily love to eat it. He liked flinging it, smearing it, and squeezing it between his fingers, but she couldn't be sure he actually got much in his belly.

In between chasing him, playing with him, and wrestling him into clothing, a bathtub, or a highchair, Margot tended to Lorelei. The woman worked feverishly, and it was exciting to hear the initial humming turn into actual songs. They were powerful and fierce, and Margot knew she had some real hits on her hands.

As an artist herself, Margot understood the creative zone. There wasn't a chance she'd interrupt her. Besides, she had to feed herself, so it really wasn't a big deal to cook for two.

Her heart really did go out to the singer. In addition to the pain of betrayal (times three), she had the additional burden of her heartache played out in the public eye. Just yesterday, a story hit the media. Someone had caught Lorelei's ex and former best friend in a convenience store in Washington state. They'd taken a grainy close-up of a ring on the drummer's left hand, and that set off a whirlwind of speculation and photographs "proving" the couple had had a Vegas wedding.

Margot hoped—maybe naively—that the singer was too immersed in writing songs to bother with social media.

Now, with Colt napping, Margot had a moment to herself. She sat on the living room floor, her back against the couch and her phone perched on the coffee table as she waited for her daughter to answer the video call.

And there she was. Emerson's beautiful face filled up the screen. "Hey, Mom. Where's the cowboy hat and shitkicker boots?"

"Ha ha. That's not what it's like out here. Though I hear there's a mechanical bull in one of the bars in town."

Emerson laughed. "Now, that I have to see. Have your cowboy take a video for me."

"I didn't say I'd ride it, and he's not a cowboy. He owns a gold mine."

"That's just so Wild Wild West. Does he look like an outlaw?"

No, but he acts like one in bed. She grinned. "No, my favorite daughter. So, what's going on? Give me an update on the wedding plans."

"How much time do you have?"

"Colt just went down for a nap, so I've got about two hours."

"Does it feel weird to be dropped into somebody else's family, taking care of someone else's kid?" Her daughter talked as she walked from the front desk to her room at the hotel. Margot could see the lush tropical plants and turquoise blue pool with waterfalls. A breeze tousled her daughter's long blond bangs.

"I'm getting settled in, and he's a good boy." *No, don't lie to her. She might be getting married in a few days, but you matter, too.* "Well, actually, yeah. It's a little weird." She'd barely had time with Beau before he'd run off to handle the crisis.

"Who's going to watch him when you come here?"

"Oh, I'm sure things will settle down by then."

"Actually, I was going to ask if you could change your ticket and come a few days earlier. So far, Noah's family's doing everything. Which is great. I love them, but I want my mom here. You have to do my hair. Remember prom?"

"Of course." They'd scored an appointment at one of the top salons in the city, and Emerson had been so excited, but the stylist did some avant-garde thing that looked awful. So, Margot had fixed it, and in the end, her daughter had achieved the look she'd wanted. Her heart squeezed at the memory. "I want to be there."

"If we pay to change your ticket, will you come? All these plans are being made, and I want you here with me. I love his family—I do—but I want—"

"An advocate. I get it."

"Like, we'd planned to have the ceremony on the beach, but all along his parents have been pushing for us to have it at the church on their property. It's really tiny, and it's been there for generations, so it matters to them. We finally gave in."

"But you still prefer the beach?"

"I had to weigh it, you know? The beach versus his family's traditions? Put it this way. It was upsetting his grandmothers and aunts. His dad was acting really distant, and you know, I want them to be happy. I'm going to be part of their lives, and that's a lot more important to me than where I marry him, so I'm fine with it."

Okay, she was definitely going early. She'd dip into her savings to pay the change fee. She had no doubt Noah's family was good and kind, but no one was there to represent Emerson. "What about the reception? Is it still in his parents' backyard?"

Emerson lowered the phone so she could unlock her room. "Yes. Everyone's bringing something. It'll be a big potluck." Once inside, she kicked off her shoes and unclasped the barrette that held her hair back. It spilled forward, all sun-kissed and wavy. "Why are you smiling like that?"

"Because I remember you at fourteen, crying when I wouldn't let you buy Manolo Blahnik stilettos for middle school graduation. I remember cleaning out your backpack when you were fifteen and finding makeup hidden in every pocket. Sophomore year, you must've missed the bus a dozen times because you couldn't get your hair the way you wanted."

Her daughter groaned. "Don't remind me."

"For junior prom, I ordered seven gowns from Neiman Marcus because you couldn't decide which one to wear. And look at you now. No makeup, no hair products. Just my beautiful girl, more relaxed than I've ever seen you. And you're getting *married*." Emotion crashed over her. Her daughter was joining a family that lived three thousand miles away. She would miss so much of her life.

"I tried so hard in high school, you know? To keep up with my friends, to dress like them and talk like them, and I think back to how much energy went into looking a certain way—the Greenwich way—and I can't believe how unhappy I was. I know you think I dropped out of college because you guys stopped paying for it, but I'd been considering it the whole time. Maybe it was the wrong school for me, but it just felt like high school all over again. You know what my moment was?"

"No. Tell me."

"I had just finished rush, and it was the night of initiation. I was upstairs in one of the bedrooms—there were three beds all smashed in this little room—and everyone was getting ready. I was listening to them talk about how they slept with their makeup on in case a frat raided them at night, and I just felt so tired. Like, there's *never* a break from being 'on?' None?"

"Yeah, that does sound exhausting. You didn't have to stay in a sorority, though. You don't regret not getting an education?"

"But I get one every day. I have the best manager in the world. She teaches me every aspect of this business. I'm meeting the most interesting, successful people, and Noah's family's amazing. They have a totally different attitude than what I grew up with. They work to live. They don't live to work like Dad did."

She'd always presented their father as a hero, and she wouldn't speak badly of him now. "Your dad worked to give us a good life."

"Yeah, I'm not so sure about that anymore. I think it fed his ego to be Managing Director. Because now that I've seen another way to live, I see it's all about the choices we make."

"And what choices do you and Noah want to make?"

"We're going to make sure we get in a surf every day because it centers us. And we're going to save our money so we can open a surf shop one day."

"Are you worried about seeing your dad at the wedding?"

"I am. I wasn't going to invite him because, really, fuck him for what he did to you, but Owen said I might regret it later. He said, 'You don't have to fake anything and pretend like he didn't screw Mom over, but twenty years from now, when you've got kids, and you're looking back at your wedding pictures, you might regret icing him out.'"

"That's very wise for a snot-nosed kid brother."

Emerson smiled. "Yeah, he's not so annoying anymore." But the smile faded. "Are you okay, Mom? The main reason I didn't want to invite him is because I don't want you to see him with the skank."

Her new plan of making her emotional needs a priority hit a bump. She couldn't put a damper on her daughter's wedding, but she also had to be real. "To be honest, I'd be happy if I never saw either of them again, but you don't have to worry about tension between us because I just don't care enough."

"It's funny that you don't even ask questions. Don't you want to know if he's happy? If they got the funding?"

"Oh, I don't know. Part of me hopes he's miserable and misses the effort I put into our relationship." Because she was damn sure Petra didn't put in half as much. "But the money part...I guess I don't let myself go there. We're divorced, so I'm not going to benefit from his success or be impacted by his failure."

For a moment, she really looked at her beautiful daughter, and instead of seeing the teenager who'd come home shouting, "Mom?" and kicking off her shoes and dropping her coat on the foyer floor, she saw a woman.

And the only way to bridge the unavoidable physical distance was to establish a deep and true emotional one. "To be honest, it's a relief not to be responsible for his moods. He's great when he's happy, but the moment things go sideways, he gets—"

"Depressed. Yeah, I saw that. His mood swings were always scary. We kind of tiptoed around him."

"I didn't know you noticed."

"Oh, absolutely. Owen and I would lay low till it passed.

I used to say there was only room for Dad's emotions in our house."

"Isn't it funny how I tried to shield you from something so obvious?"

"To be honest, it would've helped if you'd talked to us about stuff like that since we were too young to understand what was going on. We only knew something was off." She grinned. "In any event, I can't wait to see Dad's face when you show up with your hot cowboy. What do you bet Petra's going to flirt her ass off?"

"Ah, well, unfortunately, Beau can't come."

"Are you serious? Why not?"

"He's got a crisis at the mine."

Her daughter didn't look disappointed or concerned, as Margot expected. She looked resigned. "Why does this sound so familiar?"

"What do you mean? He's nothing like your dad. He'd come with me if he could. He *wants* to."

"Okay. But you can't blame me for being worried about you. You met this guy a week ago, and now, you're *living* with him. I just don't want a repeat of your marriage, where his life takes over yours."

It rang a bell inside her, and she had to wonder if it was true.

"You just got your freedom. I don't want you putting aside your work so Beau can handle his, you know?" Emerson's gaze cut toward the door, and she broke into a huge smile. "Noah's here. We're going surfing." She looked back at the screen. "I've got to go, Mom. I'm sorry if I upset you. I just want you to be happy, and if you tell me this guy's right for you, then I'll support you all the way."

"Thank you." She gave an uneasy smile. "That means a lot."

"So, can you come early?"

"Yes, absolutely. After we get off the phone, I'll see what I can do."

"Thanks, Mom. Talk to you later."

"Can't wait to hug you. Bye, sweetie."

Unnerved, she got up and headed into Beau's office so she could check out the flights on his computer. It was a warm, cozy space with dark paneling, built-in bookcases, and Beau's scent filling every crevice.

Why does this sound so familiar?

Because, to an outsider, it was. Her daughter didn't know Beau's honesty, didn't see their intense connection. She didn't know Beau treated her so well.

For God's sake, he might lose the mine. Of course, he had to be there.

Her fingers fumbled on the keyboard, and she had to retype the airline's website.

Her ex was always in crisis. The markets crashed, he didn't get the bonus he'd earned, someone had presented his idea to the board... It was a constant refrain. *I can't go on vacation, to the party, to the game, to dinner.*

I don't want you putting your work aside so Beau can handle his.

For three days, she'd taken care of Colt, fed Lorelei, and cleaned the kitchen countless times. But she hadn't worked. She'd put her business on hold while Beau dealt with *his* crisis.

The airline could wait. Opening a new tab, she logged into her store's dashboard and found a good number of sales she'd ignored. Against the wall, she had a stack of boxes she hadn't mailed yet. How could she carry them into the post office with a two-year-old? She'd told herself it was the holidays, so everyone would understand.

She glanced at the unfulfilled orders. One was a commissioned piece that would bring in real money.

I'm doing it again. I'm putting my needs, my work, on hold for someone else.

Only this time, it wasn't her own children. It wasn't her husband.

It was for someone else's family.

It's okay. Don't get upset.

It's only been a few days.

Beau hadn't asked her to do anything. No, she'd stepped right in. She'd offered to watch Colt.

What should I have done, though? He couldn't take a two-year-old to work with him. He was literally going into a mine shaft.

But that wasn't the right question because her default setting was helping others reach *their* goals. The correct question was: what would a person who prioritized herself and her business have done?

She would've taken Colt that first morning and then looked for babysitters and daycare facilities to help her out. This family had lived here for decades, so they had to have plenty of recommendations. She'd have found a balance between her work and taking care of her lover's grandson.

If my work isn't my top priority, what will my future look like? If she couldn't support herself, she'd be at the mercy of her children.

That will never happen. I'm not their problem.

She couldn't believe how easily she'd fallen into her old pattern.

But it was all right because she'd noticed. She could do something about it.

Talk to him. She called Beau. When he didn't answer, she calmly left a message. "Hey, I hate to bother you at work, but we need to talk. I'm going to need some help with babysitting so I can get my work done. Give me some guidance, okay?"

There. See? No big deal. Beau would hire someone, and everything would be fine.

Much calmer now, she went back to the airline's page. When she saw the change fee, she was relieved. It wasn't bad at all. But just as she went to purchase it, she heard a scream. Leaping from the chair, she tore down the hallway and threw open Colt's bedroom door.

She found the little boy pressed against the wall, blankets askew. "I'm here, baby. I'm here." Desperate to comfort him, she reached out, but he twisted away, shrieking. "Are you okay? Sweetie, tell me what's wrong." Was he hurt? It was impossible to tell. He wouldn't let her touch him. "Baby, I can't help if you don't talk to me."

"Ga-ga. Want Ga-ga."

"I know you do, doll. Of course, you do. Grandpa's at work right now, but I'm here, and I can help you. Will you let me?"

"No. Ga-ga. Want my ga-ga."

"All right. I'm going to call him, okay?" Dammit, she'd left her phone in the office. "Here, come with me." She held out her hand, but he refused to take it. The abject fear in his eyes made her frantic to comfort him. *I can't leave him alone like this.* "If you want me to call Grandpa, you have to come with me."

Tears streaked his flushed cheeks, and he kicked out his legs. He looked so miserable she could hardly stand it.

"What about Aunt Lorelei? Can I get her?"

"*No.*" In all the time she'd spent with him, he'd never had a tantrum. He'd never been distressed. "Ga-ga." It was a mournful plea that ripped her heart into a thousand pieces.

She had no choice but to leave him. "Okay, I'll be right back. I'm just getting my phone." On her way down the hallway, she knocked on Lorelei's door. "I need your help." How had the woman not heard the plaintive cries? She didn't have time to wait, so she let herself in, only to find the room empty. "Dammit." She dashed into the office, grabbed her cell, and hurried back to Colt.

"Okay, sweetie. I'm calling him right now." Her hand was shaking because she didn't know if he was all right. She didn't see blood, and he seemed more scared than in pain. When Beau didn't answer, she grew enraged.

He knows I'm watching his grandson. He has to be available to me.

Okay, distraction. That always worked with her kids. "Come on. Let's get some hot chocolate while we wait for Grandpa to call us back, okay?"

"No," he screamed. "No shocklet. Ga-ga."

"I know, baby. I know. But he's not here. I am. Will you please let me help you?" *My God.* The boy was inconsolable.

She hit redial. This time, finally, Beau answered. "What's up?" He sounded tense, impatient.

"Colt had a nightmare, and all he wants is his grandpa."

With the boy so close, she kept her tone light. "He misses you."

"Margot, I'm in the middle of a firefight here. I need you to handle that. There's a fifty-fifty chance we're going to lose the mine."

"I know." In the background, people talked, and she knew she didn't have his full attention. Which sucked because this little boy was literally cowering in a corner and wanted nothing to do with a woman who'd been in his life a total of five days. "But Beau, listen to me. Your grandson needs you." *Can't you hear him sobbing?*

"I'm sorry to put you in this position, but I need you to step up for me right now."

"*What?*" That was not the response she'd expected.

"Margot."

Oh, she hated that patronizing tone. The one that said, *You can't possibly understand what I'm going through/how important this crisis is/how significant my role is.* "No. Don't *Margot* me. Your grandson is terrified, and he doesn't want me. He wants you. You need to take a break from what you're doing and come home and reassure him."

"I can't do that. I'll be home as soon as I can, but right now, I have to go."

The line went dead. He'd hung up on her.

Cold seeped under her skin. She'd made it clear his grandson was shaken by a nightmare, and the only person he wanted was Beau.

And he'd hung up on her.

This is bullshit.

No. *No.*

I'm not doing it again.

Not for anything.

Dropping her phone on the mattress, she sat down. The boy might not want her, but she wouldn't leave him alone. So, she stretched out on his bed. She'd keep him company, let him know she was there.

What else could she do?

After the boy calmed down, they'd had a snack in the kitchen and then sat on the couch to watch a movie. He'd quickly lost interest, of course, so she'd taken him and a few trucks into Beau's office while she changed her ticket.

Her session had timed out, but she was glad she hadn't hit Purchase. Because she was leaving even earlier.

She was leaving now.

It hurt. Oh, God, it hurt. The grip of loss squeezed so hard she couldn't draw a breath.

Beau.

She wanted him. So badly.

She craved him. It was more than attraction. More than affection. The roots were so deep, the idea of leaving him shook her.

But she wasn't ready yet. She wasn't in the right headspace to be in a relationship.

I meet a guy, he asks me to move in, and I immediately become the same woman I was for my twenty-seven-year marriage.

And so, she did it. She changed her ticket to a flight that left tomorrow.

She just couldn't understand how she'd given up her life again. So easily.

And why is Lorelei's comeback more important than mine?

The singer had walked in the front door about an hour ago. With a distracted wave, she'd ducked back into her room. Margot got it. She recognized the intense look in the singer's eyes, like she'd received a massive gift of inspiration and had to get it down before she lost it.

Margot didn't want to interrupt her, but she had no choice. She had a taxi coming.

"I have to go see Aunt Lorelei, and I need you to come with me, so please choose one truck." The boy clutched a bright yellow school bus to his chest. "Awesome. Let's go." With Colt in her arms, she headed down the hallway. At her knock, she heard a muffled, "Come in." When she entered, she found Lorelei on the floor surrounded by photographs. "What're you doing? With that look on your face when you came home, I assumed you were writing a song." *Not reminiscing.*

"I am, yeah. Everything I've written so far is angry, and I was like, up to my eyeballs in ugliness, and I thought about what you said. About how it was an endless loop. And I wanted out, you know?"

"I do."

"So, I took a long walk, and it hit me." She lifted a few photos. "A lot more than betrayal has happened to me this year."

She gestured to them. "What are they?"

"All my life, my mom told me my dad didn't care about anything but the mine. That he was a narcissist, obsessed with his work."

Margot sat down beside her, settling Colt in her lap.

"Did he tell you about the lawsuits?" the singer asked.

"A little." But it was all over the media. Everyone knew what Courtney had done. "He said she signed a lot of contracts that weren't necessarily in your best interests, and when you finally became successful, she walked away from them."

Lorelei nodded. "She acted like the deals were nothing but pieces of paper. But all those people put their hearts and souls into helping me move my career along. *She's* the narcissist. I only found out when we got sued. I spent the summer with my dad and brother and sister, and it was amazing. I had the best time. And I found all this stuff in a closet in his office. He'd saved pictures and posters...memorabilia from my entire life." She glanced at the photos. "He's been there all along, every step of the way. And all those years that I was surrounded by shitty people like my ex and my friend, and my mom, I missed out on my *dad*. I needed him. I needed a brother and sister. And that's worth writing about."

"It is. You're absolutely right. I'm glad you can see beyond what those people did to you. For me, that's when the healing began. Now, I have to talk to you."

Lorelei set the photos down. "What's wrong?"

"Remember I told you my daughter's getting married?"

She nodded, clearly sensing more was going on.

"Well, I'm leaving early. I'm leaving today." Before Beau got home. She had a reservation at an airport hotel because she knew if she talked to him, he'd convince her that he was the only one who could make the critical decisions to save the mine. And she'd believe him. Because it was true—he wasn't exaggerating. She knew that. "And I need you to take care of your nephew until your dad gets home. Can you do that?"

"Um, yes. Of course." She gathered the photographs and slid them back into the large file folder. "Is he on his way? Because I know he's trying to set everything up so he can go with you."

"No, he's not coming." *God, this hurt.* It hurt worse than when her ex dumped her. But she couldn't go back to the woman she used to be. She had to stay on this new path. "I need to go without him." A hard knot formed in her throat, making it painful to swallow. "Because I'm not coming back. I'm sorry, Lorelei, but this is goodbye."

———

Beau was issuing instructions to the hydrologist when he heard the knock on the door.

Only when his assistant peeked in and waved did he shift his attention to her. "Your daughter called," she whispered. "She's been trying to reach you on your cell, but she says you're not answering."

Even as he asked, "Lorelei?" he was unearthing his phone from the pile of schematics and 3-D imaging cluttering the table.

She nodded.

Found it. He swiped the screen and found missed calls. His first thought was Colt. He felt like shit for hanging up on Margot, but he'd been in a board meeting, his team watching, waiting for him to give their marching orders.

Maybe it was more than a nightmare. Was he *hurt*? "Excuse me. I have to take this." Anxiety ripped through him as he strode out of the conference room and tapped the screen.

"Dad?" Lorelei sounded like she was barely holding on to her composure.

"Yeah, honey. What's going on?"

"Margot's leaving."

He ignored the stab of fear in his heart. "What do you mean leaving?" He needed facts. Information.

"She's packing right now."

"Hang on. What happened?"

"I guess her daughter called and asked her to come sooner. She wants her mom there for the wedding."

"Okay. That's fine." He wouldn't begrudge her that time with Emerson. He just wished he could go with her. "What time is she leaving? I'd like to take her to the airport."

"No, Dad. You're not getting it. She's *leaving*. She's not coming back. You have to come home. You can't lose her."

"I don't understand. What's going on?" But even as the words left his mouth, he knew. Worse than hearing his grandson crying and hanging up on her, he'd been completely out of touch. He'd barely talked to her the last few days.

Holy shit.

She's leaving me.

"Don't let her go. I'm on my way." His thumb was on the button to disconnect, when he said, "Lor?"

"Yeah?"

"Thank you. For letting me know.

"Of course, Dad." She paused. "I've got Colt, so don't worry about that. Just…hurry."

He headed back into the conference room and found

nine sets of eyes on him. Decisions needed to be made, and only the owner could make them. "I'm sorry. I have to go."

"Are you serious?" the geologist asked.

"Yes. There's a family situation I have to take care of." He pointed to his Vice President of Operations. "Arturo's in charge. He'll take it from here."

The man nodded. They had a plan in place, and Beau had been in the process of giving everyone on the team their marching orders. Arturo could do it.

He shot a text to Margot before shoving the file folder into his briefcase and heading out the door.

Beau: On my way home. Please don't go until I get there. We need to talk.

She didn't respond, which meant the entire drive home, his fear escalated. He had to get to her before she left. He had to apologize. He had to fix what he'd done wrong.

Was it so bad she had to leave him? What happened to them talking through things?

Or maybe... Was her daughter pregnant? He knew she and her fiancé didn't make much money, so maybe they needed childcare. Margot wouldn't want to miss out on knowing her first grandchild.

What if Emerson had called off the wedding? Margot would go to her, for sure. That wouldn't be permanent, though. That would just be for a few weeks. Margot would come back to him.

No, it's me. She's leaving me. He hadn't intended on being away longer than a day—but now, three had gone by. Did she think he was a workaholic like her ex? That he got his ego stroked from owning a gold mine? Because that wasn't the case. Sure, there were always problems in his industry. Pricing fluctuations were a constant issue, but he had experts in place to handle everything. This was a unique situation and required decision-making from him, the owner. No one else could shoulder the responsibility when the viability of the entire operation was at stake.

But why would she leave without talking to him?

Because she's fed up. She came here less than a week ago and spent a total of two days with me. That's not what she signed up for.

How could she acclimate to a new place and get her work done while caring full-time for a two-year-old? He left a voice message for his son. "With everything going on at the mine, I can't watch Colt right now. We need to talk about childcare. Think about which options you're comfortable with and call me."

Next, he called Margot. It went right to voicemail, so he left a message. "I'm on my way home. Don't leave until I get there. Margot—*Jesus*—whatever's going on, we can handle it together."

The moment he pulled up to the house, he parked, cut the ignition, and ran to the front door.

When he opened it, he tripped over her suitcase in the entryway. "Margot?" He hollered like he'd lost a child at the mall.

Turned out, she was right there, pulling her coat out of the hall closet. "Hi."

She looked lost, scared, and almost haunted.

"What's going on? Is your daughter all right?"

"Everything's fine. I think Emerson's voice got lost in Noah's big family, and she wants me there."

"Okay. That makes sense. So, you're going early, but you'll be back?" He looked down at the bulging suitcase. "You're coming back to me, right?" His voice sounded strange, like it had been bound in rope, the air squeezed out of it.

She watched him for a moment, a helpless look in her eyes. Finally, she let out a breath. "No. I'm not coming back."

Panic like he'd never known exploded in his chest. "Why? What happened?"

Looking away, she pressed her lips together. "I just...I can't do this anymore."

"Do what? I don't understand. You said you loved me."

"And I do." Her eyes went glossy. She reached out to touch him but pulled her arm back. "I *do*. But I've been here what? Five days? And what have I done? I'm taking care of your grandson, your daughter, and your household, but I'm not running my business. I'm not even working on the mall."

"That's my fault. I never should've left you alone with Colt. I didn't know it would go on this long."

"This is all just so familiar, you know? But it's my problem. Not yours. Look, everyone has some kind of drama going on, and if I let them, their needs will always come before my own. Because everyone's needs are the most important thing in the world to them. But you know something? Even if mailing my orders isn't as important as saving the mine, it has to be my priority. If it's not, then who the hell am I?"

He wanted to fight for her. He wanted to promise not to burden her with his household issues, to help her make herself a priority, but that wasn't the point, was it? She was telling him she needed to get to that place on her own.

And he loved her enough to let her go.

Even if it shredded his heart and stripped him of his happiness.

He didn't want to go back to a world without color. Without laughter and passion. A life without Margot... *Fuck.*

No.

"Look, there's always going to be a crisis at the mine or with one of your kids, and I get it. That comes first. But come on, when am I going to come first? When am I going to put myself first?"

Every day of his marriage, he'd come home to a tirade just like this. How many times had he gotten the call that his wife had taken the kids to a hotel in town? He'd race home just like he'd done today. And what was the point? In the end, his wife belonged somewhere else. And Margot? She wasn't asking for anything but her freedom.

Meanwhile, he had a business to run. Employees to support. He had obligations and commitments. "I understand." He could tell by the way she flinched that his tone surprised her. It sounded dead, flat as a coin that had been run over a hundred times.

"It's not your fault, Beau. I just can't lose myself inside your life. I'm sorry."

The tension was torturous, and he realized he was blocking the door. He stepped aside. When she didn't go, when she watched him with a helpless expression, he realized she'd expected him to fight for her. "I can tell you how much you mean to me, I can make promises about how we'll work on this together, but I can't make you stay. I can't make you happy to be here with me."

"I'm happy here. I love you."

But not enough to stay. Not enough to work through their problems. *Yep. Been there done that.* "Where will you go?"

"I'm going back to Merry Falls. I need to focus on my work. Just...no distractions. I have to build my own life. Not get lost in someone else's."

Now, she was just repeating herself. There was nothing more to say, so he nodded. "Goodbye, Margot."

Chapter Sixteen

A PLUMERIA-SCENTED BREEZE RUFFLED THE GAUZE curtains of the tiny church. Perched on top of a hill, it overlooked the ocean, and Margot couldn't think of a more perfect spot for a wedding.

She was so glad she'd come early. Emerson had shown her around the resort where she worked and her fiancé's lush, tropical property. At this point, she'd met the entire family and knew her daughter was in good hands.

Still, her heart was shattered. She kept a smile on her face, but she'd never felt a despair like this, as big and deep as the ocean.

She'd left for the right reason—she had to make herself a priority and grow her business. She had to.

Okay, but why did she have to give up Beau? Couldn't she have it all?

Sweetheart, whatever's going on, we can handle it together.

His words played on repeat in her mind. Night and day, they ran like a river right through the heart of her.

She put the finishing touches on her daughter's hair—

and really, why did they ever think some random stylist could do a better job than Margot? She'd touched the fine down on Emerson's scalp when they'd first placed her in her arms. She'd brushed out her tangled toddler curls, and she'd given the first cut. She knew exactly how the cowlick whorled and how to twist the brush to blow it out straight.

"Mom?" Emerson's soft voice cut through her thoughts. "I'm sorry for comparing your situation with Dad to Beau. I can see how upset you are, and I wish I'd never said anything."

She pressed her daughter's hand. "It's not your fault. I would've been upset, too, if you'd run off with someone you just met." *I did it twice. With him, and away from him.* She shook her head. "I'm not exactly myself right now. But I'm back on track. I'll be okay."

"It's not that you ran off with him because I fell for Noah right away. I get that part. Sometimes, when you know, you know."

I know.

"Just one look at him, and I felt something," Emerson said. "It's hard to explain."

But Margot knew. "It's this feeling that you recognize someone you know you've never seen in your life." She could feel her daughter's eyes on her, but she couldn't stop. "It's almost like a click inside you. Your body understands before your mind has a chance to catch up."

"Mom." Her daughter's voice was rich with compassion.

She took a step back to admire her little girl. Wow. *Wow.* She stroked her daughter's cheek with the back of her hand. "Look at you. You're the most beautiful bride I've ever seen."

Emerson didn't need a couture gown or a makeup artist to glow with inner peace and beauty.

Her daughter reached for her hand. "Thank you, Mom. I'm so glad you're here with me."

"Me, too."

Emerson got up. "When I told you I didn't want you to put Beau's life in front of yours, I didn't mean for you to break up with him."

"Oh, honey, this is not your fault. It's mine. The fact that I could fall back so easily into my old pattern was a red flag. It's just too soon. I need more time alone."

"But what if Beau's your person?"

"He is." She could barely get the words out. But she couldn't break down in front of her daughter on her wedding day. *Keep it together.* "When your dad left me, I could hardly get out of bed. Once I calmed down, I could see I didn't miss him at all. Mostly, I was just scared about money since I'd never made any. Well, terrified, honestly. But walking away from Beau...I've never experienced this kind of pain. And it's not tied to me being alone again. It's about losing an essential part of me." She shook her head. "I know that sounds dramatic. I just met him."

"Mom, no. Seriously, I knew Noah was The One the first day I saw him on the beach. I hadn't even talked to him. He and his friends were waxing their boards, and when the other guys headed out into the ocean, Noah stayed behind because there was this little boy who'd been watching them. The other guys ignored him, but Noah took the time to teach him what to do. He was so kind and gentle to this boy he didn't know. Well, it was more than that. It was the way he noticed me, too. It was like our eyes locked, and I felt a chemical reaction right here." She patted her chest. "Mom, if Beau's the one for you, go back to him. Like, really, we only get so much time on this earth. Shouldn't we be doing the things that make us happy?"

"Yes," she whispered, no longer afraid to share the truth with her little girl who'd turned into an exceptional young woman. "But I need to work, and I'm afraid I won't have enough money to see me through to the end of my life. I've never fully supported myself."

"Okay, but what does Beau have to do with that? And how will fear help you make more money? Fear's the very thing that blocks us."

"You're right. I just…I got scared. I lost myself in Beau's life. That's the kind of thing that will ensure I don't have enough money."

In a rush, her daughter hugged her. Margot breathed in her soft, floral scent. "Mom, that's just who you are. Why do you think my friends wanted to come over to my house? Why do you think Johanna would sit on the counter while you were cooking dinner? Because you listened to her problems and tried to help her. That's the essence of you, and it will never change. Why would you want it to? So what if Beau asked you to watch his grandson for a few days?"

"He didn't ask. I offered."

"Of course, you offered. You wouldn't be you if you'd gone into your office and back to work knowing your man had a crisis and couldn't take his grandson with him. It was a couple of days. So what? And if you have a crisis at the same time as Beau, then you find someone to step in and help. You don't give up the best thing that's ever happened to you.

Mom, you're a caring person. You put your whole heart and soul into relationships. That's a good thing. You don't need to be alone the rest of your life to make sure you're productive. That's just crazy-talk." Emerson stood. "Now, can I get married or what?"

Margot entered the church alone. An older man played "The Wedding March" on a ukelele, and everyone wore leis. Since the bride and groom didn't want any separation between families, people sat anywhere they wanted.

As she headed down the aisle to find her seat in the first pew, her gaze landed on the back of her ex's head—the first time she'd seen him in nine months, and it hit like a baseball bat to the chest. It was muscle memory, the sense that they should be seated together, parents of the bride, celebrating this momentous occasion.

Instead, he had a thirty-eight-year-old girlfriend. He'd become a total caricature of the successful Greenwich husband who dumped his wife for a younger woman. Of course, he'd never have a child with Petra but that meant he got it all. Money, a hot young girlfriend who was as driven as he was, and the recovery of his reputation.

Oddly, Petra wasn't sitting beside him. Had her ex decided it would be best for his daughter if his sidepiece didn't come?

You know what? I don't care. After the initial blow of seeing him, she realized she didn't feel much of anything. She wouldn't want him back. Not for anything.

The man was exhausting. And the passion? It was never there. And she only knew that now because she had Beau.

Did she have Beau?

God, he'd been so cold. She'd never forget that moment he'd stepped aside to let her out the door or the finality in his words. *"Goodbye, Margot."* With a flick of a switch, he'd gone from panicked to stone cold.

She knew her daughter had entered when a gasp passed through the church and everyone got to their feet. Emerson hadn't wanted her dad to walk her down the aisle—in fact, she'd preferred to have her mom do it, but she hadn't wanted the fallout—so she walked alone.

Her gaze was fixed on her groom, her eyes lit with a lifetime of possibilities with this man who cared for her so deeply.

Her ex had tossed her aside, and Beau said *I love you* one day and *Goodbye, Margot* the next, so what were feelings anyway but a momentary response to a situation? Sure, Beau had massive stress. His entire livelihood plus that of his employees was threatened—and no, she didn't take that lightly—but to shut down his emotions for her so completely? That was scary.

She hoped with all her heart Emerson didn't experience the end of Noah's love.

Oh, my God. Stop it.

It's her wedding.

Her daughter was absolutely radiant, her whole being focused on her groom, and there was no room for negativity. Today was about joy and love, and she would put aside her own heartache to be fully here for her daughter.

A young woman sang "Simply The Best," and the lyrics resonated with her deeply. She could relate to each and every sentiment.

My heart's on fire.

Take my heart and make it strong.

She'd walked away from Beau and left behind her heart and soul.

What have I done?

How could I leave the only man who sees me, knows me, and truly loves me?

He hadn't gone cold because he'd lost feelings, but because she'd hurt him. She'd given up. She saw him as this sturdy, powerful man, but he was broken, too. His wife had walked away, taking their children.

Well, there you go. We did it again. They'd let their past wounds kill their future together. Margot had assigned Beau with the same self-focus she'd experienced from her ex, but where Scott had taken everything she'd offered, Beau gave her the tools to succeed. He was helping her fulfill her dreams. He'd given her a studio—*who else has ever done that?* She hadn't even done it for herself.

Awareness hit, arming her with certainty. Emerson was right. It *was* her nature to take care of people. It wasn't a flaw. In any conversation, she went right to the heart of the matter. Some people liked it, while others found it off-putting. They thought she was nosy, but they misunderstood. She truly cared about their relationships, their hopes and dreams.

She wanted her life with Beau. Fiercely. Would he take her back? Or by pressing the bruise his ex had left, had she lost his trust for good?

Emerson reached the first pew. As she handed the bridal bouquet to her mom, her dad got up from his seat across the aisle to come and kiss her on the cheek. Her daughter stiffened—she'd made it clear she didn't want her dad involved in any way—and Margot wouldn't tolerate her sweet girl's discomfort, so she took the bouquet and smiled, nodding for her to continue to the altar. Emerson turned away as though her dad was nothing but a ghost.

As Margot watched the couple exchange vows, the scent of the pale pink, orange, and yellow plumeria filled her senses, and the velvety petals of the bright pink stargazer stretched open as if it couldn't contain its joy.

She thought about something her daughter had said right before they'd left the bridal suite.

"If a career was so important to you, you wouldn't have been a stay-at-home mom. You want to know who you are? Look at your actions. Look at your choices. You love to take care of people, and that's a beautiful thing."

Her daughter was a smart woman.

She closed her eyes and breathed in the sweetly scented flowers.

How do I fix this? Beau lives three thousand miles away. I can't fly all the way back, rent a car, show up on his doorstep, and beg him to take me back.

She'd start with a phone call. An apology. It was just his tone had been so final. So intimidating.

A swish of fabric got her attention, and she opened her eyes to find a man sitting down next to her, his big body forcing her to scoot over. His khakis whispered on the wooden bench.

Margot's heart heaved, and joy exploded in her chest.

Beau.

He's here.

Focused on the bride and groom, he reached for her

hand and clasped it. All the words came rushing in, and the force it took to keep silent had her breath catching in her throat.

I'm sorry.

I was an idiot.

I got scared.

I'm trying really hard but the wounds go deep, and sometimes, I don't react well.

I'm scared I'm going to get hurt again.

But he just smiled and squeezed her hand because he already knew all that, didn't he?

And she could read him, too.

I'm sorry.

I need time to think before I react. So, I let you go.

I gave us both space. And now, I'm back.

I'm putting you first.

I will always put you first.

Oh, yeah. She could read his every thought.

After the ceremony, they filed out of the church and headed for the reception. Golf carts drove the guests down the sloping hill to a big, grassy lawn. Tablecloths billowed in the breeze, and tiki torches stood sentry by each table.

All through dinner, Margot and Beau held hands, but they couldn't talk. They were at the head table with the bride, groom, and her now-in-laws. But once the speeches ended, once the married couple finished their first dance, Margot tugged him toward the shelter of a banyan tree. Her happiness was electric. She was pretty sure a satellite could spot her as a glowing object. Once alone, she threw her arms around his neck. "I can't believe you came here."

"Are you sure about that?" He tipped her chin, gazing into her eyes. "Did you really think I'd let you go?"

"My fear did. I had some sleepless nights imagining a future without you, but my heart knew it was wrong. Because I've been lying to myself. I keep thinking I'm afraid of not having enough money to support myself, but that's just a cover for the real truth. I'm scared to love someone so completely, and then have him abandon me. It's so hard to trust again."

"It is. It's terrifying. But what we have is nothing like our past relationships. I know myself and my feelings, and I know we're going to be together for the rest of our lives. And Margot, our lives are going to be stunning."

In a single brushstroke, she got a flash of their future— the peaceful mornings sharing breakfast in the banquette, the passion in the bedroom, the family dinners, the laughter, and the feeling of being loved, accepted, and of finally finding her true home with Beau.

Elated, she kissed him, scraping her fingers across his scalp and losing herself in the soft, slick heat of his mouth.

He pulled away, cupping her cheeks, and leaning his forehead against hers. "I don't want you to lose yourself in my world. If you need an office outside the house—"

"I don't. I'd be miserable separated from the heart of our family. I understand myself now. Honestly, I needed my daughter to remind me I'm a woman who loves hard and takes care of the people who matter to her. If I'd wanted to be a business maven, that's what I would've done."

"You have no idea how badly I need to be loved the way

you love. But I made a mistake, too. I was so relieved to finally have a partner, someone I can count on to be there through all the hard times, that I lost sight of your experience in all this."

She shook her head. "It's not your fault, Beau. I think we touched a hot button that threw us back to our marriages. When you hung up on me, it triggered the countless times my ex discarded me because work came first. And when you walked in the door, you got Courtney all over again."

"I know you're scared. It's *because* you give your whole heart, and that means it'll hurt like hell when it breaks. But I won't break it. I promise you, I will take care of you, heart, body, and soul." He gripped her wrists. "I will not break you, Margot Rhodes. I will love you with every fiber of my being."

She kissed him. Right there under the tree with the ocean breezes and the DJ calling all couples onto the dance floor, she healed her heart and made a promise to her future. And it was going to be a good one.

When the kiss got too heated, she pulled away. "I can't believe I almost lost you. Lost something so precious and rare and perfect."

He shook his head emphatically. "Not a chance. I knew when I watched you get into the cab that this was never going to end. I watched Courtney go, too, because she had my kids with her, but I didn't give a shit about her. I was relieved to have her gone. But you? I panicked. I wanted to drop to my knees and beg you to stay. But you had your daughter's wedding, and I couldn't ruin that for you. I knew, though, I'd do anything to win you back." He paused, searching her eyes. "Even if it means selling the mine."

"Oh, hell no. *Hell. No.* I love your passion, I love your hard work, and I am your *partner*. I'm here to support you. Just the way you support me."

"I love you, Margot. I love you like I've never loved anyone before in my life, and I'm so damn thankful I get to spend the rest of it with you at my side."

"*Mom.*" With wicked delight in her eyes, Emerson raced over to them. "You're going to die when you see this. You know how Petra didn't come to the ceremony? Dad said she wasn't feeling well, so she stayed in the hotel room?"

Margot didn't know the details, but she'd obviously noticed her missing, so she nodded.

"Guess why she wasn't feeling well?" Her daughter turned, and both she and Beau followed her gaze to the dance floor where her ex and Petra stood facing each other but not touching.

Because Petra's belly was swollen. She was *pregnant*.

At that exact moment, her ex glanced over. His eyes locked with Margot's and held. In their depths, she saw misery, helplessness, and profound regret.

The moment he started to move toward her, Beau's body went hard. He didn't move, but his expression stopped her ex cold. Wrapping his arm around her, Beau brought her in close and kissed her temple.

Her ex watched the loving gesture with a tormented mix of jealousy and grief.

She hoped Scott could read her as easily as she did him: *You wanted me to find my own exit ramp, and boy, did I ever.*

"Talk about karma," her daughter said, breaking the intense but silent exchange. "Can you even imagine? It's the one thing he swore would never happen, and now he's going to be changing diapers and waking up for midnight feedings. I'm dying." She dashed off to join her husband.

Margot took one more glance at her ex. The tension between the couple was like a forcefield. Of all the outcomes, Scott having a *baby* just didn't compute.

"Are you okay?" Beau asked.

"I don't know what I am."

"It must be hard to see him after what he's done. But to see him with Petra, to know you won't be the only mother of his children...it has to be hard."

She appreciated that he didn't laugh along with her daughter, because while she would love to find it hilarious that her ex got to live his worst nightmare...she didn't. "I think enough time has passed, and I've done enough work to actually feel sorry for him. Well, for both of them."

"What do you mean?"

The kindness in his eyes, the absolute patience and interest in hearing her thoughts, filled her with a sense of... well, utter peace. She felt safe with him. She could just be herself. "Petra thought she had a master of the universe ready to kick ass and make it rain money. And since he's wearing the same suit he wore the day he left me, they clearly didn't get any investors. Which means she's become the caretaker of his emotional state, and I don't think that's what she signed up for."

"And him?"

"He was looking for a solution to his financial problems. Instead, he has the burden of not only figuring out how to keep a roof over his own head but a second family to support."

He made his bed, and now he had to lie in it. But

enough about them. She had everything she needed right here in her arms.

"What's that look for?"

She smiled. "Well, if karma's a thing, then I must've been a very good girl."

"You're good, all right." His hands slid down to her ass and squeezed. "And also, very bad. Just how I like you."

Epilogue

HANDS GRIPPED HER THIGHS, AND A HOT TONGUE licked inside her. Margot stretched luxuriously in her bed before throwing back the covers to find a head of dark shiny hair between her legs. "Well, hello."

Her sweetheart, the love of her life, only took a break from pleasuring her to say, "Happy birthday."

"Mm. Best one ever." She spread her legs wider, and he reached for her breasts. He knew just how to make her dissolve into the most blissful sensations. Over a year and a half together, and this man had kissed, touched, caressed, and stroked, every inch of her body. He'd taken the time to explore her and learn her sensitive spots. "*Yes.*"

He ran his palm across her nipples, pinching them, ramping up her need. Her hips rocked against his mouth, and her fingernails scraped across his scalp. When she grabbed a fistful of his hair, he said, "You want to come on my mouth or my cock?"

"Do I have to choose?"

He laughed. "Never." His tongue found her clit, his

fingers slid inside her slick core, and electric heat shot through her.

"God, Beau. *God.*" She closed her eyes, losing herself in the inexorable swirl of his tongue and the rhythmic caress of his fingers on that sensitive inner patch. As the erotic tension peaked, the world went black…and just when she didn't think she could stand it another second, stars exploded behind her eyelids.

She soared into a universe made up of a euphoric love only soul mates understood. Before she could come down to earth, he surged forward. His mouth covered hers in a desperate, devouring kiss.

One hand slid under her ass, tilting her, and he thrust inside. Her legs wrapped around his hips, and she hugged him to her, so full of love for this man. His insatiable need for her made her feel like an absolute queen.

Pulling out, he sat back on his heels and dragged her onto his lap. His shiny, wet cock stood at full attention as he took in her naked body. "Fuck. You're so hot." His hands glided up her belly, her rib cage, until he grabbed handfuls of her breasts. He lunged forward to lick her nipples and suck them into his mouth.

He made her feel like a sexual goddess, and she threw her arms over her head and basked in the way he worshipped her. He sat back up and got a hold of his cock, and heat streamed through her at the feral look in his eyes. Slowly, he pushed back inside, and he let out a shaky breath.

And then, with those big hands on her hips, he used her body for his pleasure. Yanking her on and off his cock, he fucked her. His cries grew frantic, and he watched her breasts bounce. She knew he wanted them in his hands, his mouth, but couldn't do both at once, so she cupped them, pressing them together and keeping them on full display.

"*Fuck*." Pushing her off his lap, he stretched out over her. He tucked his face into her neck, slamming into her again and again, faster, harder, until the tension grew so unbearable, she cried out. She came hard and fast, one peak hitting after another.

He let out a roar, fusing their hips together, and fucking her with powerful, short thrusts. "Fuck." Spent, he rolled to her side, kissed the tip of her breast, and fell onto his back. "You're going to kill me."

"I literally didn't do a thing," she teased. "You manhandled me."

He chuckled. "Yeah, I felt real bad about that. Until you came a second time."

She loved the way he'd helped her see her body in a whole new light. "You should wake me up like this every day. Why save it for special occasions?"

Since today was the opening of the mall, they didn't have plans to celebrate, but she was okay with that. It was only seven in the morning, and he'd already given her two orgasms.

After the unconditional love he'd shown her and the hard work he consistently put into their relationship, what would a bouquet of flowers or a tennis bracelet mean? She had everything she could ever want right here in this bed, in this cabin, with this man.

She let out a satisfied sigh. "I love you."

He rolled onto his side and hitched up on an elbow. Worry gripped his features. "As much as I want to say it back—"

Excuse me?

What the hell, Beau?

Had his feelings changed? Her mind hurtled back to two birthdays ago, to the day she'd expected a surprise party and instead gotten dumped.

But even before he could finish his sentence, she gave the ridiculous insecurities the boot. Because she knew him. Knew what they were to each other. She had no doubt he adored her.

He brushed the hair off her forehead. "Sometimes, I wake up before you and just watch you sleep, and my heart can hardly stand how lucky I am. How did I get a woman who cares so deeply about me and my children? Who understands what the mine means to me—this land, the history, the geology? You just get it. You get *me*. Saying *I love you* feels as bland as a greeting card. What I feel is so much more. I need you, I crave you. I miss you when you're in the other room, and there are never enough hours in the day to spend with you, exploring your thoughts, your body, your heart. I want more and more and more of you."

She turned onto her side, so they were face-to-face. "I more than love you, too. You are the piece of my soul that was missing, and now, with you, I'm complete."

Her kids had called in the morning, so Beau headed off to the mall without her to help the artists and caterers with their last-minute setup. Now, though, she was on her way, and she couldn't be more excited.

Once she, Callie, and Phinny had met, everything had come together. They'd gone with her idea of filling the spaces with artists-in-residents from around the world, and to their surprise, they'd discovered a huge interest in living in Jackson Hole, Wyoming, for a year and working and selling their art in this little mall just outside of Calamity.

It had taken eighteen months to pull it all together, but today, they'd open their doors and visitors from around the world would come to see gallery-worthy art.

For months, Margot had worried about losing money for Beau—what if no one showed up? But it hadn't been just the three of them marketing the mall. It was the artists, the tourism board, and local business owners who would benefit from this new draw to the area. So, when the lodge started booking gallery owners from London, New York, Paris, and Miami, she knew they'd be just fine. Better than fine.

All dressed up on this gorgeous June afternoon, Margot parked and got out of her Mercedes SUV—a Christmas gift from Beau because he wanted her safe on these snowy mountain roads—and headed to the building. They'd turned the entire mall into an art installation—inside and out—and the setting sun glanced off the copper and steel sculptures, making it look like it was on fire.

She was sincerely fine without a birthday celebration, but she did wish her kids could be here to see what she'd accomplished. Emerson was pregnant and still working full time, and her son's unit had moved to Okinawa. Both were busy, and neither could take the time off to fly out to this remote spot on the map. She totally understood that. At least she'd gotten to talk to them on the phone.

One day, they'd come and see her new life.

She reached the door to find it locked. That was odd. Maybe they didn't want people wandering in before the food stations were set up and the artists were ready to go. She texted the group chat.

Margot: Door's locked! Let me in!

A few moments later, she heard the click. She stepped back, assuming someone would open it, but no one did. *Okay, now, it's getting weirder.* She pulled it open herself and heard, "Surprise!"

Navy, silver, and gold balloons floated to the ground, and she walked through a celebration of twisting crepe paper.

People rushed to her, surrounding and hugging her: Callie and Fin Bowie, Phinny and her hockey coach husband Declan, Jessa, Walker, and Colt, all the artists, crew, catering staff, and townspeople who'd supported her over the past year.

Finally, she saw the beloved faces of her two children, and tears sprang to her eyes.

"Emerson! Oh, my God, you're here." She wrapped her daughter up in her arms and felt her pregnant belly between them. She held out her arm for her son. "*Owen.* I can't believe it. You said you couldn't get leave." She brought her son in for a bear hug.

"*I* couldn't." He gave her a cocky smirk. "But Beau's friends with the senator, so he made it happen." And then, he gripped her tightly. He'd always been a mama's boy.

"Beau did this?" She pulled away to ask. "He brought you both out here?"

In unison, they nodded, both with big grins.

"Dad sends his apologies," Owen teased. "But one of the

twins has a cold, and the other's still not sleeping through the night."

She didn't want to laugh at her ex's misfortune—the birth of two healthy babies would be a bounty of joy to anyone other than him—but she couldn't help it. She'd seen pictures of his "happy" family, and he looked resentful and tense. But really, forget him. She had her children *right here*.

"I can't believe it. This is the best birthday ever." It had been years since she'd had both of them together at the same time, and it filled the parts of her that still mourned the family she'd lost.

Beau joined them, leaning in to kiss her cheek.

"I can't believe you did this for me. Thank you." She included him in the group hug. "I have everything I could ever want right here in my arms."

"Do you mind if I steal your mom for a moment?" he asked her kids.

Clearly, they knew what he was up to because they didn't even conceal their delight and released her right away.

He took her hand and led her through the clusters of people grabbing drinks, sampling the food the caterers were setting out, and chatting. It was a small town, so everyone pretty much knew each other.

As they headed down the long corridor, the afternoon light filtered through the hanging orbs and landed in bright blue splotches, making the floor glow like an aquarium. All along the center of the mall, they'd arranged various styles of landscaping from English garden to Mojave Desert and everything in between. The sculptures within each setting had no relationship to the design, which made them stand out.

"I can't believe how great this place looks," she said.

"You did it. It's all your vision."

"Hardly. It was a collaboration. I had the best team in the world." And she could now call them her friends. It had been a very long time since she'd had people she genuinely liked to hang out with. "Where are we going?" It looked like he was taking her to her office.

At first, she'd loved the idea of having her own studio, but the work involved in creating the mall took most of her time. She'd even had to narrow her personal business down to just ornaments. She'd never give up making those.

"There's something I wanted to discuss with you privately."

"Okay." She'd go anywhere this man wanted, but she suspected he had a gift for her. "You realize bringing my kids to Calamity is the best birthday present I could ever want, right?"

"I do. Yes."

"Okay, Mr. Man of Few Words." *Wait a minute.* Was he nervous? She'd been so carried away by seeing her kids and the excitement of the opening that she hadn't noticed the bead of sweat over his lip. "What's going on?"

But he didn't need words to explain anything. He'd stopped in front of her office.

Only, he'd transformed it. "What have you done?" She could hardly believe what she was seeing. He'd framed the window with dangling ornaments in a heart-shaped design. She hurried inside to see hundreds of her glass globes hanging from the ceiling by silver ribbons.

He'd set up an easel, brushes, watercolors... Every tool

an artist could dream of having. On the walls, he'd hung some of her paintings.

And on a table, she found a stack of familiar boxes. Tears filled her eyes, and she slapped her hand over her mouth so he wouldn't see her ugly cry. She hurried over and ripped off the packing tape, pulling out the first tattered and worn box of her family's ornaments. "Beau." Her voice broke.

He came up from behind and wrapped his arms around her. "I'm here, sweetheart."

"I can't believe you did this."

"I'm glad you like it. It was presumptuous of me to turn your office into a studio, and if it's not something you want, I can switch it back. I don't want you to feel pressure to paint—"

She turned within the shelter of his embrace. "Pressure? I've been missing it like air. I just haven't had the mental space." She couldn't create when she was so preoccupied. "You're the most amazing man I've ever known. How on earth did I get so lucky?"

He kissed her. "I ask myself the same thing about you every single day."

She reached inside the box and pulled out an angel ornament. "This was my great-grandmother's." She held it out for him to see. "How did you get these?"

"I asked Emerson to check with her dad. She said my timing couldn't have been more perfect because he'd already stopped payment on the storage unit, and the contents were going up for auction."

That fucker. He knew she could afford it now, and he hadn't bothered to let her know. "You bought everything, didn't you?"

"You're damn right I did. I want to make sure you have a chance to go through it and keep what you want. You must have baby books and photo albums, important stuff like that."

"I do." She set the ornament back in its padded cubby and threw herself into his arms. "I love you so much."

"I'm glad to hear you say that. Because…" Reaching for her hand, he got down on one knee. "Margot Sophia Rhodes—" His cheeks flushed a deep red, and his breath caught. He lowered his gaze and took a moment to pull himself together before turning those bright blue eyes on her. "I love you. I love everything about you, and I want you forever. I know we haven't talked about marriage. We've both signed the pieces of paper before, and they didn't even amount to kindling for the fireplace. But marrying *you* means stitching our families together, and there's nothing I want more than to be woven into the fabric of your life."

She dropped to her knees. "My *life*? Beau, you're woven into my *heart*. I can't separate you from me in here." She brought his hand to her chest. "But yes, I'll marry you. Of course, I will."

"I haven't asked yet."

She grinned. "Then, what was that whole speech for?"

"I was getting there." They cracked up, and he pulled a box out of his pocket. He popped it open to reveal a ring. "Margot Rhodes, will you marry me?"

"Oh, my God." She pulled it out of the box. "What in the world is this?"

"It's called fire opal."

When she held it under the lights, it gave a spectral display of yellows, oranges, and reds. Set in a gold band and surrounded by shiny yellow-green peridot, it was an absolute showstopper. "I can't believe you made this."

"It's us. In a ring." With a shaky hand, he slid it onto her finger. And then, he kissed her.

It didn't seem real to have such a bounty of goodness in her life, but the press of his lips, the clutch of his hand at the back of her neck, and the heat of his body was all the proof she needed.

It had been a long road to get here, but she'd landed in a place she could finally call her forever home.

And the address was Beau.

Thank you for reading ALL I WANT FOR CHRISTMAS IS YOU! Are you dying to know what's going on with Lorelei?!! Well, don't worry—I got you! Here's how she found out her closest friends in the world were cheating on her and how she handled it: Lorelei Calloway: Unwrapped.

Up next in the Calamity Falls series (and don't worry—they can all be read as standalones!) is the final book in the hockey series. And guess who plays a starring role? Lorelei! Booker's finally coming home, and thanks to the pop star, he's in for a HUGE surprise! Preorder NEVER IN MY WILDEST DREAMS. #surprisebaby #hockey #sportsromance #holidayromance

. . .

Subscribe to my newsletter to find out when NEVER IN MY WILDEST DREAMS will be released. It says July 2024, but it'll be sooner than that!

Want to get caught up on the whole Calamity Falls series?

KEEP ON LOVING YOU
WE BELONG TOGETHER
THE VERY THOUGHT OF YOU
JUST THE WAY YOU ARE
IT WAS ALWAYS YOU
CAN'T HELP FALLING IN LOVE
COME AWAY WITH ME
WHOLE LOTTA LOVE
YOU'RE STILL THE ONE
THE DEEPER I FALL
LOVE ME LIKE YOU DO
TRULY, MADLY, DEEPLY
ALL I WANT FOR CHRISTMAS IS YOU
NEVER IN MY WILDEST DREAMS

Have you read the Rock Star Romance series? Come meet the sexy rockers of Blue Fire:

YOU REALLY GOT ME
I WANT YOU TO WANT ME
TAKE ME HOME TONIGHT
MORE THAN A FEELING

Look for NEVER IN MY WILDEST DREAMS coming soon! Grab a FREE copy of PLANES, TRAINS, AND HEAD OVER HEELS. And come hang out with me on Facebook, TikTok, Twitter, Instagram, Goodreads, and Pinterest or in my private reader group.

To get caught up on the four hockey friends, start with THE DEEPER I FALL, about a grumpy, tatted hockey player who falls head over heels in love with the spoiled socialite he's forced to live with for a month. This one's Declan's book!

Read an excerpt from THE DEEPER I FALL

Aim your cell phone camera at the QR code to get links to all the places you can find me!

Excerpt of The Deeper I Fall

PROLOGUE

Ten Months Ago

TONIGHT, SERAPHINA MAUD CRUTCHLEY WAS A superstar.

She didn't feel like one very often. Rarely, in fact. But at this moment, with the spotlight trained on her as she stood in the middle of the ballroom surrounded by every single luminary in London's elite, she felt a wild mix of emotion: pride, certainly, but also the teensiest sense of imposter syndrome.

Honestly, she didn't know what to do with all the attention, so she smiled and kept her focus on the stage.

"The Lumley Foundation has hosted this ball for over a century." The CEO, in his black tailcoat and white bow tie, addressed the crowd of glittering donors. "Thanks to the addition of Phinny to our team, we've seen our donations quadruple. With her sparkling personality and boundless compassion, she is most certainly a bright star among us. Thank you, Phinny, for putting together such a spectacular array of auction items." He gave her a nod, and the audience broke into applause.

Her stepfather squeezed her shoulder, and her mum whispered in her ear, "I'm so proud of you, darling."

It was the most glorious moment of her life. Thanks to the blinding light in her eyes, she couldn't see the audience, so she just waved her appreciation. When the applause didn't die down, she began to wonder what was going on. The acknowledgment was lovely, but surely, she hadn't done anything *that* exceptional.

She supposed scoring a reclusive billionaire's superyacht for a week was quite a coup, but still…

This response is a bit much.

It was only when the spotlight turned away from her that she discovered the reason for the crowd's enthusiasm. Cameron Lumley had taken the stage. Shaking the CEO's hand, he grabbed the microphone. Then, her elegant, handsome boyfriend flashed his movie star smile. "Good evening."

Even though his family ran the foundation, he had no reason to be on stage right then. He might not run events, but he sure was an impressive sight. His custom-made suit hugged his broad shoulders and muscular thighs while his commanding presence captured the attention of everyone in the room. "On behalf of my family, I'd like to thank you all for your support this evening. As you know, the charity is my life's work, so it's only fitting that the woman who owns my heart now plays such a central role in it."

Surprise jolted her.

I own his heart?

They'd been together a while, but they hardly had some grand love affair. Not even close.

What's he going on about?

Her parents moved to stand on either side of her, enormous smiles stretching across their faces.

Cameron extended a hand. "Darling, please come up here."

She almost shouted *Why?* She didn't need to get up on stage. The band should start playing, and the patrons should go back to dancing. That was the order of events.

Her mum took the champagne flute out of her hand. "Don't just stand there."

With all eyes on her, what choice did Phinny have? But while her brain sent the signal to her legs, they refused to cooperate. A wave of nausea hit, and she went hot all over.

Her stepfather set his hand on the small of her back and gave her a nudge. "Go on now. Don't embarrass us."

That got her moving. As the crowd parted, she made her way to the steps. On some level, she knew what was happening, but her mind was racing, and she couldn't think clearly.

Please don't do this.

We're nowhere near ready for this. They'd grown up together but had only begun dating during their last year at university.

Casually dating.

Cameron stood center stage, while the CEO reached for her hand and helped her up the stairs. It was hard enough to move in her ball gown and shapewear bodysuit, but with her legs shaking, she moved like a newborn foal.

Which was fitting since her heart was positively *galloping*.

"Darling…" Cameron reached for her hand, kissing her palm.

And then, he dropped to a knee.

In the middle of the grandest charity event of the year, her boyfriend—emphasis on *friend*—was about to propose. "I have loved you my entire life, but it was only when I saw you coming out of Trinity Hall that I knew it was time to start our future together. Every day has gotten better, and I can't wait to spend my life with you. Seraphina, will you do me the honor of becoming my wife?"

With the audience's collective gasp, the air was sucked out of the room.

She couldn't breathe. Blood roared in her ears, and her vision blurred around the edges.

In the silence, she had the strangest sensation of floating. She could picture herself grabbing a handful of helium balloons and drifting off the stage, out the window, and sailing over the rooftops of London.

Cameron's smile faltered, and it jerked her back to the moment. She couldn't embarrass him. "Yes. Of course, yes."

Relief washed over his handsome features, and he stood to his full height. He wrapped an arm around her and faced the ballroom, raising their clasped hands as though she were a trophy.

In the middle of the audience, Phinny found her parents. She'd never seen them so happy.

But why? The moment felt surreal. She'd never gushed about him to her parents. Never once talked about marriage or babies or any kind of future with him. They were two people from similar backgrounds who had fun together. *We're just dating.*

Marriage?

Standing on that stage, she felt like a paper doll cut out.

With a tug, she was led back down the stairs. Immediately, well-wishers swarmed them. His family, their friends…everyone was gleeful.

And it was all a lie.

Because she couldn't marry him.

Flee. It wasn't a thought so much as an alarm that rang through her body. She wrenched her hand out of his grip and made her way out of the ballroom. When she saw a sign for a powder room, she ducked inside and locked the door.

Oh, God. What is happening?

As she ran cold water over her hands, she looked up at her wild-eyed reflection. Her pulse pounded violently. Why had he proposed publicly? Now, calling it off would create a scandal.

It didn't have to be like this.

A hard rap jerked her attention from the mirror.

"Phinny?" *Cameron.* "Open up."

Angry that he'd put her in a terrible position, she opened the door, grabbed his wrist, and pulled him inside the lavender-scented bathroom. "What was that?"

His eyes flickered with hurt. "What do you mean, what was that? It was a marriage proposal."

"But why? Cameron, we're not ready for that."

"We've been dating for three years. When did you think we'd be ready?"

"I don't know." *Never.* "We haven't talked about it."

"What on earth do you think we've been doing all this time?"

"We've been *dating*."

"Yes, on a course toward marriage. Why else would I be exclusive with someone if not with the intention to marry her? Why are you acting like this came out of nowhere? You can't pretend you didn't know it was the path we've been on."

She couldn't argue his point, and it flustered her. Because, really, it uncovered a truth that would only hurt his feelings. *I don't love you.* "I can't possibly get married now. I haven't done anything with my life."

His jaw snapped shut like he was trying to contain his anger. "Whatever you want to do, what better way to do it than as Cameron Lumley's wife?"

Obviously, that made perfect sense. Marrying into one of the wealthiest families in the United Kingdom would afford her any opportunity her heart desired. And it wasn't like Cameron cared what she did. That wouldn't change once they got married. He'd still go off with his mates on trips, and she'd go clubbing with hers. Sometimes, they'd do the holidays together, while other times, they'd be with their own families.

She knew exactly what her life with him would look like because that was the kind of marriage his parents had. And she didn't want to wind up like his mum, spending more time with her wine than her husband.

She pulled off the engagement ring. "I'm sorry, but I'm not ready to get married."

He just stared at her as though waiting for her to laugh

and say *Gotcha. Of course, I'll marry you, silly!* "Are you serious?"

"Quite." His presumption that she'd just fall in line with some plan he'd never voiced irked her. "Cameron, come on. Do you even love me?"

"Of course I do." He seemed calmer as if they could now settle things. "I like you better than anyone else we know."

Well, there's a ringing endorsement for marriage. "And I like you. But I need more time."

"How much time?"

"I don't know."

"Are we talking about a few weeks?"

Weeks? "I'm twenty-four. What's the rush?"

His expression shuttered. "Waiting these three years has cost me nearly two million pounds."

She flinched as if he'd flicked cold water at her face. As soon as he married, he'd tap into his trust fund. With each child he added to his family, the monthly allowance would go up.

Quite the incentive to keep the Lumley line going.

She'd known that. So, why did it sound so ugly to hear him say it out loud?

He must not have liked her crestfallen expression because he reached for her elbows and bent his knees to look her in the eyes. "Darling, there's no one I'd rather spend my life with than you. You make me laugh...you make me happy."

"Well, yes, because I don't require anything of you."

He chuckled. "Most definitely, that's one for the plus column. But it works both ways. We give each other room to live our lives. Trust me, that's a good thing. We'll never grow restless or resentful."

I want more.

And what a bombshell revelation that was. She'd just been going along, having fun, not questioning anything, and she'd given no thought to where she was heading. Now that he'd forced her to think about it, she had to accept she hadn't done a damn thing with her life.

She couldn't say what she wanted to do exactly, but for the first time, she felt something missing. Something between the phases of parties, clubs, and shopping and getting married and popping out babies. "I need more time."

The smile vanished. He straightened. "No."

Fear sliced through her. She might not be ready to marry him, but she'd never contemplated a life without him. Like her parents, he was a major cog in the machine of her world, and she didn't know how to operate without all of them. "No, you won't wait?"

"I have waited. Three years is more than enough." He softened. "Look, you'd make a smashing stylist. Or you and your mum could open a boutique. Once we're married, you can use a portion of the extra fifty thousand pounds a month to do whatever you want. It doesn't matter to me, but we either get married now or it's done."

"It's done? Or we're done?"

"We're done. If you're not ready to marry me after three years, then I've got no reason to believe you'll be ready by four years or even five."

"I can't imagine my life without you, but I can't marry you because you've run out of patience with me. I'm sorry, Cameron." She took in the proud jut of his chin and the look in his eyes that screamed *Are you seriously going to walk away from me?* She liked him very much. They'd had a lot of fun together. But she didn't love him.

And so, she walked out the door.

Cut from her mooring, she felt adrift...uneasy. She hustled toward the exit as though the manor were on fire. The tight silk liner of her dress and the five-inch stilettos hampered her progress, though, as people rushed toward her, eager to share the happy occasion.

She couldn't talk to anyone right then, so she hurried on. Pulling out her phone, she tried to text her parents' driver, but her trembling fingers kept tapping the wrong pads, making her delete and start over.

"Seraphina?" Her mum glided along the hallway.

"Where are you going?" her stepfather asked. "We've just opened the bubbly to toast your wonderful news. Let's find Cameron. Come along."

The moment her mum reached her, the smile faded. "What's going on?"

Phinny handed over her phone. "Can you please ask Fergus to come 'round?"

Her stepfather snatched it. "We'll do no such thing. All of our friends are here to celebrate with you."

"There's nothing to celebrate." Phinny let out a tight breath. "We're not getting married."

"Of course, you are." Andrew's eyebrows shot up. "Don't be ridiculous."

When she'd met him as a little girl, she'd called him by his first name, but since she couldn't pronounce Andrew, she'd wound up saying Dewzy. For the first time since he'd come into her life, that term of endearment didn't fit. At this moment, when he cared more about his reputation than her feelings, he was purely her stepfather. "I gave the ring back. I'm not marrying him."

"Seraphina." Her mother sounded appalled.

"I told him I needed more time, and he said he wouldn't give me any."

Clasping her wrist, Andrew led them to an alcove. "You've known each other your entire lives. How much more time could you possibly need?"

"There are things I still want to do."

"Like what?" her mum whispered harshly. "You want to shop more? Travel more? Have more spa days? What exactly are you so eager to do?"

Like a can on the road flattened by a tire, Phinny's spirit compressed under the weight of her mum's words. She'd never considered herself frivolous. She'd been living the only life she'd ever known. "I don't know. But I would rather find out than get married to a man I don't love."

Her stepfather had always indulged her, and in return, she'd tried very hard to please him. So, to see the tick in his jaw, the color flood his cheeks, truly upset her. "What on earth do you think we've been doing, Seraphina?"

"What do you mean?" A sickening feeling rolled through her.

"You don't have a proper job, you live in an apartment we own, and you use a credit card we've given you...why do you think we've been supporting you all this time?"

The great beast of fear loomed over her like a dark, menacing shadow. "I—" Her mind went blank.

"We've supported you because you were going to marry Cameron," her mum said. "And Lumleys do philanthropy, just as I've done. Just as you've been doing. *That* has been our expectation. If we thought for a moment you had no intention of marrying him, you'd have been polishing your CV and applying for jobs your last year at university. You'd have been paying your own bills upon graduation."

"Now, go and find your fiancé," her stepfather said. "And get things back on track. Or the locks to your Knightsbridge apartment will be changed by morning."

"What?" She could barely process his words. He couldn't possibly mean to throw her out onto the streets?

"Darling, please." Her mum patted his arm.

Oh, thank God. Her mum would always take care of her. They were a team. Her parents were upset. She understood that. But they'd never make her marry a man she didn't love.

But then her mum's features hardened. "Let her make some calls, see which of her friends will allow her to sleep on their couch until she gets a job."

About the Author

Award-winning author Erika Kelly writes sexy and emotional small town romance. Married to the love of her life and raising four children, she lives in the southwest, drinks a lot of tea, and is always waiting for her cats to get off her keyboard.

erikakellybooks.com

facebook.com/ErikaKelly

x.com/ErikaKellyBooks

instagram.com/erikakellyauthor

goodreads.com/Erika_Kelly

pinterest.com/erikakellybooks

amazon.com/Erika-Kelly/e/B00L0MLWUY

bookbub.com/authors/erika-kelly

Made in the USA
Monee, IL
02 December 2023

48023380R00192